DIRK GENTLY'S HOLISTIC DETECTIVE AGENCY

DOUGLAS ADAMS created all the various and contradictory manifestations of *The Hitchhiker's Guide to the Galaxy*: radio, novels, TV, computer game, stage adaptations, comic book and bath towel. He lectured and broadcast around the world and was a patron of the Dian Fossey Gorilla Fund and Save the Rhino International. Douglas Adams was born in Cambridge, UK and lived with his wife and daughter in Islington, London, before moving to Santa Barbara, California, where he died suddenly in 2001.

BOOKS BY DOUGLAS ADAMS

The Hitchhiker trilogy

The Hitchhiker's Guide to the Galaxy

The Restaurant at the End of the Universe

Life, the Universe and Everything

So Long, and Thanks for All the Fish

Mostly Harmless

The Hitchhiker's Guide to the Galaxy:
The Original Radio Scripts

The Hitchhiker's Guide to the Galaxy Radio Scripts:
the Tertiary, Quandary and Quintessential Phases

The Dirk Gently series

Dirk Gently's Holistic Detective Agency

The Long Dark Tea-time of the Soul

Collected works

The Salmon of Doubt

With John Lloyd

The Meaning of Liff

The Deeper Meaning of Liff

With Mark Carwardine

Last Chance to See . . .

*By Terry Jones, based on a
story/computer game by Douglas Adams*

Douglas Adams's Starship Titanic

DOUGLAS ADAMS

DIRK GENTLY'S HOLISTIC DETECTIVE AGENCY

PAN BOOKS

First published 1987 by William Heinemann Ltd

This edition published 2021 by Pan Books
an imprint of Pan Macmillan
The Smithson, 6 Briset Street, London EC1M 5NR
EU representative: Macmillan Publishers Ireland Limited,
Mallard Lodge, Lansdowne Village, Dublin 4
Associated companies throughout the world
www.panmacmillan.com

ISBN 978-1-5290-3458-5

1 3 5 7 9 8 6 4 2

A CIP catalogue record for this book is available from
the British Library.

Printed and bound by CPI Group (UK) Ltd, Croydon, CR0 4YY

Visit **www.panmacmillan.com** to read more about all our books
and to buy them. You will also find features, author interviews and
news of any author events, and you can sign up for e-newsletters
so that you're always first to hear about our new releases.

Author's Note

The physical descriptions of St Cedd's College in this book, in so far as they are specific at all, owe a little to my memories of St John's College, Cambridge, although I've also borrowed indiscriminately from other colleges as well. Sir Isaac Newton was at Trinity College in real life, and Samuel Taylor Coleridge was at Jesus.

The point is that St Cedd's College is a completely fictitious assemblage, and no correspondence is intended between any institutions or characters in this book and any real institutions or people, living, dead, or wandering the night in ghostly torment.

This book was written and typeset on an Apple Macintosh Plus computer and LaserWriter Plus printer using MacAuthor word-processing software.

The completed document was then printed using a Linotron 100 at The Graphics Factory, London SW3, to produce a final high-resolution image of the text. My thanks to Mike Glover of Icon Technology for his help with this process.

Finally, my very special thanks are due to Sue Freestone for all her help in nursing this book into existence.

Douglas Adams
London, 1987

1

This time there would be no witnesses.

This time there was just the dead earth, a rumble of thunder, and the onset of that interminable light drizzle from the north-east by which so many of the world's most momentous events seem to be accompanied.

The storms of the day before, and of the day before that, and the floods of the previous week, had now abated. The skies still bulged with rain, but all that actually fell in the gathering evening gloom was a dreary kind of prickle.

Some wind whipped across the darkening plain, blundered through the low hills and gusted across a shallow valley where stood a structure, a kind of tower, alone in a nightmare of mud, and leaning.

It was a blackened stump of a tower. It stood like an extrusion of magma from one of the more pestilential pits of hell, and it leaned at a peculiar angle, as if oppressed by something altogether more terrible than its own considerable weight. It seemed a dead thing, long ages dead.

The only movement was that of a river of mud that moved sluggishly along the bottom of the valley past the tower. A mile or so further on, the river ran down a ravine and disappeared underground.

But as the evening darkened it became apparent that the tower was not entirely without life. There was a single dim red light guttering deep within it.

The light was only just visible – except of course that there was no one to see, no witnesses, not this time, but it was nevertheless a light. Every few minutes it grew a little stronger and a little brighter and then faded slowly away almost to nothing. At the same time a low keening noise drifted out on the wind, built up to a kind of wailing climax, and then it too faded, abjectly, away.

Time passed, and then another light appeared, a smaller, mobile light. It emerged at ground level and moved in a single bobbing circuit of the tower, pausing occasionally on its way around. Then it, and the shadowy figure that could just be discerned carrying it, disappeared inside once more.

An hour passed, and by the end of it the darkness was total. The world seemed dead, the night a blankness.

And then the glow appeared again near the tower's peak, this time growing in power more purposefully. It quickly reached the peak of brightness it had previously attained, and then kept going, increasing, increasing. The keening sound that accompanied it rose in pitch and stridency until it became a wailing scream. The scream screamed on and on till it became a blinding noise and the light a deafening redness.

And then, abruptly, both ceased.

There was a millisecond of silent darkness.

An astonishing pale new light billowed and bulged from deep within the mud beneath the tower. The sky clenched, a mountain of mud convulsed, earth and sky bellowed at each other, there was a horrible pinkness, a sudden greenness, a lingering orangeness that stained the clouds, and then the light sank and the night at last was deeply, hideously dark. There was no further sound other than the soft tinkle of water.

But in the morning the sun rose with an unaccustomed sparkle on a day that was, or seemed to be, or at least would have seemed to be if there had been anybody there to whom it could seem to be anything at all, warmer, clearer and brighter – an altogether livelier day than any yet known. A clear river ran through the shattered remains of the valley.

And time began seriously to pass.

3

2

[faint text from previous page showing through]

High on a rocky promontory sat an Electric Monk on a
bored horse. From under its rough woven cowl the
Monk gazed unblinkingly down into another valley,
with which it was having a problem.

The day was hot, the sun stood in an empty hazy sky
and beat down upon the grey rocks and the scrubby,
parched grass. Nothing moved, not even the Monk. The
horse's tail moved a little, swishing slightly to try and
move a little air, but that was all. Otherwise, nothing
moved.

The Electric Monk was a labour-saving device, like a
dishwasher or a video recorder. Dishwashers washed
tedious dishes for you, thus saving you the bother of
washing them yourself; video recorders watched tedious
television for you, thus saving you the bother of looking
at it yourself; Electric Monks believed things for you,
thus saving you what was becoming an increasingly
onerous task, that of believing all the things the world
expected you to believe.

Unfortunately this Electric Monk had developed a
fault, and had started to believe all kinds of things, more
or less at random. It was even beginning to believe
things they'd have difficulty believing in Salt Lake City.
It had never heard of Salt Lake City, of course. Nor had
it ever heard of a quingigillion, which was roughly the
number of miles between this valley and the Great Salt
Lake of Utah.

The problem with the valley was this. The Monk currently believed that the valley and everything in the valley and around it, including the Monk itself and the Monk's horse, was a uniform shade of pale pink. This made for a certain difficulty in distinguishing any one thing from any other thing, and therefore made doing anything or going anywhere impossible, or at least difficult and dangerous. Hence the immobility of the Monk and the boredom of the horse, which had had to put up with a lot of silly things in its time but was secretly of the opinion that this was one of the silliest.

How long did the Monk believe these things?

Well, as far as the Monk was concerned, for ever. The faith which moves mountains, or at least believes them against all the available evidence to be pink, was a solid and abiding faith, a great rock against which the world could hurl whatever it would, yet it would not be shaken. In practice, the horse knew, twenty-four hours was usually about its lot.

So what of this horse, then, that actually held opinions, and was sceptical about things? Unusual behaviour for a horse, wasn't it? An unusual horse perhaps?

No. Although it was certainly a handsome and well-built example of its species, it was none the less a perfectly ordinary horse, such as convergent evolution has produced in many of the places that life is to be found. They have always understood a great deal more than they let on. It is difficult to be sat on all day, every day, by some other creature, without forming an opinion about them.

On the other hand, it is perfectly possible to sit all day, every day, on top of another creature and not have the slightest thought about them whatsoever.

When the early models of these Monks were built, it was felt to be important that they be instantly

5

recognisable as artificial objects. There must be no danger of their looking at all like real people. You wouldn't want your video recorder lounging around on the sofa all day while it was watching TV. You wouldn't want it picking its nose, drinking beer and sending out for pizzas.

So the Monks were built with an eye for originality of design and also for practical horse-riding ability. This was important. People, and indeed things, looked more sincere on a horse. So two legs were held to be both more suitable and cheaper than the more normal primes of seventeen, nineteen or twenty-three; the skin the Monks were given was pinkish-looking instead of purple, soft and smooth instead of crenellated. They were also restricted to just the one mouth and nose, but were given instead an additional eye, making for a grand total of two. A strange-looking creature indeed. But truly excellent at believing the most preposterous things.

This Monk had first gone wrong when it was simply given too much to believe in one day. It was, by mistake, cross-connected to a video recorder that was watching eleven TV channels simultaneously, and this caused it to blow a bank of illogic circuits. The video recorder only had to watch them, of course. It didn't have to believe them all as well. This is why instruction manuals are so important.

So after a hectic week of believing that war was peace, that good was bad, that the moon was made of blue cheese, and that God needed a lot of money sent to a certain box number, the Monk started to believe that thirty-five per cent of all tables were hermaphrodites, and then broke down. The man from the Monk shop said that it needed a whole new motherboard, but then pointed out that the new improved Monk Plus models were twice as powerful, had an entirely new multi-tasking Negative Capability feature that allowed them to hold up to sixteen entirely different and contradictory ideas in memory simultaneously without generating any irritating system errors, were twice as fast and at least three times as glib, and you could have a whole new one for less than the cost of replacing the motherboard of the old model.

That was it. Done.

The faulty Monk was turned out into the desert where it could believe what it liked, including the idea that it had been hard done by. It was allowed to keep its horse, since horses were so cheap to make.

For a number of days and nights, which it variously believed to be three, forty-three, and five hundred and ninety-eight thousand seven hundred and three, it roamed the desert, putting its simple Electric trust in rocks, birds, clouds and a form of non-existent elephant-asparagus, until at last it fetched up here, on this high rock, overlooking a valley that was not, despite the deep fervour of the Monk's belief, pink. Not even a little bit.

Time passed.

3

Time passed.

Susan waited.

The more Susan waited, the more the doorbell didn't ring. Or the phone. She looked at her watch. She felt that now was about the time that she could legitimately begin to feel cross. She was cross already, of course, but that had been in her own time, so to speak. They were well and truly into his time now, and even allowing for traffic, mishaps, and general vagueness and dilatoriness, it was now well over half an hour past the time that he had insisted was the latest time they could possibly afford to leave, so she'd better be ready.

She tried to worry that something terrible had happened to him, but didn't believe it for a moment. Nothing terrible ever happened to him, though she was beginning to think that it was time it damn well did. If nothing terrible happened to him soon maybe she'd do it herself. Now there was an idea.

She threw herself crossly into the armchair and watched the news on television. The news made her cross. She flipped the remote control and watched something on another channel for a bit. She didn't know what it was, but it also made her cross.

Perhaps she should phone. She was damned if she was going to phone. Perhaps if she phoned he would phone her at the same moment and not be able to get through.

She refused to admit that she had even thought that.

Damn him, where was he? Who cared where he was anyway? She didn't, that was for sure.

Three times in a row he'd done this. Three times in a row was enough. She angrily flipped channels one more time. There was a programme about computers and some interesting new developments in the field of things you could do with computers and music.

That was it. That was really it. She knew that she had told herself that that was it only seconds earlier, but this was now the final real ultimate it.

She jumped to her feet and went to the phone, gripping an angry Filofax. She flipped briskly through it and dialled a number.

'Hello, Michael? Yes, it's Susan. Susan Way. You said I should call you if I was free this evening and I said I'd rather be dead in a ditch, remember? Well, I suddenly discover that I am free, absolutely, completely and utterly free, and there isn't a decent ditch for miles around. Make your move while you've got your chance is my advice to you. I'll be at the Tangiers Club in half an hour.'

She pulled on her shoes and coat, paused when she remembered that it was Thursday and that she should put a fresh, extra-long tape on the answering machine, and two minutes later was out of the front door. When at last the phone did ring the answering machine said sweetly that Susan Way could not come to the phone just at the moment, but that if the caller would like to leave a message, she would get back to them as soon as possible. Maybe.

4

It was a chill November evening of the old-fashioned type.

The moon looked pale and wan, as if it shouldn't be up on a night like this. It rose unwillingly and hung like an ill spectre. Silhouetted against it, dim and hazy through the dampness which rose from the unwholesome fens, stood the assorted towers and turrets of St Cedd's, Cambridge, a ghostly profusion of buildings thrown up over centuries, medieval next to Victorian, Odeon next to Tudor. Only rising through the mist did they seem remotely to belong to one another.

Between them scurried figures, hurrying from one dim pool of light to another, shivering, leaving wraiths of breath which folded themselves into the cold night behind them.

It was seven o'clock. Many of the figures were heading for the college dining hall which divided First Court from Second Court, and from which warm light, reluctantly, streamed. Two figures in particular seemed ill-matched. One, a young man, was tall, thin and angular; even muffled inside a heavy dark coat he walked a little like an affronted heron.

The other was small, roundish, and moved with an ungainly restlessness, like a number of elderly squirrels trying to escape from a sack. His own age was on the older side of completely indeterminate. If you picked a number at random, he was probably a little older than that, but – well, it was impossible to tell. Certainly his face was heavily lined, and the small amount of hair that escaped from under his red woollen skiing hat was thin, white, and had very much its own ideas about how it wished to arrange itself. He too was muffled inside a heavy coat, but over it he wore a billowing gown with very faded purple trim, the badge of his unique and peculiar academic office.

As they walked the older man was doing all the talking. He was pointing at items of interest along the way, despite the fact that it was too dark to see any of them. The younger man was saying 'Ah yes,' and 'Really? How interesting . . .' and 'Well, well, well,' and 'Good heavens.' His head bobbed seriously.

They entered, not through the main entrance to the hall, but through a small doorway on the east side of the court. This led to the Senior Combination Room and a dark-panelled anteroom where the Fellows of the college assembled to slap their hands and make 'brrrrrr' noises before making their way through their own entrance to the High Table.

They were late and shook off their coats hurriedly. This was complicated for the older man by the necessity first of taking off his professorial gown, and then of putting it back on again once his coat was off, then of stuffing his hat in his coat pocket, then of wondering where he'd put his scarf, and then of realising that he hadn't brought it, then of fishing in his coat pocket for his handkerchief, then of fishing in his other coat pocket for his spectacles, and finally of finding them quite unexpectedly wrapped in his scarf, which it turned out he had brought after all but hadn't been wearing despite the damp and bitter wind blowing in like a witch's breath from across the fens.

He bustled the younger man into the hall ahead of

him and they took the last two vacant seats at the High Table, braving a flurry of frowns and raised eyebrows for interrupting the Latin grace to do so.

Hall was full tonight. It was always more popular with the undergraduates in the colder months. More unusually, the hall was candlelit, as it was now only on very few special occasions. Two long, crowded tables stretched off into the glimmering darkness. By candle-light, people's faces were more alive, the hushed sounds of their voices, the clink of cutlery and glasses, seemed more exciting, and in the dark recesses of the great hall, all the centuries for which it had existed seemed present at once. High Table itself formed a crosspiece at the top, and was raised about a foot above the rest. Since it was a guest night, the table was set on both sides to accom-modate the extra numbers, and many diners therefore sat with their backs to the rest of the hall.

'So, young MacDuff,' said the Professor once he was seated and flapping his napkin open, 'pleasure to see you again, my dear fellow. Glad you could come. No idea what all this is about,' he added, peering round the hall in consternation. 'All the candles and silver and business. Generally means a special dinner in honour of someone or something no one can remember anything about except that it means better food for a night.'

He paused and thought for a moment, and then said, 'It seems odd, don't you think, that the quality of the food should vary inversely with the brightness of the lighting. Makes you wonder what culinary heights the kitchen staff could rise to if you confined them to perpetual dark-ness. Could be worth a try, I think. Got some good vaults in the college that could be turned over to the purpose. I think I showed you round them once, hmmm? Nice brickwork.'

All this came as something of a relief to his guest. It

was the first indication his host had given that he had the faintest recollection who he was. Professor Urban Chronotis, the Regius Professor of Chronology, or 'Reg' as he insisted on being called, had a memory that he himself had once compared to the Queen Alexandra Birdwing Butterfly, in that it was colourful, flitted prettily hither and thither, and was now, alas, almost completely extinct.

When he had telephoned with the invitation a few days previously, he had seemed extremely keen to see his former pupil, and yet when Richard had arrived this evening, a little on the late side, admittedly, the Professor had thrown open the door apparently in anger, had started in surprise on seeing Richard, demanded to know if he was having emotional problems, reacted in annoyance to being reminded gently that it was now ten years since he had been Richard's college tutor, and finally agreed that Richard had indeed come for dinner, whereupon he, the Professor, had started talking rapidly and at length about the history of the college architecture, a sure sign that his mind was elsewhere entirely.

'Reg' had never actually taught Richard, he had only been his college tutor, which meant in short that he had had charge of his general welfare, told him when the exams were and not to take drugs, and so on. Indeed, it was not entirely clear if Reg had ever taught anybody at all and what, if anything, he would have taught them. His professorship was an obscure one, to say the least, and since he dispensed with his lecturing duties by the simple and time-honoured technique of presenting all his potential students with an exhaustive list of books that he knew for a fact had been out of print for thirty years, then flying into a tantrum if they failed to find them, no one had ever discovered the precise nature of his academic discipline. He had, of course, long ago taken the precaution of removing the only extant copies of the books on his reading list from the university and college libraries, as a result of which he had plenty of time to, well, to do whatever it was he did.

Since Richard had always managed to get on reasonably well with the old fruitcake, he had one day plucked up courage to ask him what, exactly, the Regius Professorship of Chronology was. It had been one of those light summery days when the world seems about to burst with pleasure at simply being itself, and Reg had been in an uncharacteristically forthcoming mood as they had walked over the bridge where the River Cam divided the older parts of the college from the newer.

'Sinecure, my dear fellow, an absolute sinecure,' he had beamed. 'A small amount of money for a very small, or shall we say non-existent, amount of work. That puts me permanently just ahead of the game, which is a comfortable if frugal place to spend your life. I recommend it.' He leaned over the edge of the bridge and started to point out a particular brick that he found interesting.

'But what sort of study is it supposed to be?' Richard had pursued. 'Is it history? Physics? Philosophy? What?'

'Well,' said Reg, slowly, 'since you're interested, the chair was originally instituted by King George III, who, as you know, entertained a number of amusing notions, including the belief that one of the trees in Windsor Great Park was in fact Frederick the Great.

'It was his own appointment, hence "Regius". His own idea as well, which is somewhat more unusual.'

Sunlight played along the River Cam. People in punts happily shouted at each other to fuck off. Thin natural scientists who had spent months locked away in their rooms growing white and fishlike, emerged blinking into the light. Couples walking along the bank got so excited about the general wonderfulness of it all that they had to pop inside for an hour.

'The poor beleaguered fellow,' Reg continued, 'George III, I mean, was, as you may know, obsessed with time. Filled the palace with clocks. Wound them incessantly. Sometimes would get up in the middle of the night and prowl round the palace in his nightshirt winding clocks. He was very concerned that time continued to go forward, you see. So many terrible things had occurred in his life that he was terrified that any of them might happen again if time were ever allowed to slip backwards even for a moment. A very understandable fear, especially if you're barking mad, as I'm afraid to say, with the very greatest sympathy for the poor fellow, he undoubtedly was. He appointed me, or rather I should say, my office, this professorship, you understand, the post that I am now privileged to hold to – where was I? Oh yes. He instituted this, er, Chair of Chronology to see if there was any particular reason why one thing happened after another and if there was any way of stopping it. Since the answers to the three questions were, I knew immediately, yes, no, and maybe, I realised I could then take the rest of my career off.'

'And your predecessors?'

'Er, were much of the same mind.'

'But who were they?'

'Who were they? Well, splendid fellows of course, splendid to a man. Remind me to tell you about them some day. See that brick? Wordsworth was once sick on that brick. Great man.'

All that had been about ten years ago.

Richard glanced around the great dining hall to see what had changed in the time, and the answer was, of course, absolutely nothing. In the dark heights, dimly seen by the flickering candlelight, were the ghostly portraits of prime ministers, archbishops, political reformers and poets, any of whom might, in their day, have been sick on that same brick.

'Well,' said Reg, in a loudly confidential whisper, as if introducing the subject of nipple-piercing in a nunnery, 'I hear you've suddenly done very well for yourself, at last, hmmm?'

'Er, well, yes, in fact,' said Richard, who was as surprised at the fact as anybody else, 'yes, I have.'

Around the table several gazes stiffened on him.

'Computers,' he heard somebody whisper dismissively to a neighbour further down the table. The stiff gazes relaxed again, and turned away.

'Excellent,' said Reg. 'I'm so pleased for you, so pleased.

'Tell me,' he went on, and it was a moment before Richard realised that the Professor wasn't talking to him any more, but had turned to the right to address his other neighbour, 'what's all this about, this,' he flourished a vague hand over the candles and college silver, '. . . stuff?'

His neighbour, an elderly wizened figure, turned very slowly and looked at him as if he was rather annoyed at being raised from the dead like this.

'Coleridge,' he said in a thin rasp, 'it's the Coleridge Dinner, you old fool.' He turned very slowly back until he was facing the front again. His name was Cawley, he was a Professor of Archaeology and Anthropology, and it was frequently said of him, behind his back, that he regarded it not so much as a serious academic study, more as a chance to relive his childhood.

'Ah, is it,' murmured Reg, 'is it?' and turned back to Richard. 'It's the Coleridge Dinner,' he said knowledgeably. 'Coleridge was a member of the college, you know,' he added after a moment. 'Coleridge. Samuel Taylor.

Poet. I expect you've heard of him. This is his Dinner. Well, not literally, of course. It would be cold by now.' Silence. 'Here, have some salt.'

'Er, thank you, I think I'll wait,' said Richard, surprised. There was no food on the table yet.

'Go on, take it,' insisted the Professor, proffering him the heavy silver salt cellar.

Richard blinked in bemusement but with an interior shrug he reached to take it. In the moment that he blinked, however, the salt cellar had completely vanished.

He started back in surprise.

'Good one, eh?' said Reg as he retrieved the missing cruet from behind the ear of his deathly right-hand neighbour, provoking a surprisingly girlish giggle from somewhere else at the table. Reg smiled impishly. 'Very irritating habit, I know. It's next on my list for giving up after smoking and leeches.'

Well, that was another thing that hadn't changed. Some people pick their noses, others habitually beat up old ladies on the streets. Reg's vice was a harmless if peculiar one – an addiction to childish conjuring tricks. Richard remembered the first time he had been to see Reg with a problem – it was only the normal *Angst* that periodically takes undergraduates into its grip, particularly when they have essays to write, but it had seemed a dark and savage weight at the time. Reg had sat and listened to his outpourings with a deep frown of concentration, and when at last Richard had finished, he pondered seriously, stroked his chin a lot, and at last leaned forward and looked him in the eye.

'I suspect that your problem,' he said, 'is that you have too many paper clips up your nose.'

Richard stared at him.

'Allow me to demonstrate,' said Reg, and leaning

across the desk he pulled from Richard's nose a chain of eleven paper clips and a small rubber swan.

'Ah, the real culprit,' he said, holding up the swan. 'They come in cereal packets, you know, and cause no end of trouble. Well, I'm glad we've had this little chat, my dear fellow. Please feel free to disturb me again if you have any more such problems.'

Needless to say, Richard didn't.

Richard glanced around the table to see if there was anybody else he recognised from his time at the college.

Two places away to the left was the don who had been Richard's Director of Studies in English, who showed no signs of recognising him at all. This was hardly surprising since Richard had spent his three years here assiduously avoiding him, often to the extent of growing a beard and pretending to be someone else.

Next to him was a man whom Richard had never managed to identify. Neither, in fact, had anyone else. He was thin and vole-like and had the most extraordinarily long bony nose – it really was very, very long and bony indeed. In fact it looked a lot like the controversial keel which had helped the Australians win the America's Cup in 1983, and this resemblance had been much remarked upon at the time, though not of course to his face. No one had said anything to his face at all.

No one.

Ever.

Anyone meeting him for the first time was too startled and embarrassed by his nose to speak, and the second time was worse because of the first time, and so on. Years had gone by now, seventeen in all. In all that time he had been cocooned in silence. In hall it had long been the habit of the college servants to position a separate set of salt, pepper and mustard on either side of him, since no one could ask him to pass them, and to ask someone sitting on the other side of him was not only rude but completely impossible because of his nose being in the way.

The other odd thing about him was a series of gestures he made and repeated regularly throughout every evening. They consisted of tapping each of the fingers of his left hand in order, and then one of the fingers of his right hand. He would then occasionally tap some other part of his body, a knuckle, an elbow or a knee. Whenever he was forced to stop this by the requirements of eating he would start blinking each of his eyes instead, and occasionally nodding. No one, of course, had ever dared to ask him why he did this, though all were consumed with curiosity.

Richard couldn't see who was sitting beyond him.

In the other direction, beyond Reg's deathly neighbour, was Watkin, the Classics Professor, a man of terrifying dryness and oddity. His heavy rimless glasses were almost solid cubes of glass within which his eyes appeared to lead independent existences like goldfish. His nose was straight enough and ordinary, but beneath it he wore the same beard as Clint Eastwood. His eyes gazed swimmingly around the table as he selected who was going to be spoken at tonight. He had thought that his prey might be one of the guests, the newly appointed Head of Radio Three, who was sitting opposite – but unfortunately he had already been ensnared by the Music Director of the college and a Professor of Philosophy. These two were busy explaining to the harassed man that the phrase 'too much Mozart' was, given any reasonable definition of those three words, an inherently self-contradictory expression, and that any sentence which contained such a phrase would be thereby rendered meaningless and could not, consequently, be advanced as part of an argument in favour of any given programme-scheduling strategy. The poor man was already beginning to grip his cutlery too tightly. His eyes darted about desperately looking for rescue, and made the mistake of lighting on those of Watkin.

'Good evening,' said Watkin with smiling charm, nodding in the most friendly way, and then letting his gaze settle glassily on to his bowl of newly arrived soup, from which position it would not allow itself to be moved. Yet. Let the bugger suffer a little. He wanted the rescue to be worth at least a good half-dozen radio talk fees.

Beyond Watkin, Richard suddenly discovered the source of the little girlish giggle that had greeted Reg's conjuring trick. Astonishingly enough it was a little girl. She was about eight years old with blonde hair and a glum look. She was sitting occasionally kicking pettishly at the table leg.

'Who's that?' Richard asked Reg in surprise.

'Who's what?' Reg asked Richard in surprise.

Richard inclined a finger surreptitiously in her direction. 'The girl,' he whispered, 'the very, very little girl. Is it some new maths professor?'

Reg peered round at her. 'Do you know,' he said in astonishment, 'I haven't the faintest idea. Never known anything like it. How extraordinary.'

At that moment the problem was solved by the man from the BBC, who suddenly wrenched himself out of the logical half-nelson into which his neighbours had got him, and told the girl off for kicking the table. She stopped kicking the table, and instead kicked the air with redoubled vigour. He told her to try and enjoy herself, so she kicked him. This did something to bring a brief glimmer of pleasure into her glum evening, but it didn't last. Her father briefly shared with the table at large his feelings about baby-sitters who let people down, but nobody felt able to run with the topic.

'A major season of Buxtehude,' resumed the Director of Music, 'is of course clearly long overdue. I'm sure you'll be looking forward to remedying this situation at the first opportunity.'

'Oh, er, yes,' replied the girl's father, spilling his soup, 'er, that is . . . he's not the same one as Gluck, is he?'

The little girl kicked the table leg again. When her father looked sternly at her, she put her head on one side and mouthed a question at him.

'Not now,' he insisted at her as quietly as he could.

'When, then?'

'Later. Maybe. Later, we'll see.'

She hunched grumpily back in her seat. 'You always say later,' she mouthed at him.

'Poor child,' murmured Reg. 'There isn't a don at this table who doesn't behave exactly like that inside. Ah, thank you.' Their soup arrived, distracting his attention, and Richard's.

'So tell me,' said Reg, after they had both had a couple of spoonsful and arrived independently at the same conclusion, that it was not a taste explosion, 'what you've been up to, my dear chap. Something to do with computers, I understand, and also to do with music. I thought you read English when you were here – though only, I realise, in your spare time.' He looked at Richard significantly over the rim of his soup spoon. 'Now wait,' he interrupted before Richard even had a chance to start, 'don't I vaguely remember that you had some sort of computer when you were here? When was it? 1977?'

'Well, what we called a computer in 1977 was really a kind of electric abacus, but . . .'

'Oh, now, don't underestimate the abacus,' said Reg. 'In skilled hands it's a very sophisticated calculating device. Furthermore it requires no power, can be made with any materials you have to hand, and never goes bing in the middle of an important piece of work.'

'So an electric one would be particularly pointless,' said Richard.

'True enough,' conceded Reg.

'There really wasn't a lot this machine could do that you couldn't do yourself in half the time with a lot less trouble,' said Richard, 'but it was, on the other hand, very good at being a slow and dim-witted pupil.'

Reg looked at him quizzically.

'I had no idea they were supposed to be in short supply,' he said. 'I could hit a dozen with a bread roll from where I'm sitting.'

'I'm sure. But look at it this way. What really is the point of trying to teach anything to anybody?'

This question seemed to provoke a murmur of sympathetic approval from up and down the table.

Richard continued, 'What I mean is that if you really want to understand something, the best way is to try and explain it to someone else. That forces you to sort it out in your own mind. And the more slow and dim-witted your pupil, the more you have to break things down into more and more simple ideas. And that's really the essence of programming. By the time you've sorted out a complicated idea into little steps that even a stupid machine can deal with, you've certainly learned something about it yourself. The teacher usually learns more than the pupil. Isn't that true?'

'It would be hard to learn much less than my pupils,' came a low growl from somewhere on the table, 'without undergoing a pre-frontal lobotomy.'

'So I used to spend days struggling to write essays on this 16K machine that would have taken a couple of hours on a typewriter, but what was fascinating to me was the process of trying to explain to the machine what it was I wanted it to do. I virtually wrote my own word processor in BASIC. A simple search and replace routine would take about three hours.'

'I forget, did you ever get any essays done at all?'

'Well, not as such. No actual essays, but the reasons why not were absolutely fascinating. For instance, I discovered that . . .'

He broke off, laughing at himself.

'I was also playing keyboards in a rock group, of course,' he added. 'That didn't help.'

'Now, that I didn't know,' said Reg. 'Your past has murkier things in it than I dreamed possible. A quality, I might add, that it shares with this soup.' He wiped his mouth with his napkin very carefully. 'I must go and have a word with the kitchen staff one day. I would like to be sure that they are keeping the right bits and throwing the proper bits away. So. A rock group, you say. Well, well, well. Good heavens.'

'Yes,' said Richard. 'We called ourselves The Reasonably Good Band, but in fact we weren't. Our intention was to be the Beatles of the early eighties, but we got much better financial and legal advice than the Beatles ever did, which was basically "Don't bother", so we didn't. I left Cambridge and starved for three years.'

'But didn't I bump into you during that period,' said Reg, 'and you said you were doing very well?'

'As a road sweeper, yes. There was an awful lot of mess on the roads. More than enough, I felt, to support an entire career. However, I got the sack for sweeping the mess on to another sweeper's patch.'

Reg shook his head. 'The wrong career for you, I'm sure. There are plenty of vocations where such behaviour would ensure rapid preferment.'

'I tried a few – none of them much grander, though. And I kept none of them very long, because I was always too tired to do them properly. I'd be found asleep slumped over the chicken sheds or filing cabinets – depending on what the job was. Been up all night with the computer you see, teaching it to play "Three Blind Mice". It was an important goal for me.'

'I'm sure,' agreed Reg. 'Thank you,' he said to the college servant who took his half-finished plate of soup from him, 'thank you very much. "Three Blind Mice", eh? Good. Good. So no doubt you succeeded eventually, and this accounts for your present celebrated status. Yes?'

'Well, there's a bit more to it than that.'

'I feared there might be. Pity you didn't bring it with you, though. It might have cheered up the poor young lady who is currently having our dull and crusty company forced upon her. A swift burst of "Three Blind Mice" would probably do much to revive her spirits.' He leaned forward to look past his two right-hand neighbours at the girl, who was still sitting sagging in her chair.

'Hello,' he said.

She looked up in surprise, and then dropped her eyes shyly, swinging her legs again.

'Which do you think is worse,' enquired Reg, 'the soup or the company?'

She gave a tiny, reluctant laugh and shrugged, still looking down.

'I think you're wise not to commit yourself at this stage,' continued Reg. 'Myself, I'm waiting to see the carrots before I make any judgements. They've been boiling them since the weekend, but I fear it may not be enough. The only thing that could possibly be worse than the carrots is Watkin. He's the man with the silly glasses sitting between us. My name's Reg, by the way. Come over and kick me when you have a moment.'

The girl giggled and glanced up at Watkin, who stiffened and made an appallingly unsuccessful attempt to smile good-naturedly.

'*Well*, little girl,' he said to her awkwardly, and she had desperately to suppress a hoot of laughter at his glasses. Little conversation therefore ensued, but the girl had an ally, and began to enjoy herself a tiny little bit. Her father gave her a relieved smile.

Reg turned back to Richard, who said, suddenly, 'Do you have any family?'

'Er . . . no,' said Reg, quietly. 'But tell me. After "Three Blind Mice", what then?'

'Well, to cut a long story short, Reg, I ended up working for WayForward Technologies . . .'

'Ah, yes, the famous Mr Way. Tell me, what's he like?' Richard was always faintly annoyed by this question, probably because he was asked it so often.

'Both better and worse than he's represented in the press. I like him a lot, actually. Like any driven man he can be a bit trying at times, but I've known him since the very early days of the company when neither he nor I had a bean to our names. He's fine. It's just that it's a good idea not to let him have your phone number unless you possess an industrial-grade answering machine.'

'What? Why's that?'

'Well, he's one of those people who can only think when he's talking. When he has ideas, he has to talk them out to whoever will listen. Or, if the people themselves are not available, which is increasingly the case, their answering machines will do just as well. He just phones them up and talks at them. He has one secretary whose sole job is to collect tapes from people he might have phoned, transcribe them, sort them and give him the edited text the next day in a blue folder.'

'A blue one, eh?'

'Ask me why he doesn't simply use a tape recorder,' said Richard with a shrug.

Reg considered this. 'I expect he doesn't use a tape recorder because he doesn't like talking to himself,' he said. 'There is a logic there. Of a kind.'

He took a mouthful of his newly arrived *porc au poivre* and ruminated on it for a while before gently laying his knife and fork aside again for the moment.

'So what,' he said at last, 'is the role of young MacDuff in all this?'

'Well, Gordon assigned me to write a major piece of software for the Apple Macintosh. Financial spreadsheet, accounting, that sort of thing, powerful, easy to use, lots of graphics. I asked him exactly what he wanted in it, and he just said, "Everything. I want the top piece of all-singing, all-dancing business software for that machine." And being of a slightly whimsical turn of mind I took him literally.

'You see, a pattern of numbers can represent anything you like, can be used to map any surface, or modulate any dynamic process – and so on. And any set of company accounts are, in the end, just a pattern of numbers. So I sat down and wrote a program that'll take those numbers and do what you like with them. If you just want a bar graph it'll do them as a bar graph, if you want them as a pie chart or scatter graph it'll do them as a pie chart or scatter graph. If you want dancing girls jumping out of the pie chart in order to distract attention from the figures the pie chart actually represents, then the program will do that as well. Or you can turn your figures into, for instance, a flock of seagulls, and the formation they fly in and the way in which the wings of each gull beat will be determined by the performance of each division of your company. Great for producing animated corporate logos that actually *mean* something.

'But the silliest feature of all was that if you wanted your company accounts represented as a piece of music, it could do that as well. Well, I thought it was silly. The corporate world went bananas over it.'

Reg regarded him solemnly from over a piece of carrot poised delicately on his fork in front of him, but did not interrupt.

'You see, any aspect of a piece of music can be expressed as a sequence or pattern of numbers,' enthused Richard. 'Numbers can express the pitch of notes, the length of notes, patterns of pitches and lengths . . .'

'You mean tunes,' said Reg. The carrot had not moved yet.

Richard grinned.

'Tunes would be a very good word for it. I must remember that.'

'It would help you speak more easily.' Reg returned the carrot to his plate, untasted. 'And this software did well, then?' he asked.

'Not so much here. The yearly accounts of most British companies emerged sounding like the Dead March from *Saul*, but in Japan they went for it like a pack of rats. It produced lots of cheery company anthems that started well, but if you were going to criticise you'd probably say that they tended to get a bit loud and squeaky at the end. Did spectacular business in the States, which was the main thing, commercially. Though the thing that's interesting me most now is what happens if you leave the accounts out of it. Turn the numbers that represent the way a swallow's wings beat directly into music. What would you hear? Not the sound of cash registers, according to Gordon.'

'Fascinating,' said Reg, 'quite fascinating,' and popped the carrot at last into his mouth. He turned and leaned forward to speak to his new girlfriend.

'Watkin loses,' he pronounced. 'The carrots have achieved a new all-time low. Sorry, Watkin, but awful as you are, the carrots, I'm afraid, are world-beaters.'

The girl giggled more easily than last time and she smiled at him. Watkin was trying to take all this good-naturedly, but it was clear as his eyes swam at Reg that he was more used to discomfiting than being discomfited.

'Please, Daddy, can I now?' With her new-found, if slight, confidence, the girl had also found a voice.

'Later,' insisted her father.

'This is already later. I've been timing it.'

'Well . . .' He hesitated, and was lost.

'We've been to Greece,' announced the girl in a small but awed voice.

'Ah, have you indeed,' said Watkin, with a little nod. 'Well, well. Anywhere in particular, or just Greece generally?'

'Patmos,' she said decisively. 'It was beautiful. I think Patmos is the most beautiful place in the whole world. Except the ferry never came when it said it would. Never, ever. I timed it. We missed our flight but I didn't mind.'

'Ah, Patmos, I see,' said Watkin, who was clearly roused by the news. 'Well, what you have to understand, young lady, is that the Greeks, not content with dominating the culture of the Classical world, are also responsible for the greatest, some would say the only, work of true creative imagination produced this century as well. I refer of course to the Greek ferry timetables. A work of the sublimest fiction. Anyone who has travelled in the Aegean will confirm this. Hmm, yes. I think so.'

She frowned at him.

'I found a pot,' she said.

'Probably nothing,' interrupted her father hastily. 'You

know the way it is. Everyone who goes to Greece for the first time thinks they've found a pot, don't they? Ha, ha.'

There were general nods. This was true. Irritating, but true.

'I found it in the harbour,' she said, 'in the water. While we were waiting for the damn ferry.'

'Sarah! I've told you . . .'

'It's just what you called it. And worse. You called it words I didn't think you knew. Anyway, I thought that if everyone here was meant to be so clever, then someone would be able to tell me if it was a proper ancient Greek thing or not. I think it's *very* old. Will you please let them see it, Daddy?'

Her father shrugged hopelessly and started to fish about under his chair.

'Did you know, young lady,' said Watkin to her, 'that the Book of Revelation was written on Patmos? It was indeed. By Saint John the Divine, as you know. To me it shows very clear signs of having been written while waiting for a ferry. Oh, yes, I think so. It starts off, doesn't it, with that kind of dreaminess you get when you're killing time, getting bored, you know, just making things up, and then gradually grows to a sort of climax of hallucinatory despair. I find that very suggestive. Perhaps you should write a paper on it.' He nodded at her.

She looked at him as if he were mad.

'Well, here it is,' said her father, plonking the thing down on the table. 'Just a pot, as you see. She's only six,' he added with a grim smile, 'aren't you, dear?'

'Seven,' said Sarah.

The pot was quite small, about five inches high and four inches across at its widest point. The body was almost spherical, with a very narrow neck extending about an inch above the body. The neck and about half of the surface area were encrusted with hard-caked earth, but the parts of the pot that could be seen were of a rough, ruddy texture.

Sarah took it and thrust it into the hands of the don sitting on her right.

'You look clever,' she said. 'Tell me what you think.'

The don took it, and turned it over with a slightly supercilious air. 'I'm sure if you scraped away the mud from the bottom,' he remarked wittily, 'it would probably say "Made in Birmingham".'

'That old, eh?' said Sarah's father with a forced laugh. 'Long time since anything was made there.'

'Anyway,' said the don, 'not my field, I'm a molecular biologist. Anyone else want to have a look?'

This question was not greeted with wild yelps of enthusiasm, but nevertheless the pot was passed from hand to hand around the far end of the table in a desultory fashion. It was goggled at through pebble glasses, peered at through horn-rims, gazed at over half-moons, and squinted at by someone who had left his glasses in his other suit, which he very much feared had now gone to the cleaner's. No one seemed to know how old it was, or to care very much. The young girl's face began to grow downhearted again.

'Sour lot,' said Reg to Richard. He picked up a silver salt cellar again and held it up.

'Young lady,' he said, leaning forward to address her.

'Oh, not again, you old fool,' muttered the aged archaeologist Cawley, sitting back and putting his hands over his ears.

'Young lady,' repeated Reg, 'regard this simple silver salt cellar. Regard this simple hat.'

'You haven't got a hat,' said the girl sulkily.

'Oh,' said Reg, 'a moment please,' and he went and fetched his woolly red one.

'Regard,' he said again, 'this simple silver salt cellar. Regard this simple woolly hat. I put the salt cellar in the hat, thus, and I pass the hat to you. The next part of the trick, dear lady . . . is up to you.'

He handed the hat to her, past their two intervening neighbours, Cawley and Watkin. She took the hat and looked inside it.

'Where's it gone?' she asked, staring into the hat.

'It's wherever you put it,' said Reg.

'Oh,' said Sarah, 'I see. Well . . . that wasn't very good.'

Reg shrugged. 'A humble trick, but it gives me pleasure,' he said, and turned back to Richard. 'Now, what were we talking about?'

Richard looked at him with a slight sense of shock. He knew that the Professor had always been prone to sudden and erratic mood swings, but it was as if all the warmth had drained out of him in an instant. He now wore the same distracted expression Richard had seen on his face when first he had arrived at his door that evening, apparently completely unexpected. Reg seemed then to sense that Richard was taken aback and quickly reassembled a smile.

'My dear chap!' he said. 'My dear chap! My dear, dear chap! What was I saying?'

'Er, you were saying "My dear chap".'

'Yes, but I feel sure it was a prelude to something. A sort of short toccata on the theme of what a splendid fellow you are prior to introducing the main subject of my discourse, the nature of which I currently forget. You have no idea what I was about to say?'

'No.'

'Oh. Well, I suppose I should be pleased. If everyone knew exactly what I was going to say, then there would be no point in my saying it, would there? Now, how's our young guest's pot doing?'

In fact it had reached Watkin, who pronounced himself no expert on what the ancients had made for themselves to drink out of, only on what they had written as a result. He said that Cawley was the one to whose knowledge and experience they should all bow, and attempted to give the pot to him,

'I said,' he repeated, 'yours was the knowledge and experience to which we should bow. Oh, for heaven's sake, take your hands off your ears and have a look at the thing.'

Gently, but firmly, he drew Cawley's right hand from his ear, explained the situation to him once again, and handed him the pot. Cawley gave it a cursory, but clearly expert examination.

'Yes,' he said, 'about two hundred years old, I would think. Very rough. Very crude example of its type. Utterly without value, of course.'

He put it down peremptorily and gazed off into the old minstrel gallery, which appeared to anger him for some reason.

The effect on Sarah was immediate. Already discouraged, she was thoroughly downcast by this. She bit her lip and threw herself back against her chair, feeling once again thoroughly out of place and childish. Her father gave her a warning look about misbehaving, and then apologised for her again.

'Well, Buxtehude,' he hurried on to say, 'yes, good old Buxtehude. We'll have to see what we can do. Tell me . . .'

'Young lady,' interrupted a voice, hoarse with astonishment, 'you are clearly a magician and enchantress of prodigious powers!'

All eyes turned to Reg, the old show-off. He was gripping the pot and staring at it with manic fascination. He turned his eyes slowly to the little girl, as if for the first time assessing the power of a feared adversary.

'I bow to you,' he whispered. 'I, unworthy though I am to speak in the presence of such a power as yours, beg leave to congratulate you on one of the finest feats of the conjurer's art it has been my privilege to witness!'

Sarah stared at him with widening eyes.

'May I show these people what you have wrought?' he asked earnestly.

Very faintly she nodded, and he fetched her formerly precious, but now sadly discredited, pot a sharp rap on the table.

It split into two irregular parts, the caked clay with which it was surrounded falling in jagged shards on the table. One side of the pot fell away, leaving the rest standing.

Sarah's eyes goggled at the stained and tarnished but clearly recognisable silver college salt cellar standing jammed in the remains of the pot.

'Stupid old fool,' muttered Cawley.

After the general disparagement and condemnation of this cheap parlour trick had died down – none of which could dim the awe in Sarah's eyes – Reg turned to Richard and said, idly:

'Who was that friend of yours when you were here, do you ever see him? Chap with an odd East European name. Svlad something. Svlad Cjelli. Remember the fellow?'

Richard looked at him blankly for a moment.

'Svlad?' he said. 'Oh, you mean Dirk. Dirk Cjelli. No. I never stayed in touch. I've bumped into him a couple of times in the street but that's all. I think he changes his name from time to time. Why do you ask?'

5

High on his rocky promontory the Electric Monk continued to sit on a horse which was going quietly and
uncomplainingly spare. From under its rough woven
cowl the Monk gazed unblinkingly down into the valley,
with which it was having a problem, but the problem
was a new and hideous one to the Monk, for it was this –
Doubt.

He never suffered it for long, but when he did, it
gnawed at the very root of his being.

The day was hot; the sun stood in an empty hazy sky
and beat down upon the grey rocks and the scrubby,
parched grass. Nothing moved, not even the Monk. But
strange things were beginning to fizz in its brain, as they
did from time to time when a piece of data became
misaddressed as it passed through its input buffer.

But then the Monk began to believe, fitfully and nervously at first, but then with a great searing white flame
of belief which overturned all previous beliefs, including
the stupid one about the valley being pink, that somewhere down in the valley, about a mile from where he
was sitting, there would shortly open up a mysterious
doorway into a strange and distant world, a doorway
through which he might enter. An astounding idea.

Astoundingly enough, however, on this one occasion
he was perfectly right.

The horse sensed that something was up.

It pricked up its ears and gently shook its head. It had

gone into a sort of trance looking at the same clump of rocks for so long, and was on the verge of imagining them to be pink itself. It shook its head a little harder.

A slight twitch on the reins, and a prod from the Monk's heels, and they were off, picking their way carefully down the rocky incline. The way was difficult. Much of it was loose shale – loose brown and grey shale, with the occasional brown and green plant clinging to a precarious existence on it. The Monk noticed this without embarrassment. It was an older, wiser Monk now, and had put childish things behind it. Pink valleys, hermaphrodite tables, these were all natural stages through which one had to pass on the path to true enlightenment.

The sun beat hard on them. The Monk wiped the sweat and dust off its face and paused, leaning forward on the horse's neck. It peered down through the shimmering heat haze at a large outcrop of rock which stood out on to the floor of the valley. There, behind that outcrop, was where the Monk thought, or rather passionately believed to the core of its being, the door would appear. It tried to focus more closely, but the details of the view swam confusingly in the hot rising air.

As it sat back in its saddle, and was about to prod the horse onward, it suddenly noticed a rather odd thing.

On a flattish wall of rock nearby, in fact so nearby that the Monk was surprised not to have noticed it before, was a large painting. The painting was crudely drawn, though not without a certain stylish sweep of line, and seemed very old, possibly very, very old indeed. The paint was faded, chipped and patchy, and it was difficult to discern with any clarity what the picture was. The Monk approached the picture more closely. It looked like a primitive hunting scene.

The group of purple, multi-limbed creatures were

clearly early hunters. They carried rough spears, and were in hot pursuit of a large horned and armoured creature, which appeared to have been wounded in the hunt already. The colours were now so dim as to be almost non-existent. In fact, all that could be clearly seen was the white of the hunters' teeth, which seemed to shine with a whiteness whose lustre was undimmed by the passage of what must have been many thousands of years. In fact they even put the Monk's own teeth to shame, and he had cleaned them only that morning.

The Monk had seen paintings like this before, but only in pictures or on the TV, never in real life. They were usually to be found in caves where they were protected from the elements, otherwise they would not have survived.

The Monk looked more carefully at the immediate environs of the rock wall and noticed that, though not exactly in a cave, it was nevertheless protected by a large overhang and was well sheltered from the wind and rain. Odd, though, that it should have managed to last so long. Odder still that it should appear not to have been discovered. Such cave paintings as there were were all famous and familiar images, but this was not one that he had ever seen before.

Perhaps this was a dramatic and historic find he had made. Perhaps if he were to return to the city and announce this discovery he would be welcomed back, given a new motherboard after all and allowed to believe – to believe – believe what? He paused, blinked, and shook his head to clear a momentary system error.

He pulled himself up short.

He believed in a door. He must find that door. The door was the way to . . . to . . .

The Door was The Way.

Good.

Capital letters were always the best way of dealing with things you didn't have a good answer to.

Brusquely he tugged the horse's head round and urged it onward and downward. Within a few minutes more of tricky manoeuvring they had reached the valley floor, and he was momentarily disconcerted to discover that the fine top layer of dust that had settled on the brown parched earth was indeed a very pale brownish pink, particularly on the banks of the sluggish trickle of mud which was all that remained, in the hot season, of the river that flowed through the valley when the rains came. He dismounted and bent down to feel the pink dust and run it through his fingers. It was very fine and soft and felt pleasant as he rubbed it on his skin. It was about the same colour, perhaps a little paler.

The horse was looking at him. He realised, a little belatedly perhaps, that the horse must be extremely thirsty. He was extremely thirsty himself, but had tried to keep his mind off it. He unbuckled the water flask from the saddle. It was pathetically light. He unscrewed the top and took one single swig. Then he poured a little into his cupped hand and offered it to the horse, who slurped at it greedily and briefly.

The horse looked at him again.

The Monk shook his head sadly, resealed the bottle and replaced it. He knew, in that small part of his mind where he kept factual and logical information, that it would not last much longer, and that, without it, neither would they. It was only his Belief that kept him going, currently his Belief in The Door.

He brushed the pink dust from his rough habit, and then stood looking at the rocky outcrop, a mere hundred yards distant. He looked at it not without a slight, tiny trepidation. Although the major part of his mind was firm in its eternal and unshakeable Belief that there would be a Door behind the outcrop, and that the Door would be The Way, yet the tiny part of his brain that understood about the water bottle could not help but recall past disappointments and sounded a very tiny but jarring note of caution.

If he elected not to go and see The Door for himself, then he could continue to believe in it for ever. It would be the lodestone of his life (what little was left of it, said the part of his brain that knew about the water bottle).

If on the other hand he went to pay his respects to the Door and it wasn't there . . . what then?

The horse whinnied impatiently.

The answer, of course, was very simple. He had a whole board of circuits for dealing with exactly this problem, in fact this was the very heart of his function. He would continue to believe in it whatever the facts turned out to be, what else was the meaning of Belief?

The Door would still be there, even if the door was not.

He pulled himself together. The Door would be there, and he must now go to it, because The Door was The Way.

Instead of remounting his horse, he led it. The Way was but a short way, and he should enter the presence of the Door in humility.

He walked, brave and erect, with solemn slowness. He approached the rocky outcrop. He reached it. He turned the corner. He looked.

The Door was there.

The horse, it must be said, was quite surprised.

The Monk fell to his knees in awe and bewilderment. So braced was he for dealing with the disappointment that was habitually his lot that, though he would never know to admit it, he was completely unprepared for this. He stared at The Door in sheer, blank system error.

It was a door such as he had never seen before. All the doors he knew were great steel-reinforced things, because of all the video recorders and dishwashers that were kept behind them, plus of course all the expensive Electric Monks that were needed to believe in it all. This one was simple, wooden and small, about his own size. A Monk-size door, painted white, with a single, slightly dented brass knob slightly less than halfway up one side. It was set simply in the rock face, with no explanation as to its origin or purpose.

Hardly knowing how he dared, the poor startled Monk staggered to his feet and, leading his horse, walked nervously forward towards it. He reached out and touched it. He was so startled when no alarms went off that he jumped back. He touched it again, more firmly this time.

He let his hand drop slowly to the handle – again, no alarms. He waited to be sure, and then he turned it, very, very gently. He felt a mechanism release. He held his breath. Nothing. He drew the door towards him, and it came easily. He looked inside, but the interior was so dim in contrast with the desert sun outside that he could see nothing. At last, almost dead with wonder, he entered, pulling the horse in after him.

A few minutes later, a figure that had been sitting out of sight around the next outcrop of rock finished rubbing dust on his face, stood up, stretched his limbs and made his way back towards the door, patting his clothes as he did so.

6

'In Xanadu did Kubla Khan
A stately pleasure-dome decree:'

The reader clearly belonged to the school of thought which holds that a sense of the seriousness or greatness of a poem is best imparted by reading it in a silly voice. He soared and swooped at the words until they seemed to duck and run for cover.

'Where Alph, the sacred river ran
Through caverns measureless to man
  Down to a sunless sea.'

Richard relaxed back into his seat. The words were very, very familiar to him, as they could not help but be to any English graduate of St Cedd's College, and they settled easily into his mind.

The association of the college with Coleridge was taken very seriously indeed, despite the man's well-known predilection for certain recreational pharmaceuticals under the influence of which this, his greatest work, was composed, in a dream.

The entire manuscript was lodged in the safe-keeping of the college library, and it was from this itself, on the regular occasion of the Coleridge Dinner, that the poem was read.

'So twice five miles of fertile ground
With walls and towers were girdled round:
And there were gardens bright with sinuous rills,
Where blossomed many an incense-bearing tree;

And here were forests ancient as the hills,
Enfolding sunny spots of greenery.'

Richard wondered how long it took. He glanced sideways at his former Director of Studies and was disturbed
by the sturdy purposefulness of his reading posture. The
singsong voice irritated him at first, but after a while it
began to lull him instead, and he watched a rivulet of
wax seeping over the edge of a candle that was burning
low now and throwing a guttering light over the carnage
of dinner.

'But oh! that deep romantic chasm which slanted
Down the green hill athwart a cedarn cover!
A savage place! as holy and enchanted
As e'er beneath a waning moon was haunted
By woman wailing for her demon-lover!'

The small quantities of claret that he had allowed
himself during the course of the meal seeped warmly
through his veins, and soon his own mind began to
wander, and provoked by Reg's question earlier in the
meal, he wondered what had lately become of his former ... was friend the word? He seemed more like a
succession of extraordinary events than a person. The
idea of him actually having friends as such seemed not
so much unlikely, more a sort of mismatching of concepts,
like the idea of the Suez crisis popping out for a bun.

Svlad Cjelli. Popularly known as Dirk, though, again,
'popular' was hardly right. Notorious, certainly; sought
after, endlessly speculated about, those too were true.
But popular? Only in the sense that a serious accident
on the motorway might be popular – everyone slows
down to have a good look, but no one will get too close
to the flames. Infamous was more like it, Svlad Cjelli,
infamously known as Dirk.

...an the average undergraduate and
...at is to say, there was just the one
...ually wore, but he wore it with a
...are in one so young. The hat was
...and, with a very flat brim, and it
...e as if balanced on gimbals, which
...ct horizontality at all times, however
... his head. As a hat it was a remarkable
rather than ... rely successful piece of personal decor-
ation. It would make an elegant adornment, stylish,
shapely and flattering, if the wearer were a small bedside lamp, but not otherwise.

People gravitated around him, drawn in by the stories
he denied about himself, but what the source of these
stories might be, if not his own denials, was never
entirely clear.

The tales had to do with the psychic powers that he'd
supposedly inherited from his mother's side of the family who, he claimed, had lived at the smarter end of
Transylvania. That is to say, he didn't make any such
claim at all, and said it was the most absurd nonsense.
He strenuously denied that there were bats of any kind
at all in his family and threatened to sue anybody who
put about such malicious fabrications, but he affected
nevertheless to wear a large and flappy leather coat, and
had one of those machines in his room which are supposed to help cure bad backs if you hang upside down
from them. He would allow people to discover him
hanging from this machine at all kinds of odd hours of
the day, and more particularly of the night, expressly so
that he could vigorously deny that it had any significance whatsoever.

By means of an ingenious series of strategically
deployed denials of the most exciting and exotic things,
he was able to create the myth that he was a psychic,

mystic, telepathic, fey, clairvoyant, psychosassic vampire bat.

What did 'psychosassic' mean?

It was his own word and he vigorously denied that it meant anything at all.

'And from this chasm, with ceaseless turmoil
      seething,
As if this earth in fast thick pants were breathing,
A mighty fountain momently was forced:
Amid whose swift half-intermitted burst
Huge fragments vaulted . . .'

Dirk had also been perpetually broke. This would change.

It was his room-mate who started it, a credulous fellow called Mander, who, if the truth were known, had probably been specially selected by Dirk for his credulity.

Steve Mander noticed that if ever Dirk went to bed drunk he would talk in his sleep. Not only that, but the sort of things he would say in his sleep would be things like, 'The opening up of trade routes to the mumble mumble burble was the turning point for the growth of empire in the snore footle mumble. Discuss.'

'. . . like rebounding hail,
Or chaffy grain beneath the thresher's flail:'

The first time this happened Steve Mander sat bolt upright in bed. This was shortly before prelim exams in the second year, and what Dirk had just said, or judiciously mumbled, sounded remarkably like a very likely question in the Economic History paper.

Mander quietly got up, crossed over to Dirk's bed and listened very hard, but other than a few completely disconnected mumblings about Schleswig–Holstein and the Franco–Prussian war, the latter being largely directed by Dirk into his pillow, he learned nothing more.

News, however, spread – quietly, discreetly, and like wildfire.

> 'And 'mid these dancing rocks at once and ever
> It flung up momently the sacred river.'

For the next month Dirk found himself being constantly wined and dined in the hope that he would sleep very soundly that night and dream-speak a few more exam questions. Remarkably, it seemed that the better he was fed, and the finer the vintage of the wine he was given to drink, the less he would tend to sleep facing directly into his pillow.

His scheme, therefore, was to exploit his alleged gifts without ever actually claiming to have them. In fact he would react to stories about his supposed powers with open incredulity, even hostility.

> 'Five miles meandering with a mazy motion
> Through wood and dale the sacred river ran,
> Then reached the caverns measureless to man,
> And sank in tumult to a lifeless ocean:
> And 'mid this tumult Kubla heard from far
> Ancestral voices prophesying war!'

Dirk was also, he denied, a clairaudient. He would sometimes hum tunes in his sleep that two weeks later would turn out to be a hit for someone. Not too difficult to organise, really.

In fact, he had always done the bare minimum of research necessary to support these myths. He was lazy, and essentially what he did was allow people's enthusiastic credulity to do the work for him. The laziness was essential – if his supposed feats of the paranormal had been detailed and accurate, then people might have been suspicious and looked for other explanations. On the other hand, the more vague and ambiguous his 'predictions', the more other people's own wishful thinking would close the credibility gap.

Dirk never made much out of it – at least, he appeared not to. In fact, the benefit to himself, as a student, of being continually wined and dined at other people's expense was more considerable than anyone would expect unless they sat down and worked out the figures.

And, of course, he never claimed – in fact, he actively denied – that any of it was even remotely true.

He was therefore well placed to execute a very nice and tasty little scam come the time of finals.

> 'The shadow of the dome of pleasure
> Floated midway on the waves;
> Where was heard the mingled measure
> From the fountain and the caves.
> It was a miracle of rare device,
> A sunny pleasure-dome with caves of ice!'

'Good heavens . . . !' Reg suddenly seemed to awake with a start from the light doze into which he had gently slipped under the influence of the wine and the reading, and glanced about himself with blank surprise, but nothing had changed. Coleridge's words sang through a warm and contented silence that had settled on the great hall. After another quick frown, Reg settled back into another doze, but this time a slightly more attentive one.

> 'A damsel with a dulcimer
> In a vision once I saw:
> It was an Abyssinian maid,
> And on her dulcimer she played,
> Singing of Mount Abora.'

Dirk allowed himself to be persuaded to make, under hypnosis, a firm prediction about what questions would be set for examination that summer.

He himself first planted the idea by explaining exactly the sort of thing that he would never, under any circumstances, be prepared to do, though in many ways he would like to, just to have the chance to disprove his alleged and strongly disavowed abilities.

And it was on these grounds, carefully prepared, that he eventually agreed – only because it would once and for all scotch the whole silly – immensely, tediously silly – business. He would make his predictions by means of automatic writing under proper supervision, and they would then be sealed in an envelope and deposited at the bank until after the exams.

Then they would be opened to see how accurate they had been *after* the exams.

He was, not surprisingly, offered some pretty hefty bribes from a pretty hefty number of people to let them see the predictions he had written down, but he was absolutely shocked by the idea. That, he said, would be *dishonest* . . .

> 'Could I revive within me
> Her symphony and song,
> To such a deep delight 'twould win me,
> That with music loud and long,
> I would build that dome in air,
> That sunny dome! Those caves of ice!'

Then, a short time later, Dirk allowed himself to be seen around town wearing something of a vexed and solemn expression. At first he waved aside enquiries as to what it was that was bothering him, but eventually he let slip that his mother was going to have to undergo some extremely expensive dental work which, for reasons that he refused to discuss, would have to be done privately, only there wasn't the money.

From here, the path downward to accepting donations for his mother's supposed medical expenses in return for quick glances at his written exam predictions proved to be sufficiently steep and well-oiled for him to be able to slip down it with a minimum of fuss.

Then it further transpired that the only dentist who could perform this mysterious dental operation was an East European surgeon now living in Malibu, and it was in consequence necessary to increase the level of donations rather sharply.

He still denied, of course, that his abilities were all that they were cracked up to be, in fact he denied that they existed at all, and insisted that he would never have embarked on the exercise at all if it wasn't to disprove the whole thing – and also, since other people seemed, at their own risk, to have a faith in his abilities that he himself did not, he was happy to indulge them to the extent of letting them pay for his sainted mother's operation.

He could only emerge well from this situation.

Or so he thought.

> 'And all who heard should see them there,
> And all should cry, Beware! Beware!
> His flashing eyes, his floating hair!'

The exam papers Dirk produced under hypnosis, by means of automatic writing, he had, in fact, pieced together simply by doing the same minimum research that any student taking exams would do, studying previous exam papers and seeing what, if any, patterns emerged, and making intelligent guesses about what might come up. He was pretty sure of getting (as anyone would be) a strike rate that was sufficiently high to satisfy the credulous, and sufficiently low for the whole exercise to look perfectly innocent.

As indeed it was.

What completely blew him out of the water, and caused a furore which ended with him being driven out of Cambridge in the back of a Black Maria, was the fact that all the exam papers he sold turned out to be the same as the papers that were actually set.

Exactly. Word for word. To the very comma.

> 'Wave a circle round him thrice,
> And close your eyes with holy dread,
> For he on honey-dew hath fed,
> And drunk the milk of Paradise . . .'

And that, apart from a flurry of sensational newspaper reports which exposed him as a fraud, then trumpeted him as the real thing so that they could have another round of exposing him as a fraud again and then trumpeting him as the real thing again, until they got bored and found a nice juicy snooker player to harass instead, was that.

In the years since then, Richard had run into Dirk from time to time and had usually been greeted with that kind of guarded half smile that wants to know if you think it owes you money before it blossoms into one that hopes you will lend it some. Dirk's regular name changes suggested to Richard that he wasn't alone in being treated like this.

He felt a tug of sadness that someone who had seemed so shiningly alive within the small confines of a university community should have seemed to fade so much in the light of common day. And he wondered at Reg's asking after him like that, suddenly and out of the blue, in what seemed altogether too airy and casual a manner.

He glanced around him again, at his lightly snoring

neighbour, Reg; at little Sarah rapt in silent attention; at the deep hall swathed in darkly glimmering light; at the portraits of old prime ministers and poets hung high in the darkness with just the odd glint of candlelight gleaming off their teeth; at the Director of English Studies standing reading in his poetry-reading voice; at the book of 'Kubla Khan' that the Director of English Studies held in his hand; and finally, surreptitiously, at his watch. He settled back again.

The voice continued, reading the second, and altogether stranger part of the poem . . .

7

This was the evening of the last day of Gordon Way's life, and he was wondering if the rain would hold off for the weekend. The forecast had said changeable – a misty night tonight followed by bright but chilly days on Friday and Saturday with maybe a few scattered showers towards the end of Sunday when everyone would be heading back into town.

Everyone, that is, other than Gordon Way.

The weather forecast hadn't mentioned that, of course, that wasn't the job of the weather forecast, but then his horoscope had been pretty misleading as well. It had mentioned an unusual amount of planetary activity in his sign and had urged him to differentiate between what he thought he wanted and what he actually needed, and suggested that he should tackle emotional or work problems with determination and complete honesty, but had inexplicably failed to mention that he would be dead before the day was out.

He turned off the motorway near Cambridge and stopped at a small filling station for some petrol, where he sat for a moment, finishing off a call on his car phone.

'OK, look, I'll call you tomorrow,' he said, 'or maybe later tonight. Or call me. I should be at the cottage in half an hour. Yes, I know how important the project is to you. All right, I know how important it is, full stop. You want it, I want it. Of course I do. And I'm not saying that we won't continue to support it. I'm just saying it's expensive and we should look at the whole thing with determination and complete honesty. Look, why don't you come out to the cottage, and we can talk it through. OK, yeah, yes, I know. I understand. Well, think about it, Kate. Talk to you, later. Bye.'

He hung up and continued to sit in his car for a moment.

It was a large car. It was a large silver-grey Mercedes of the sort that they use in advertisements, and not just advertisements for Mercedes. Gordon Way, brother of Susan, employer of Richard MacDuff, was a rich man, the founder and owner of WayForward Technologies II. WayForward Technologies itself had of course gone bust, for the usual reason, taking his entire first fortune with it.

Luckily, he had managed to make another one.

The 'usual reason' was that he had been in the business of computer hardware when every twelve-year-old in the country had suddenly got bored with boxes that went bing. His second fortune had been made in software instead. As a result of two major pieces of software, one of which was *Anthem* (the other, more profitable one had never seen the light of day), WFT-II was the only British software company that could be mentioned in the same sentence as such major U.S. companies as Microsoft or Lotus. The sentence would probably run along the lines of 'WayForward Technologies, unlike such major U.S. companies as Microsoft or Lotus . . .' but it was a start. WayForward was in there. And he owned it.

He pushed a tape into the slot on the stereo console. It accepted it with a soft and decorous click, and a moment or two later Ravel's *Boléro* floated out of eight perfectly matched speakers with fine-meshed matte-black grilles. The stereo was so smooth and spacious you could almost sense the whole ice-rink. He tapped his fingers lightly on the padded rim of the steering wheel. He gazed at the dashboard. Tasteful illuminated figures and tiny, immaculate lights gazed dimly back at him. After a while he suddenly realised this was a self-service station and got out to fill the tank.

This took a minute or two. He stood gripping the filler nozzle, stamping his feet in the cold night air, then walked over to the small grubby kiosk, paid for the petrol, remembered to buy a couple of local maps, and then stood chatting enthusiastically to the cashier for a few minutes about the directions the computer industry was likely to take in the following year, suggesting that par-allel processing was going to be the key to really intuitive productivity software, but also strongly doubting whether artificial intelligence research *per se*, particularly artificial intelligence research based on the ProLog language, was really going to produce any serious commercially viable products in the foreseeable future, at least as far as the office desk top environment was concerned, a topic that fascinated the cashier not at all.

'The man just liked to talk,' he would later tell the police. 'Man, I could have walked away to the toilet for ten minutes and he would've told it all to the till. If I'd been fifteen minutes the till would have walked away too. Yeah, I'm sure that's him,' he would add when shown a picture of Gordon Way. 'I only wasn't sure at first because in the picture he's got his mouth closed.'

'And you're absolutely certain you didn't see anything else suspicious?' the policeman insisted. 'Nothing that struck you as odd in any way at all?'

'No, like I said, it was just an ordinary customer on an ordinary night, just like any other night.'

The policeman stared at him blankly. 'Just for the sake of argument,' he went on to say, 'if I were suddenly to do this . . .' – he made himself go cross-eyed, stuck his tongue out of the corner of his mouth and danced up and down twisting his fingers in his ears – 'would anything strike you about that?'

'Well, er, yeah,' said the cashier, backing away nervously. 'I'd think you'd gone stark raving mad.'

'Good,' said the policeman, putting his notebook away. 'It's just that different people sometimes have a different idea of what "odd" means, you see, sir. If last night was an ordinary night just like any other night, then I am a pimple on the bottom of the Marquess of Queensbury's aunt. We shall be requiring a statement later, sir. Thank you for your time.'

That was all yet to come.

Tonight, Gordon pushed the maps in his pocket and strolled back towards his car. Standing under the lights in the mist it had gathered a finely beaded coat of matte moisture on it, and looked like – well, it looked like an extremely expensive Mercedes-Benz. Gordon caught himself, just for a millisecond, wishing that he had something like that, but he was now quite adept at fending off that particular line of thought, which only led off in circles and left him feeling depressed and confused.

He patted it in a proprietorial manner, then, walking around it, noticed that the boot wasn't closed properly and pushed it shut. It closed with a good healthy clunk. Well, that made it all worth it, didn't it? Good healthy clunk like that. Old-fashioned values of quality and workmanship. He thought of a dozen things he had to talk to Susan about and climbed back into the car, pushing the auto-dial code on his phone as soon as the car was prowling back on to the road.

'. . . so if you'd like to leave a message, I'll get back to you as soon as possible. Maybe.'

Beep.

'Oh, Susan, hi, it's Gordon,' he said, cradling the phone awkwardly on his shoulder. 'Just on my way to the cottage. It's, er, Thursday night, and it's, er . . . 8.47. Bit misty on the roads. Listen, I have those people from the States coming over this weekend to thrash out the distribution on *Anthem* Version 2.00, handling the promotion, all that stuff, and look, you know I don't like to ask you this sort of thing, but you know I always do anyway, so here it is.

'I just need to know that Richard is on the case. I mean *really* on the case. I can ask him, and he says, Oh sure, it's fine, but half the time – shit, that lorry had bright lights, none of these bastard lorry drivers ever dips them properly, it's a wonder I don't end up dead in the ditch, that would be something, wouldn't it, leaving your famous last words on somebody's answering machine, there's no reason why these lorries shouldn't have automatic light-activated dipper switches. Look, can you make a note for me to tell Susan – not you, of course, secretary Susan at the office – to tell her to send a letter from me to that fellow at the Department of the Environment saying we can provide the technology if he can provide the legislation? It's for the public good, and anyway he owes me a favour plus what's the point in having a CBE if you can't kick a little ass? You can tell I've been talking to Americans all week.

'That reminds me, God, I hope I remembered to pack the shotguns. What is it with these Americans that they're always so mad to shoot my rabbits? I bought them some maps in the hope that I can persuade them to go on long healthy walks and take their minds off shooting rabbits. I really feel quite sorry for the creatures. I think I should put one of those signs on my lawn when the Americans are coming, you know, like they have in Beverly Hills, saying "Armed Response".

'Make a note to Susan, would you please, to get an "Armed Response" sign made up with a sharp spike on the bottom at the right height for rabbits to see. That's secretary Susan at the office, not you, of course.

'Where was I?

'Oh yes. Richard and *Anthem* 2.00. Susan, that thing has got to be in beta testing in two weeks. He tells me it's fine. But every time I see him he's got a picture of a sofa spinning on his computer screen. He says it's an important concept, but all I see is furniture. People who want their company accounts to sing to them do not want to buy a revolving sofa. Nor do I think he should be turning the erosion patterns of the Himalayas into a flute quintet at this time.

'And as for what Kate's up to, Susan, well, I can't hide the fact that I get anxious at the salaries and computer time it's eating up. Important long-term research and development it might be, but there is also the possibility, only a possibility, I'm saying, but nevertheless a possibility which I think we owe it to ourselves fully to evaluate and explore, which is that it's a lemon. That's odd, there's a noise coming from the boot, I thought I'd just closed it properly.

'Anyway, the main thing's Richard. And the point is that there's only one person who's really in a position to know if he's getting the important work done, or if he's just dreaming, and that one person is, I'm afraid, Susan.

'That's you, I mean, of course, not secretary Susan at the office.

'So can you, I don't like to ask you this, I really don't, can you really get on his case? Make him see how important it is? Just make sure he realises that Way-Forward Technologies is meant to be an expanding commercial business, not an adventure playground for crunch-heads. That's the problem with crunch-heads –

they have one great idea that actually works and then they expect you to carry on funding them for years while they sit and calculate the topographies of their navels. I'm sorry. I'm going to have to stop and close the boot properly. Won't be a moment.'

He put the telephone down on the seat beside him, pulled over on to the grass verge, and got out. As he went to the boot, it opened, a figure rose out of it, shot him through the chest with both barrels of a shotgun and then went about its business.

Gordon Way's astonishment at being suddenly shot dead was nothing to his astonishment at what happened next.

8

'Come in, dear fellow, come in.'

The door to Reg's set of rooms in college was up a winding set of wooden stairs in the corner of Second Court, and was not well lit, or rather it was perfectly well lit when the light was working, but the light was not working, so the door was not well lit and was, furthermore, locked. Reg was having difficulty in finding the key from a collection which looked like something that a fit Ninja warrior could hurl through the trunk of a tree.

Rooms in the older parts of the college have double doors, like airlocks, and like airlocks they are fiddly to open. The outer door is a sturdy slab of grey painted oak, with no features other than a very narrow slit for letters, and a Yale lock, to which suddenly Reg at last found the key.

He unlocked it and pulled it open. Behind it lay an ordinary white-panelled door with an ordinary brass doorknob.

'Come in, come in,' repeated Reg, opening this and fumbling for the light switch. For a moment only the dying embers of a fire in the stone grate threw ghostly red shadows dancing around the room, but then electric light flooded it and extinguished the magic. Reg hesitated on the threshold for a moment, oddly tense, as if wishing to be sure of something before he entered, then bustled in with at least the appearance of cheeriness.

It was a large panelled room, which a collection of gently shabby furniture contrived to fill quite comfortably. Against the far wall stood a large and battered old mahogany table with fat ugly legs, which was laden with books, files, folders and teetering piles of papers. Standing in its own space on the desk, Richard was amused to note, was actually a battered old abacus.

There was a small Regency writing desk standing nearby which might have been quite valuable had it not been knocked about so much, also a couple of elegant Georgian chairs, a portentous Victorian bookcase, and so on. It was, in short, a don's room. It had a don's framed maps and prints on the walls, a threadbare and faded don's carpet on the floor, and it looked as if little had changed in it for decades, which was probably the case because a don lived in it.

Two doors led out from either end of the opposite wall, and Richard knew from previous visits that one led to a study which looked much like a smaller and more intense version of this room – larger clumps of books, taller piles of paper in more imminent danger of actually falling, furniture which, however old and valuable, was heavily marked with myriad rings of hot tea or coffee cups, on many of which the original cups themselves were probably still standing.

The other door led to a small and rather basically equipped kitchen, and a twisty internal staircase at the top of which lay the Professor's bedroom and bathroom.

'Try and make yourself comfortable on the sofa,' invited Reg, fussing around hospitably. 'I don't know if you'll manage it. It always feels to me as if it's been stuffed with cabbage leaves and cutlery.' He peered at Richard seriously. 'Do you have a good sofa?' he enquired.

'Well, yes.' Richard laughed. He was cheered by the silliness of the question.

'Oh,' said Reg solemnly. 'Well, I wish you'd tell me where you got it. I have endless trouble with them, quite endless. Never found a comfortable one in all my life. How do you find yours?' He encountered, with a slight air of surprise, a small silver tray he had left out with a decanter of port and three glasses.

'Well, it's odd you should ask that,' said Richard. 'I've never sat on it.'

'Very wise,' insisted Reg earnestly, 'very, very wise.' He went through a palaver similar to his previous one with his coat and hat.

'Not that I wouldn't like to,' said Richard. 'It's just that it's stuck halfway up a long flight of stairs which leads up into my flat. As far as I can make it out, the delivery men got it part way up the stairs, got it stuck, turned it around any way they could, couldn't get it any further, and then found, curiously enough, that they couldn't get it back down again. Now, that should be impossible.'

'Odd,' agreed Reg. 'I've certainly never come across any irreversible mathematics involving sofas. Could be a new field. Have you spoken to any spatial geometricians?'

'I did better than that. I called in a neighbour's kid who used to be able to solve Rubik's cube in seventeen seconds. He sat on a step and stared at it for over an hour before pronouncing it irrevocably stuck. Admittedly he's a few years older now and has found out about girls, but it's got me puzzled.'

'Carry on talking, my dear fellow, I'm most interested, but let me know first if there's anything I can get you. Port perhaps? Or brandy? The port I think is the better bet, laid down by the college in 1934, one of the finest vintages I think you'll find, and on the other hand I don't actually have any brandy. Or coffee? Some more wine perhaps? There's an excellent Margaux I've been looking for an excuse to open, though it should of course be allowed to stand open for an hour or two, which is not to say that I couldn't ... no,' he said hurriedly, 'probably best not to go for the Margaux tonight.'

'Tea is what I would really like,' said Richard, 'if you have some.'

Reg raised his eyebrows. 'Are you sure?'

'I have to drive home.'

'Indeed. Then I shall be a moment or two in the kitchen. Please carry on, I shall still be able to hear you. Continue to tell me of your sofa, and do feel free in the meantime to sit on mine. Has it been stuck there for long?'

'Oh, only about three weeks,' said Richard, sitting down. 'I could just saw it up and throw it away, but I can't believe that there isn't a logical answer. And it also made me think – it would be really useful to know before you buy a piece of furniture whether it's actually going to fit up the stairs or around the corner. So I've modelled the problem in three dimensions on my computer – and so far it just says no way.'

'It says what?' called Reg, over the noise of filling the kettle.

'That it can't be done. I told it to compute the moves necessary to get the sofa out, and it said there aren't any. I said "What?" and it said there aren't any. I then asked it, and this is the really mysterious thing, to compute the moves necessary to get the sofa into its present position in the first place, and it said that it couldn't have got there. Not without fundamental restructuring of the walls. So, either there's something wrong with the fundamental structure of the matter in my walls or,' he added with a sigh, 'there's something wrong with the program. Which would you guess?'

'And are you married?' called Reg.

'What? Oh, I see what you mean. A sofa stuck on the stairs for a month. Well, no, not married as such, but yes, there is a specific girl that I'm not married to.'

'What's she like? What does she do?'

'She's a professional cellist. I have to admit that the sofa has been a bit of a talking point. In fact she's moved back to her own flat until I get it sorted out. She, well . . .'

He was suddenly sad, and he stood up and wandered around the room in a desultory sort of way and ended up in front of the dying fire. He gave it a bit of a poke and threw on a couple of extra logs to try and ward off the chill of the room.

'She's Gordon's sister, in fact,' he added at last. 'But they are very different. I'm not sure she really approves of computers very much. And she doesn't much like his attitude to money. I don't think I entirely blame her, actually, and she doesn't know the half of it.'

'Which is the half she doesn't know?'

Richard sighed.

'Well,' he said, 'it's to do with the project which first made the software incarnation of the company profitable. It was called *Reason*, and in its own way it was sensational.'

'What was it?'

'Well, it was a kind of back-to-front program. It's funny how many of the best ideas are just an old idea back-to-front. You see there have already been several programs written that help you to arrive at decisions by properly ordering and analysing all the relevant facts so that they then point naturally towards the right decision.

The drawback with these is that the decision which all the properly ordered and analysed facts point to is not necessarily the one you want.'

'Yeeeess . . .' said Reg's voice from the kitchen.

'Well, Gordon's great insight was to design a program which allowed you to specify in advance what decision you wished it to reach, and only then to give it all the facts. The program's task, which it was able to accomplish with consummate ease, was simply to construct a plausible series of logical-sounding steps to connect the premises with the conclusion.

'And I have to say that it worked brilliantly. Gordon was able to buy himself a Porsche almost immediately despite being completely broke and a hopeless driver. Even his bank manager was unable to find fault with his reasoning. Even when Gordon wrote it off three weeks later.'

'Heavens. And did the program sell very well?'

'No. We never sold a single copy.'

'You astonish me. It sounds like a real winner to me.'

'It was,' said Richard hesitantly. 'The entire project was bought up, lock, stock and barrel, by the Pentagon. The deal put WayForward on a very sound financial foundation. Its moral foundation, on the other hand, is not something I would want to trust my weight to. I've recently been analysing a lot of the arguments put forward in favour of the Star Wars project, and if you know what you're looking for, the pattern of the algorithms is very clear.

'So much so, in fact, that looking at Pentagon policies over the last couple of years I think I can be fairly sure that the US Navy is using version 2.00 of the program, while the Air Force for some reason only has the beta-test version of 1.5. Odd, that.'

'Do you have a copy?'

'Certainly not,' said Richard, 'I wouldn't have anything to do with it. Anyway, when the Pentagon bought everything, they bought everything. Every scrap of code, every disk, every notebook. I was glad to see the back of it. If indeed we have. I just busy myself with my own projects.'

He poked at the fire again and wondered what he was doing here when he had so much work on. Gordon was on at him continually about getting the new, super version of *Anthem* ready for taking advantage of the Macintosh II, and he was well behind with it. And as for the proposed module for converting incoming Dow Jones stock-market information into MIDI data in real time, he'd only meant that as a joke, but Gordon, of course, had flipped over the idea and insisted on its being implemented. That too was meant to be ready but wasn't. He suddenly knew exactly why it was he was here.

Well, it had been a pleasant evening, even if he couldn't see why Reg had been quite so keen to see him. He picked up a couple of books from the table. The table obviously doubled as a dining table, because although the piles looked as if they had been there for weeks, the absence of dust immediately around them showed that they had been moved recently.

Maybe, he thought, the need for amiable chit-chat with someone different can become as urgent as any other need when you live in a community as enclosed as a Cambridge college was, even nowadays. He was a likeable old fellow, but it was clear from dinner that many of his colleagues found his eccentricities formed rather a rich sustained diet – particularly when they had so many of their own to contend with. A thought about Susan nagged him, but he was used to that. He flipped through the two books he'd picked up.

One of them, an elderly one, was an account of the hauntings of Borley Rectory, the most haunted house in England. Its spine was getting raggedy, and the photographic plates were so grey and blurry as to be virtually indistinguishable. A picture he thought must be a very lucky (or faked) shot of a ghostly apparition turned out, when he examined the caption, to be a portrait of the author.

The other book was more recent, and by an odd coincidence was a guide to the Greek islands. He thumbed through it idly and a piece of paper fell out.

'Earl Grey or Lapsang Souchong?' called out Reg. 'Or Darjeeling? Or PG Tips? It's all tea bags anyway, I'm afraid. And none of them very fresh.'

'Darjeeling will do fine,' replied Richard, stooping to pick up the piece of paper.

'Milk?' called Reg.

'Er, please.'

'One lump or two?'

'One, please.'

Richard slipped the paper back into the book, noticing as he did so that it had a hurriedly scribbled note on it. The note said, oddly enough, 'Regard this simple silver salt cellar. Regard this simple hat.'

'Sugar?'

'Er, what?' said Richard, startled. He put the book hurriedly back on the pile.

'Just a tiny joke of mine,' said Reg cheerily, 'to see if people are listening.' He emerged beaming from the kitchen carrying a small tray with two cups on it, which he hurled suddenly to the floor. The tea splashed over the carpet. One of the cups shattered and the other bounced under the table. Reg leaned against the door frame, white-faced and staring.

A frozen instant of time slid silently by while Richard

was too startled to react, then he leaped awkwardly forward to help. But the old man was already apologising and offering to make him another cup. Richard helped him to the sofa.

'Are you all right?' asked Richard helplessly. 'Shall I get a doctor?'

Reg waved him down. 'It's all right,' he insisted, 'I'm perfectly well. Thought I heard, well, a noise that startled me. But it was nothing. Just overcome with the tea fumes, I expect. Let me just catch my breath. I think a little, er, port will revive me excellently. So sorry, I didn't mean to startle you.' He waved in the general direction of the port decanter. Richard hurriedly poured a small glass and gave it to him.

'What kind of noise?' he asked, wondering what on earth could shock him so much.

At that moment came the sound of movement upstairs and an extraordinary kind of heavy breathing noise.

'That . . .' whispered Reg. The glass of port lay shattered at his feet. Upstairs someone seemed to be stamping. 'Did you hear it?'

'Well, yes.'

This seemed to relieve the old man.

Richard looked nervously up at the ceiling. 'Is there someone up there?' he asked, feeling this was a lame question, but one that had to be asked.

'No,' said Reg in a low voice that shocked Richard with the fear it carried, 'no one. Nobody that should be there.'

'Then . . .'

Reg was struggling shakily to his feet, but there was suddenly a fierce determination about him.

'I must go up there,' he said quietly. 'I must. Please wait for me here.'

'Look, what is this?' demanded Richard, standing

between Reg and the doorway. 'What is it, a burglar? Look, I'll go. I'm sure it's nothing, it's just the wind or something.' Richard didn't know why he was saying this. It clearly wasn't the wind, or even anything like the wind, because though the wind might conceivably make heavy breathing noises, it rarely stamped its feet in that way.

'No,' the old man said, politely but firmly moving him aside, 'it is for me to do.'

Richard followed him helplessly through the door into the small hallway, beyond which lay the tiny kitchen. A dark wooden staircase led up from here; the steps seemed damaged and scuffed.

Reg turned on a light. It was a dim one that hung naked at the top of the stairwell, and he looked up it with grim apprehension.

'Wait here,' he said, and walked up two steps. He then turned and faced Richard with a look of the most profound seriousness on his face.

'I am sorry,' he said, 'that you have become involved in what is . . . the more difficult side of my life. But you are involved now, regrettable though that may be, and there is something I must ask you. I do not know what awaits me up there, do not know exactly. I do not know if it is something which I have foolishly brought upon myself with my . . . my hobbies, or if it is something to which I have fallen an innocent victim. If it is the former, then I have only myself to blame, for I am like a doctor who cannot give up smoking, or perhaps worse still, like an ecologist who cannot give up his car – if the latter, then I hope it may not happen to you.

'What I must ask you is this. When I come back down these stairs, always supposing of course that I do, then if my behaviour strikes you as being in any way odd, if I appear not to be myself, then you must leap on me and wrestle me to the ground. Do you understand? You must prevent me from doing anything I may try to do.'

'But how will I know?' asked an incredulous Richard. 'Sorry, I don't mean it to sound like that, but I don't know what . . . ?'

'You will know,' said Reg. 'Now please wait for me in the main room. And close the door.'

Shaking his head in bewilderment, Richard stepped back and did as he was asked. From inside the large untidy room he listened to the sound of the Professor's tread mounting the stairs one at a time.

He mounted them with a heavy deliberation, like the ticking of a great, slow clock.

Richard heard him reach the top landing. There he paused in silence. Seconds went by, five, maybe ten, maybe twenty. Then came again the heavy movement and breath that had first so harrowed the Professor.

Richard moved quickly to the door but did not open it. The chill of the room oppressed and disturbed him. He shook his head to try and shake off the feeling, and then held his breath as the footsteps started once again slowly to traverse the two yards of the landing and to pause there again.

After only a few seconds, this time Richard heard the long slow squeak of a door being opened inch by inch, inch by cautious inch, until it must surely now at last be standing wide agape.

Nothing further seemed to happen for a long, long time.

Then at last the door closed once again, slowly.

The footsteps crossed the landing and paused again. Richard backed a few slight paces from the door, staring fixedly at it. Once more the footsteps started to descend the stairs, slowly, deliberately and quietly, until at last they reached the bottom. Then after a few seconds more the door handle began to rotate. The door opened and Reg walked calmly in.

'It's all right, it's just a horse in the bathroom,' he said quietly.

Richard leaped on him and wrestled him to the ground.

'No,' gasped Reg, 'no, get off me, let me go, I'm perfectly all right, damn it. It's just a horse, a perfectly ordinary horse.' He shook Richard off with no great difficulty and sat up, puffing and blowing and pushing his hands through his limited hair. Richard stood over him warily, but with great and mounting embarrassment. He edged back, and let Reg stand up and sit on a chair.

'Just a horse,' said Reg, 'but, er, thank you for taking me at my word.' He brushed himself down.

'A horse,' repeated Richard.

'Yes,' said Reg.

Richard went out and looked up the stairs and then came back in.

'A *horse*?' he said again.

'Yes, it is,' said the Professor. 'Wait' – he motioned to Richard, who was about to go out again and investigate – 'let it be. It won't be long.'

Richard stared in disbelief. 'You say there's a horse in your bathroom, and all you can do is stand there naming Beatles songs?'

The Professor looked blankly at him.

'Listen,' he said, 'I'm sorry if I . . . alarmed you earlier, it was just a slight turn. These things happen, my dear fellow, don't upset yourself about it. Dear me, I've known odder things in my time. Many of them. Far odder. She's only a horse, for heaven's sake. I'll go and let her out later. Please don't concern yourself. Let us revive our spirits with some port.'

'But . . . how did it get in there?'

'Well, the bathroom window's open. I expect she came in through that.'

Richard looked at him, not for the first and certainly not for the last time, through eyes that were narrowed with suspicion.

'You're doing it deliberately, aren't you?' he said.

'Doing what, my dear fellow?'

'I don't believe there's a horse in your bathroom,' said Richard suddenly. 'I don't know what is there, I don't know what you're doing, I don't know what any of this evening means, but I don't believe there's a horse in your bathroom.' And brushing aside Reg's further prot- estations he went up to look.

The bathroom was not large.

The walls were panelled in old oak linenfold which, given the age and nature of the building, was quite probably priceless, but otherwise the fittings were stark and institutional.

There was old, scuffed, black-and-white checked lino- leum on the floor, a small basic bath, well cleaned but with very elderly stains and chips in the enamel, and also a small basic basin with a toothbrush and toothpaste in a Duralex beaker standing next to the taps. Screwed into the probably priceless panelling above the basin was a tin mirror-fronted bathroom cabinet. It looked as if it had been repainted many times, and the mirror was stained round the edges with condensation. The lavatory had an old-fashioned cast-iron chain-pull cistern. There was an old cream-painted wooden cupboard standing in the corner, with an old brown bentwood chair next to it, on which lay some neatly folded but threadbare small towels. There was also a large horse in the room, taking up most of it.

Richard stared at it, and it stared at Richard in an appraising kind of way. Richard swayed slightly. The horse stood quite still. After a while it looked at the cupboard instead. It seemed, if not content, then at least perfectly resigned to being where it was until it was put somewhere else. It also seemed . . . what was it?

It was bathed in the glow of the moonlight that streamed in through the window. The window was open but small and was, besides, on the second floor, so the notion that the horse had entered by that route was entirely fanciful.

There was something odd about the horse, but he couldn't say what. Well, there was one thing that was clearly very odd about it indeed, which was that it was standing in a college bathroom. Maybe that was all.

He reached out, rather tentatively, to pat the creature on its neck. It felt normal – firm, glossy, it was in good condition. The effect of the moonlight on its coat was a little mazy, but everything looks a little odd by moon-light. The horse shook its mane a little when he touched it, but didn't seem to mind too much.

After the success of patting it, Richard stroked it a few times and scratched it gently under the jaw. Then he noticed that there was another door into the bathroom, in the far corner. He moved cautiously around the horse and approached the other door. He backed up against it and pushed it open tentatively.

It just opened into the Professor's bedroom, a small room cluttered with books and shoes and a small single bed. This room, too, had another door, which opened out on to the landing again.

Richard noticed that the floor of the landing was newly scuffed and scratched as the stairs had been, and these marks were consistent with the idea that the horse had somehow been pushed up the stairs. He wouldn't have liked to have had to do it himself, and he would have liked to have been the horse having it done to him even less, but it was just about possible.

But why? He had one last look at the horse, which had one last look back at him, and then he returned downstairs.

'I agree,' he said. 'You have a horse in your bathroom and I will, after all, have a little port.'

He poured some for himself, and then some for Reg, who was quietly contemplating the fire and was in need of a refill.

'Just as well I did put out three glasses after all,' said Reg chattily. 'I wondered why earlier, and now I remember.

'You asked if you could bring a friend, but appear not to have done so. On account of the sofa no doubt. Never mind, these things happen. Whoa, not too much, you'll spill it.'

All horse-related questions left Richard's mind abruptly.

'I did?' he said.

'Oh yes. I remember now. You rang me back to ask me if it would be all right, as I recall. I said I would be charmed, and fully intended to be. I'd saw the thing up if I were you. Don't want to sacrifice your happiness to a sofa. Or maybe she decided that an evening with your old tutor would be blisteringly dull and opted for the more exhilarating course of washing her hair instead. Dear me, I know what I would have done. It's only lack of hair that forces me to pursue such a hectic social round these days.'

It was Richard's turn to be white-faced and staring.

Yes, he had assumed that Susan would not want to come.

Yes, he had said to her it would be terribly dull.

71

But she had insisted that she wanted to come because it would be the only way she'd get to see his face for a few minutes not bathed in the light of a computer screen, so he had agreed and arranged that he would bring her after all.

Only he had completely forgotten this. He had not picked her up.

He said, 'Can I use your phone, please?'

9

Gordon Way lay on the ground, unclear about what to do.

He was dead. There seemed little doubt about that. There was a horrific hole in his chest, but the blood that was gobbing out of it had slowed to a trickle. Otherwise there was no movement from his chest at all, or, indeed, from any other part of him.

He looked up, and from side to side, and it became clear to him that whatever part of him it was that was moving, it wasn't any part of his body.

The mist rolled slowly over him, and explained nothing. At a few feet distant from him his shotgun lay smoking quietly in the grass.

He continued to lie there, like someone lying awake at four o'clock in the morning, unable to put their mind to rest, but unable to find anything to do with it. He realised that he had just had something of a shock, which might account for his inability to think clearly, but didn't account for his ability actually to think at all.

In the great debate that has raged for centuries about what, if anything, happens to you after death, be it heaven, hell, purgatory or extinction, one thing has never been in doubt – that you would at least know the answer when you were dead.

Gordon Way was dead, but he simply hadn't the slightest idea what he was meant to do about it. It wasn't a situation he had encountered before.

He sat up. The body that sat up seemed as real to him as the body that still lay slowly cooling on the ground, giving up its blood heat in wraiths of steam that mingled with the mist of the chill night air.

Experimenting a bit further, he tried standing up, slowly, wonderingly and wobblingly. The ground seemed to give him support, it took his weight. But then of course he appeared to have no weight that needed to be taken. When he bent to touch the ground he could feel nothing save a kind of distant rubbery resistance like the sensation you get if you try and pick something up when your arm has gone dead. His arm had gone dead. His legs too, and his other arm, and all his torso and his head.

His body was dead. He could not say why his mind was not.

He stood in a kind of frozen, sleepless horror while the mist curled slowly through him.

He looked back down at the him, the ghastly, astonished-looking him-thing lying still and mangled on the ground, and his flesh wanted to creep. Or rather, he wanted flesh that could creep. He wanted flesh. He wanted body. He had none.

A sudden cry of horror escaped from his mouth but was nothing and went nowhere. He shook and felt nothing.

Music and a pool of light seeped from his car. He walked towards it. He tried to walk sturdily, but it was a faint and feeble kind of walking, uncertain and, well, insubstantial. The ground felt frail beneath his feet.

The door of the car was still open on the driver's side, as he had left it when he had leaped out to deal with the boot lid, thinking he'd only be two seconds.

That was all of two minutes ago now, when he'd been alive. When he'd been a person. When he'd thought he was going to be leaping straight back in and driving off. Two minutes and a lifetime ago.

This was insane, wasn't it? he thought suddenly.

He walked around the door and bent down to peer into the external rear-view mirror.

He looked exactly like himself, albeit like himself after he'd had a terrible fright, which was to be expected, but that was him, that was normal. This must be something he was imagining, some horrible kind of waking dream. He had a sudden thought and tried breathing on the rear-view mirror.

Nothing. Not a single droplet formed. That would satisfy a doctor, that's what they always did on television – if no mist formed on the mirror, there was no breath. Perhaps, he thought anxiously to himself, perhaps it was something to do with having heated wing mirrors. Didn't this car have heated wing mirrors? Hadn't the salesman gone on and on about heated this, electric that, and servo-assisted the other? Maybe they were digital wing mirrors. That was it. Digital, heated, servo-assisted, computer-controlled, breath-resistant wing mirrors . . .

He was, he realised, thinking complete nonsense. He turned slowly and gazed again in apprehension at the body lying on the ground behind him with half its chest blown away. That would certainly satisfy a doctor. The sight would be appalling enough if it was somebody else's body, but his own . . .

He was dead. Dead . . . dead . . . He tried to make the word toll dramatically in his mind, but it wouldn't. He was not a film soundtrack, he was just dead.

Peering at his body in appalled fascination, he gradually became distressed by the expression of asinine stupidity on its face.

It was perfectly understandable, of course. It was just such an expression as somebody who is in the middle of being shot with his own shotgun by somebody who had been hiding in the boot of his car might be expected to wear, but he nevertheless disliked the idea that anyone might find him looking like that.

He knelt down beside it in the hope of being able to rearrange his features into some semblance of dignity, or at least basic intelligence.

It proved to be almost impossibly difficult. He tried to knead the skin, the sickeningly familiar skin, but somehow he couldn't seem to get a proper grip on it, or on anything. It was like trying to model plasticine when your arm has gone to sleep, except that instead of his grip slipping off the model, it would slip through it. In this case, his hand slipped through his face.

Nauseated horror and rage swept through him at his sheer bloody blasted impotence, and he was suddenly startled to find himself throttling and shaking his own dead body with a firm and furious grip. He staggered back in amazed shock. All he had managed to do was to add to the inanely stupefied look of the corpse a twisted-up mouth and a squint. And bruises flowering on its neck.

He started to sob, and this time sound seemed to come, a strange howling from deep within whatever this thing he had become was. Clutching his hands to his face, he staggered backwards, retreated to his car and flung himself into the seat. The seat received him in a loose and distant kind of way, like an aunt who disapproves of the last fifteen years of your life and will therefore furnish you with a basic sherry, but refuses to catch your eye.

Could he get himself to a doctor?

To avoid facing the absurdity of the idea he grappled violently with the steering wheel, but his hands slipped through it. He tried to wrestle with the automatic transmission shift and ended up thumping it in rage, but not being able properly to grasp or push it.

The stereo was still playing light orchestral music into the telephone, which had been lying on the passenger seat listening patiently all this time. He stared at it and realised with a growing fever of excitement that he was still connected to Susan's telephone-answering machine. It was the type that would simply run and run until he hung up. He was still in contact with the world.

He tried desperately to pick up the receiver, fumbled, let it slip, and was in the end reduced to bending himself down over its mouthpiece. 'Susan!' he cried into it, his voice a hoarse and distant wail on the wind. 'Susan, help me! Help me for God's sake. Susan, I'm dead . . . I'm dead . . . I'm dead and . . . I don't know what to do . . .' He broke down again, sobbing in desperation, and tried to cling to the phone like a baby clinging to its blanket for comfort.

'Help me, Susan . . .' he cried again.

'*Beep*,' said the phone.

He looked down at it again where he was cuddling it. He had managed to push something after all. He had managed to push the button which disconnected the call. Feverishly he attempted to grapple the thing again, but it constantly slipped through his fingers and eventually lay immobile on the seat. He could not touch it. He could not push the buttons. In rage he flung it at the windscreen. It responded to that, all right. It hit the windscreen, careered straight back though him, bounced off the seat and then lay still on the transmission tunnel, impervious to all his further attempts to touch it.

For several minutes still he sat there, his head nodding slowly as terror began to recede into blank desolation.

A couple of cars passed by, but would have noticed nothing odd – a car stopped by the wayside. Passing swiftly in the night their headlights would probably not have picked out the body lying in the grass behind the car. They certainly would not have noticed a ghost sitting inside it crying to himself.

He didn't know how long he sat there. He was hardly aware of time passing, only that it didn't seem to pass quickly. There was little external stimulus to mark its passage. He didn't feel cold. In fact he could almost not remember what cold meant or felt like, he just knew that it was something he would have expected to feel at this moment.

Eventually he stirred from his pathetic huddle. He would have to do something, though he didn't know what. Perhaps he should try and reach his cottage, though he didn't know what he would do when he got there. He just needed something to try for. He needed to make it through the night.

Pulling himself together he slipped out of the car, his foot and knee grazing easily through part of the door frame. He went to look again at his body, but it wasn't there.

As if the night hadn't produced enough shocks already. He started, and stared at the damp depression in the grass.

His body was not there.

10

Richard made the hastiest departure that politeness would allow.

He said thank you very much and what a splendid evening it had been and that any time Reg was coming up to London he must let him, Richard, know and was there anything he could do to help about the horse. No? Well, all right then, if you're sure, and thank you again, so much.

He stood there for a moment or two after the door finally closed, pondering things.

He had noticed during the short time that the light from Reg's room flooded out on to the landing of the main staircase, that there were no marks on the floorboards there at all. It seemed odd that the horse should only have scuffed the floorboards inside Reg's room.

Well, it all seemed very odd, full stop, but here was yet another curious fact to add to the growing pile. This was supposed to have been a relaxing evening away from work.

On an impulse he knocked on the door opposite to Reg's. It took such a long time to be answered that Richard had given up and was turning to go when at last he heard the door creak open.

He had a slight shock when he saw that staring sharply up at him like a small and suspicious bird was the don with the racing-yacht keel for a nose.

'Er, sorry,' said Richard, abruptly, 'but, er, have you seen or heard a horse coming up this staircase tonight?'

The man stopped his obsessive twitching of his fingers. He cocked his head slightly on one side and then seemed to need to go on a long journey inside himself to find a voice, which when found turned out to be a thin and soft little one.

He said, 'That is the first thing anybody has said to me for seventeen years, three months and two days, five hours, nineteen minutes and twenty seconds. I've been counting.'

He closed the door softly again.

Richard virtually ran through Second Court.

When he reached First Court he steadied himself and slowed down to a walking pace.

The chill night air was rasping in his lungs and there was no point in running. He hadn't managed to talk to Susan because Reg's phone wasn't working, and this was another thing that he had been mysteriously coy about. That at least was susceptible of a rational explanation. He probably hadn't paid his phone bill.

Richard was about to emerge out on to the street when instead he decided to pay a quick visit to the porter's lodge, which was tucked away inside the great archway entrance into the college. It was a small hutchlike place filled with keys, messages and a single electric bar heater. A radio nattered to itself in the background.

'Excuse me,' he said to the large black-suited man standing behind the counter with his arms folded. 'I . . .'

'Yes, Mr MacDuff, what can I do for you?'

In his present state of mind Richard would have been hard-pressed himself to remember his own name and was startled for a moment. However, college porters are legendary for their ability to perform such feats of memory, and for their tendency to show them off at the slightest provocation.

'Is there,' said Richard, 'a horse anywhere in the college – that you know of? I mean, you would know if there was a horse in the college, wouldn't you?'

The porter didn't blink.

'No, sir, and yes, sir. Anything else I can help you with, Mr MacDuff, sir?'

'Er, no,' said Richard and tapped his fingers a couple of times on the counter. 'No. Thank you. Thank you very much for your help. Nice to see you again, er . . . Bob,' he hazarded. 'Goodnight, then.'

He left.

The porter remained perfectly still with his arms folded, but shaking his head a very, very little bit.

'Here's some coffee for you, Bill,' said another porter, a short wiry one, emerging from an inner sanctum with a steaming cup. 'Getting a bit colder tonight?'

'I think it is, Fred, thanks,' said Bill, taking the cup.

He took a sip. 'You can say what you like about people, they don't get any less peculiar. Fellow in here just now asking if there was a horse in the college.'

'Oh yes?' Fred sipped at his own coffee, and let the steam smart his eyes. 'I had a chap in here earlier. Sort of strange foreign priest. Couldn't understand a word he said at first. But he seemed happy just to stand by the fire and listen to the news on the radio.'

'Foreigners, eh.'

'In the end I told him to shoot off. Standing in front of my fire like that. Suddenly he says is that really what he must do? Shoot off? I said, in my best Bogart voice, "You better believe it, buddy."'

'Really? Sounded more like Jimmy Cagney to me.'

'No, that's my Bogart voice. This is my Jimmy Cagney voice – "You better believe it, buddy."'

Bill frowned at him. 'Is that your Jimmy Cagney voice? I always thought that was your Kenneth McKellar voice.'

'You don't listen properly, Bill, you haven't got the ear. This is Kenneth McKellar. "Oh, you take the high road and I'll take the low road . . ."'

'Oh, I see. I was thinking of the Scottish Kenneth McKellar. So what did this priest fellow say then, Fred?'

'Oh, he just looked me straight in the eyes, Bill, and said in this strange sort of . . .'

'Skip the accent, Fred, just tell me what he said, if it's worth hearing.'

'He just said he did believe me.'

'So. Not a very interesting story then, Fred.'

'Well, maybe not. I only mention it because he also said that he'd left his horse in a washroom and would I see that it was all right.'

11

Gordon Way drifted miserably along the dark road, or rather, tried to drift.

He felt that as a ghost – which is what he had to admit to himself he had become – he should be able to drift. He knew little enough about ghosts, but he felt that if you were going to be one then there ought to be certain compensations for not having a physical body to lug around, and that among them ought to be the ability simply to drift. But no, it seemed he was going to have to walk every step of the way.

His aim was to try and make it to his house. He didn't know what he would do when he got there, but even ghosts have to spend the night somewhere, and he felt that being in familiar surroundings might help. Help what, he didn't know. At least the journey gave him an objective, and he would just have to think of another one when he arrived.

He trudged despondently from lamppost to lamppost, stopping at each one to look at bits of himself.

He was definitely getting a bit wraithlike.

At times he would fade almost to nothing, and would seem to be little more than a shadow playing in the mist, a dream of himself that could just evaporate and be gone. At other times he seemed to be almost solid and real again. Once or twice he would try leaning against a lamppost, and would fall straight through it if he wasn't careful.

At last, and with great reluctance, he actually began to turn his mind to what it was that had happened. Odd, that reluctance. He really didn't want to think about it. Psychologists say that the mind will often try to suppress the memory of traumatic events, and this, he thought, was probably the answer. After all, if having a strange figure jump out of the boot of your own car and shoot you dead didn't count as a traumatic experience, he'd like to know what did.

He trudged on wearily.

He tried to recall the figure to his mind's eye, but it was like probing a hurting tooth, and he thought of other things.

Like, was his will up-to-date? He couldn't remember, and made a mental note to call his lawyer tomorrow, and then made another mental note that he would have to stop making mental notes like that.

How would his company survive without him? He didn't like either of the possible answers to that very much.

What about his obituary? There was a thought that chilled him to his bones, wherever they'd got to. Would he be able to get hold of a copy? What would it say? They'd better give him a good write-up, the bastards. Look at what he'd done. Single-handedly saved the British software industry: huge exports, charitable contributions, research scholarships, crossing the Atlantic in a solar-powered submarine (failed, but a good try) – all sorts of things. They'd better not go digging up that Pentagon stuff again or he'd get his lawyer on to them. He made a mental note to call him in the mor . . .

No.

Anyway, can a dead person sue for libel? Only his lawyer would know, and he was not going to be able to call him in the morning. He knew with a sense of creeping dread that of all the things he had left behind in the land of the living it was the telephone that he was going to miss the most, and then he turned his mind determinedly back to where it didn't want to go.

The figure.

It seemed to him that the figure had been almost like a figure of Death itself, or was that his imagination playing tricks with him? Was he dreaming that it was a cowled figure? What would any figure, whether cowled or just casually dressed, be doing in the boot of his car?

At that moment a car zipped past him on the road and disappeared off into the night, taking its oasis of light with it. He thought with longing of the warm, leather-upholstered, climate-controlled comfort of his own car abandoned on the road behind him, and then a sudden extraordinary thought struck him.

Was there any way he could hitch a lift? Could anyone actually see him? How would anyone react if they could? Well, there was only one way to find out.

He heard another car coming up in the distance behind him and turned to face it. The twin pools of hazy lights approached through the mist and Gordon gritted his phantom teeth and stuck his thumb out at them.

The car swept by regardless.

Nothing.

Angrily he made an indistinct V sign at the receding red rear lights, and realised, looking straight through his own upraised arm, that he wasn't at his most visible at the moment. Was there perhaps some effort of will he could make to render himself more visible when he wanted to? He screwed up his eyes in concentration, then realised that he would need to have his eyes open in order to judge the results. He tried again, forcing his mind as hard as he could, but the results were unsatisfactory.

Though it did seem to make some kind of rudimentary, glowing difference, he couldn't sustain it, and it faded almost immediately, however much he piled on the mental pressure. He would have to judge the timing very carefully if he was going to make his presence felt, or at least seen.

Another car approached from behind, travelling fast. He turned again, stuck his thumb out, waited till the moment was right and willed himself visible.

The car swerved slightly, and then carried on its way, only a little more slowly. Well, that was something. What else could he do? He would go and stand under a lamppost for a start, and he would practise. The next car he would get for sure.

12

'. . . so if you'd like to leave a message, I'll get back to you as soon as possible. Maybe.'

Beep.

'Shit. Damn. Hold on a minute. Blast. Look . . . er . . .'

Click.

Richard pushed the phone back into its cradle and slammed his car into reverse for twenty yards to have another look at the signpost by the road junction he'd just sped past in the mist. He had extracted himself from the Cambridge one-way system by the usual method, which involved going round and round it faster and faster until he achieved a sort of escape velocity and flew off at a tangent in a random direction, which he was now trying to identify and correct for.

Arriving back at the junction he tried to correlate the information on the signpost with the information on the map. But it couldn't be done. The road junction was quite deliberately sitting on a page divide on the map, and the signpost was revolving maliciously in the wind. Instinct told him that he was heading in the wrong direction, but he didn't want to go back the way he'd come for fear of getting sucked back into the gravitational whirlpool of Cambridge's traffic system.

He turned left, therefore, in the hope of finding better fortune in that direction, but after a while lost his nerve and turned a speculative right, and then chanced another exploratory left and after a few more such manoeuvres was thoroughly lost.

He swore to himself and turned up the heating in the car. If he had been concentrating on where he was going rather than trying to navigate and telephone at the same time, he told himself, he would at least know where he was now. He didn't actually like having a telephone in his car, he found it a bother and an intrusion. But Gordon had insisted and indeed had paid for it.

He sighed in exasperation, backed up the black Saab and turned around again. As he did so he nearly ran into someone lugging a body into a field. At least that was what it looked like for a second to his overwrought brain, but in fact it was probably a local farmer with a sackful of something nutritious, though what he was doing with it on a night like this was anyone's guess. As his headlights swung around again, they caught for a moment a silhouette of the figure trudging off across the field with the sack on his back.

'Rather him than me,' thought Richard grimly, and drove off again.

After a few minutes he reached a junction with what looked a little more like a main road, nearly turned right down it, but then turned left instead. There was no signpost.

He poked at the buttons on his phone again.

'. . . get back to you as soon as possible. Maybe.'

Beep.

'Susan, it's Richard. Where do I start? What a mess. Look, I'm sorry, sorry, sorry. I screwed up very badly, and it's all my fault. And look, whatever it takes to make up for it, I'll do it, solemn promise . . .'

He had a slight feeling that this wasn't the right tone to adopt with an answering machine, but he carried straight on.

'Honestly, we can go away, take a holiday for a week, or even just this weekend if you like. Really, this weekend. We'll go somewhere sunny. Doesn't matter how much pressure Gordon tries to put on me, and you know the sort of pressure he can muster, he is your brother, after all. I'll just ... er, actually, it might have to be next weekend. Damn, damn, damn. It's just that I really have promised to get, no, look, it doesn't matter. We'll just do it. I don't care about getting *Anthem* finished for Comdex. It's not the end of the world. We'll just go. Gordon will just have to take a running jump – Gaaarghhhh!'

Richard swerved wildly to avoid the spectre of Gordon Way which suddenly loomed in his headlights and took a running jump at him.

He slammed on the brakes, started to skid, tried to remember what it was you were supposed to do when you found yourself skidding, he knew he'd seen it on some television programme about driving he'd seen ages ago, what was the programme? God, he couldn't even remember the title of the programme, let alone – oh yes, they'd said you mustn't slam on the brakes. That was it. The world swung sickeningly around him with slow and appalling force as the car slewed across the road, spun, thudded against the grass verge, then slithered and rocked itself to a halt, facing the wrong way. He collapsed, panting, against the steering wheel.

He picked up the phone from where he'd dropped it.

'Susan,' he gasped, 'I'll get back to you,' and hung up.

He raised his eyes.

Standing full in the glare of his headlights was the spectral figure of Gordon Way staring straight in through the windscreen with ghastly horror in its eyes, slowly raising its hand and pointing at him.

*

He wasn't sure how long he just sat there. The apparition had melted from view in a few seconds, but Richard simply sat, shaking, probably for not more than a minute, until a sudden squeal of brakes and glare of lights roused him.

He shook his head. He was, he realised, stopped in the road facing the wrong way. The car that had just screeched to an abrupt halt almost bumper to bumper with him was a police car. He took two or three deep breaths and then, stiff and trembling, he climbed out and stood up to face the officer who was walking slowly towards him, silhouetted in the police car's headlights.

The officer looked him up and down.

'Er, I'm sorry, officer,' said Richard, with as much calmness as he could wrench into his voice. 'I, er, skidded. The roads are slippery and I, er . . . skidded. I spun round. As you see, I, I'm facing the wrong way.' He gestured at his car to indicate the way it was facing.

'Like to tell me why it was you skidded then, exactly, sir?' The police officer was looking him straight in the eye while pulling out a notebook.

'Well, as I said,' explained Richard, 'the roads are slippery because of the mist, and, well, to be perfectly honest,' he suddenly found himself saying, in spite of all his attempts to stop himself, 'I was just driving along and I suddenly imagined that I saw my employer throwing himself in front of my car.'

The officer gazed at him levelly.

'Guilt complex, officer,' added Richard with a twitch of a smile, 'you know how it is. I was contemplating taking the weekend off.'

The police officer seemed to hesitate, balanced on a knife edge between sympathy and suspicion. His eyes narrowed a little but didn't waver.

'Been drinking, sir?'

'Yes,' said Richard, with a quick sigh, 'but very little. Two glasses of wine max. Er ... and a small glass of port. Absolute max. It was really just a lapse of concentration. I'm fine now.'

'Name?'

Richard gave him his name and address. The policeman wrote it all down carefully and neatly in his book, then peered at the car registration number and wrote that down too.

'And who is your employer then, sir?'

'His name is Way. Gordon Way.'

'Oh,' said the policeman raising his eyebrows, 'the computer gentleman.'

'Er, yes, that's right. I design software for the company. WayForward Technologies II.'

'We've got one of your computers down the station,' said the policeman. 'Buggered if I can get it to work.'

'Oh,' said Richard wearily, 'which model do you have?'

'I think it's called a Quark II.'

'Oh, well that's simple,' said Richard with relief. 'It doesn't work. Never has done. The thing is a heap of shit.'

'Funny thing, sir, that's what I've always said.' said the policeman. 'Some of the other lads don't agree.'

'Well, you're absolutely right, officer. The thing is hopeless. It's the major reason the original company went bust. I suggest you use it as a big paperweight.'

'Well, I wouldn't like to do that, sir,' the policeman persisted. 'The door would keep blowing open.'

'What do you mean, officer?' asked Richard.

'I use it to keep the door closed, sir. Nasty draughts down our station this time of year. In the summer, of course, we beat suspects round the head with it.'

He flipped his book closed and prodded it into his pocket.

'My advice to you, sir, is to go nice and easy on the way back. Lock up the car and spend the weekend getting completely pissed. I find it's the only way. Mind how you go now.'

He returned to his car, wound down the window, and watched Richard manoeuvre his car around and drive off into the night before heading off himself.

Richard took a deep breath, drove calmly back to London, let himself calmly into his flat, clambered calmly over the sofa, sat down, poured himself a stiff brandy and began seriously to shake.

There were three things he was shaking about.

There was the simple physical shock of his near-accident, which is the sort of thing that always churns you up a lot more than you expect. The body floods itself with adrenaline, which then hangs around your system turning sour.

Then there was the cause of the skid – the extraordinary apparition of Gordon throwing himself in front of his car at that moment. Boy oh boy. Richard took a mouthful of brandy and gargled with it. He put the glass down.

It was well known that Gordon was one of the world's richest natural resources of guilt pressure, and that he could deliver a ton on your doorstep fresh every morning, but Richard hadn't realised he had let it get to him to such an unholy degree.

He took up his glass again, went upstairs and pushed open the door to his workroom, which involved shifting a stack of *BYTE* magazines that had toppled against it. He pushed them away with his foot and walked to the end of the large room. A lot of glass at this end let in views over a large part of north London, from which the mist was now clearing. St Paul's glowed in the dark distance and he stared at it for a moment or two but it didn't do anything special. After the events of the evening he found this came as a pleasant surprise.

At the other end of the room were a couple of long tables smothered in, at the last count, six Macintosh computers. In the middle was the Mac II on which a red wire-frame model of his sofa was lazily revolving within a blue wire-frame model of his narrow staircase, complete with banister rail, radiator and fuse box details, and of course the awkward turn halfway up.

The sofa would start out spinning in one direction, hit an obstruction, twist itself in another plane, hit another obstruction, revolve round a third axis until it was stopped again, then cycle through the moves again in a different order. You didn't have to watch the sequence for very long before you saw it repeat itself.

The sofa was clearly stuck.

Three other Macs were connected up via long tangles of cable to an untidy agglomeration of synthesisers – an Emulator II+ HD sampler, a rack of TX modules, a Prophet VS, a Roland JX10, a Korg DW8000, an Octapad, a left-handed Synth-Axe MIDI guitar controller, and even an old drum machine stacked up and gathering dust in the corner – pretty much the works. There was also a small and rarely used cassette tape recorder: all the music was stored in sequencer files on the computers rather than on tape.

He dumped himself into a seat in front of one of the Macs to see what, if anything, it was doing. It was displaying an 'Untitled' *Excel* spreadsheet and he wondered why.

He saved it and looked to see if he'd left himself any notes and quickly discovered that the spreadsheet contained some of the data he had previously downloaded after searching the *World Reporter* and *Knowledge* online databases for facts about swallows.

He now had figures which detailed their migratory habits, their wing shapes, their aerodynamic profile and turbulence characteristics, and some sort of rudimentary figures concerning the patterns that a flock would adopt in flight, but as yet he had only the faintest idea as to how he was going to synthesise them all together.

Because he was too tired to think particularly constructively tonight he savagely selected and copied a whole swathe of figures from the spreadsheet at random, pasted them into his own conversion program, which scaled and filtered and manipulated the figures according to his own experimental algorithms, loaded the converted file into *Performer*, a powerful sequencer program, and played the result through random MIDI channels to whichever synthesisers happened to be on at the moment.

The result was a short burst of the most hideous cacophony, and he stopped it.

He ran the conversion program again, this time instructing it to force-map the pitch values into G minor. This was a utility he was determined in the end to get rid of because he regarded it as cheating. If there was any basis to his firmly held belief that the rhythms and harmonies of music which he found most satisfying could be found in, or at least derived from, the rhythms and harmonies of naturally occurring phenomena, then satisfying forms of modality and intonation should emerge naturally as well, rather than being forced.

For the moment, though, he forced it.

The result was a short burst of the most hideous cacophony in G minor.

So much for random shortcuts.

The first task was a relatively simple one, which would be simply to plot the waveform described by the tip of a swallow's wing as it flies, then synthesise that waveform.

That way he would end up with a single note, which would be a good start, and it shouldn't take more than the weekend to do.

Except, of course, that he didn't have a weekend available to do it in because he had somehow to get Version 2 of *Anthem* out of the door sometime during the course of the next year, or 'month' as Gordon called it.

Which brought Richard inexorably to the third thing he was shaking about.

There was absolutely no way that he could take the time off this weekend or next to fulfil the promise he had made to Susan's telephone-answering machine. And that, if this evening's débâcle had not already done so, would surely spell the final end.

But that was it. The thing was done. There is nothing you can do about a message on someone else's answering machine other than let events take their course. It was done. It was irrevocable.

An odd thought suddenly struck him.

It took him by considerable surprise, but he couldn't really see what was wrong with it.

13

A pair of binoculars scanning the London night skyline, idly, curious, snooping. A little look here, a little look there, just seeing what's going on, anything interesting, anything useful.

The binoculars settle on the back of one particular house, attracted by a slight movement. One of those large late-Victorian villas, probably flats now. Lots of black iron drainpipes. Green rubber dustbins. But dark. No, nothing.

The binoculars are just moving onwards when another slight movement catches in the moonlight. The binoculars refocus very slightly, trying to find a detail, a hard edge, a slight contrast in the darkness. The mist has lifted now, and the darkness glistens. They refocus a very, very little more.

There it is. Something, definitely. Only this time a little higher up, maybe a foot or so, maybe a yard. The binoculars settle and relax – steady, trying for the edge, trying for the detail. There. The binoculars settle again – they have found their mark, straddled between a windowsill and a drainpipe.

It is a dark figure, splayed against the wall, looking down, looking for a new foothold, looking upwards, looking for a ledge. The binoculars peer intently.

The figure is that of a tall, thin man. His clothes are right for the job, dark trousers, dark sweater, but his movements are awkward and angular. Nervous. Interesting. The binoculars wait and consider, consider and judge.

The man is clearly a rank amateur.

Look at his fumbling. Look at his ineptitude. His feet slip on the drainpipe, his hands can't reach the ledge. He nearly falls. He waits to catch his breath. For a moment he starts to climb back down again, but seems to find that even tougher going.

He lunges again for the ledge and this time catches it. His foot shoots out to steady himself and nearly misses the pipe. Could have been very nasty, very nasty indeed.

But now the way is easier and progress is better. He crosses to another pipe, reaches a third-floor window ledge, flirts briefly with death as he crawls painfully on to it, and makes the cardinal error and looks down. He sways briefly and sits back heavily. He shades his eyes and peers inside to check that the room is dark, and sets about getting the window open.

One of the things that distinguish the amateur from the professional is that this is the point when the amateur thinks it would have been a good idea to bring along something to prise the window open with. Luckily for this amateur the householder is an amateur too, and the sash window slides grudgingly up. The climber crawls, with some relief, inside.

He should be locked up for his own protection, think the binoculars. A hand starts to reach for the phone. At the window a face looks back out and for a moment is caught in the moonlight, then it ducks back inside to carry on with its business.

The hand stays hovering over the phone for a moment or two, while the binoculars wait and consider, consider and judge. The hand reaches instead for the A–Z street map of London.

There is a long studious pause, a little more intent binocular work, and then the hand reaches for the phone again, lifts it and dials.

14

Susan's flat was small but spacious, which was a trick, reflected Richard tensely as he turned on the light, that only women seemed able to pull off.

It wasn't that observation which made him tense, of course – he'd thought it before, many times. Every time he'd been in her flat, in fact. It always struck him, usually because he had just come from his own flat, which was four times the size and cramped. He'd just come from his own flat this time, only via a rather eccentric route, and it was this that made his usual observation un-usually tense.

Despite the chill of the night he was sweating.

He looked back out of the window, turned and tiptoed across the room towards where the telephone and the answering machine stood on their own small table.

There was no point, he told himself, in tiptoeing. Susan wasn't in. He would be extremely interested to know where she was, in fact – just as she, he told himself, had probably been extremely interested in knowing where he had been at the beginning of the evening.

He realised he was still tiptoeing. He hit his leg to make himself stop doing it, but carried on doing it none the less.

Climbing up the outside wall had been terrifying.

He wiped his forehead with the arm of his oldest and greasiest sweater. There had been a nasty moment when his life had flashed before his eyes but he had been too preoccupied with falling and had missed all the good bits. Most of the good bits had involved Susan, he realised. Susan or computers. Never Susan *and* computers – those had largely been the bad bits. Which was why he was here, he told himself. He seemed to need convincing, and told himself again.

He looked at his watch. Eleven forty-five.

It occurred to him he had better go and wash his wet and dirty hands before he touched anything. It wasn't the police he was worried about, but Susan's terrifying cleaner. She would know.

He went into the bathroom, turned on the light switch, wiped it, and then stared at his own startled face in the bright neon-lit mirror as he ran the water over his hands. For a moment he thought of the dancing, warm candle-light of the Coleridge Dinner, and the images of it welled up out of the dim and distant past of the earlier part of the evening. Life had seemed easy then, and carefree. The wine, the conversation, simple conjuring tricks. He pictured the round pale face of Sarah, pop-eyed with wonder. He washed his own face.

He thought:

'. . . Beware! Beware!
His flashing eyes, his floating hair!'

He brushed his own hair. He thought, too, of the pictures hanging high in the darkness above their heads. He cleaned his teeth. The low buzz of the neon light snapped him back to the present and he suddenly remembered with appalled shock that he was here in his capacity as burglar.

Something made him look himself directly in the face in the mirror, then he shook his head, trying to clear it.

When would Susan be back? That, of course, would depend on what she was doing. He quickly wiped his hands and made his way back to the answering machine. He prodded at the buttons and his conscience prodded back at him. The tape wound back for what seemed to be an interminable time, and he realised with a jolt that it was probably because Gordon had been in full flood.

He had forgotten, of course, that there would be messages on the tape other than his own, and listening to other people's phone messages was tantamount to opening their mail.

He explained to himself once again that all he was trying to do was to undo a mistake he had made before it caused any irrevocable damage. He would just play the tiniest snippets till he found his own voice. That wouldn't be too bad, he wouldn't even be able to distinguish what was being said.

He groaned inwardly, gritted his teeth and stabbed at the Play button so roughly that he missed it and ejected the cassette by mistake. He put it back in and pushed the Play button more carefully.

Beep.

'Oh, Susan, hi, it's Gordon,' said the answering machine. 'Just on my way to the cottage. It's, er . . .' He wound on for a couple of seconds. '. . . need to know that Richard is on the case. I mean *really* on . . .' Richard set his mouth grimly and stabbed at the Fast Forward again. He really hated the fact that Gordon tried to put pressure on him via Susan, which Gordon always stoutly denied he did. Richard couldn't blame Susan for getting exasperated about his work sometimes if this sort of thing was going on.

Click.

'. . . Response. Make a note to Susan would you please, to get an "Armed Response" sign made up with a sharp spike on the bottom at the right height for rabbits to see.'

'*What?*' muttered Richard to himself, and his finger

hesitated for a second over the Fast Forward button. He had a feeling that Gordon desperately wanted to be like Howard Hughes, and if he could never hope to be remotely as rich, he could at least try to be twice as eccentric. An act. A palpable act.

'That's secretary Susan at the office, not you, of course,' continued Gordon's voice on the answering machine. 'Where was I? Oh yes. Richard and *Anthem* 2.00. Susan, that thing has got to be in beta testing in two . . .' Richard stabbed at the Fast Forward, tight-lipped.

'. . . point is that there's only one person who's really in a position to know if he's getting the important work done, or if he's just dreaming, and that one person . . .' He stabbed angrily again. He had promised himself he wouldn't listen to any of it, and now here he was getting angry at what he was hearing. He should really just stop this. Well, just one more try.

When he listened again he just got music. Odd. He wound forward again, and still got music. Why would someone be phoning to play music to an answering machine? he wondered.

The phone rang. He stopped the tape and answered it, then almost dropped the phone like an electric eel as he realised what he was doing. Hardly daring to breathe, he held the telephone to his ear.

'Rule One in housebreaking,' said a voice. 'Never answer the telephone when you're in the middle of a job. Who are you supposed to be, for heaven's sake?'

Richard froze. It was a moment or two before he could find where he had put his voice.

'Who is this?' he demanded at last in a whisper.

'Rule Two,' continued the voice. 'Preparation. Bring the right tools. Bring gloves. Try to have the faintest glimmering of an idea of what you're about before you start dangling from window ledges in the middle of the night.

'Rule Three. *Never* forget Rule Two.'

'Who is this?' exclaimed Richard again.

The voice was unperturbed. 'Neighbourhood Watch,' it said. 'If you just look out of the back window you'll see . . .'

Trailing the phone, Richard hurried over to the window and looked out. A distant flash startled him.

'Rule Four. Never stand where you can be photographed.

'Rule Five . . . Are you listening to me, MacDuff?'

'What? Yes . . .' said Richard in bewilderment. 'How do you know me?'

'Rule Five. *Never* admit to your name.'

Richard stood silent, breathing hard.

'I run a little course,' said the voice, 'if you're interested . . .'

Richard said nothing.

'You're learning,' continued the voice, 'slowly, but you're learning. If you were learning fast you would have put the phone down by now, of course. But you're curious – and incompetent – and so you don't. I don't run a course for novice burglars as it happens, tempting though the idea is. I'm sure there would be grants available. If we have to have them they may as well be trained.

'However, if I did run such a course I would allow you to enrol for free, because I too am curious. Curious to know why Mr Richard MacDuff who, I am given to understand, is now a wealthy young man, something in the computer industry, I believe, should suddenly be needing to resort to house-breaking.'

'Who—?'

'So I do a little research, phone Directory Enquiries

and discover that the flat into which he is breaking is that of a Miss S. Way. I know that Mr Richard MacDuff's employer is the famous Mr G. Way and I wonder if they can by any chance be related.'

'Who—?'

'You are speaking with Svlad, commonly known as "Dirk" Cjelli, currently trading under the name of Gently for reasons which it would be otiose, at this moment, to rehearse. I bid you good evening. If you wish to know more I will be at the Pizza Express in Upper Street in ten minutes. Bring some money.'

'Dirk?' exclaimed Richard. 'You . . . Are you trying to blackmail me?'

'No, you fool, for the pizzas.' There was a click and Dirk Gently rang off.

Richard stood transfixed for a moment or two, wiped his forehead again, and gently replaced the phone as if it were an injured hamster. His brain began to buzz gently and suck its thumb. Lots of little synapses deep inside his cerebral cortex all joined hands and started dancing around and singing nursery rhymes. He shook his head to try and make them stop, and quickly sat down at the answering machine again.

He fought with himself over whether or not he was going to push the Play button again, and then did so anyway before he had made up his mind. Hardly four seconds of light orchestral music had oozed soothingly past when there came the sound of a key scratching in the lock out in the hallway.

In panic Richard thumped the Eject button, popped the cassette out, rammed it into his jeans pocket and replaced it from the pile of fresh cassettes that lay next to the machine. There was a similar pile next to his own machine at home. Susan at the office provided them – poor, long-suffering Susan at the office. He must remember to feel sympathy for her in the morning, when he had the time and concentration for it.

Suddenly, without even noticing himself doing it, he changed his mind. In a flash he popped the substitute cassette out of the machine again, replaced the one he had stolen, rammed down the rewind button and made a lunge for the sofa where, with two seconds to go before the door opened, he tried to arrange himself into a nonchalant and winning posture. On an impulse he stuck his left hand up behind his back where it might come in useful.

He was just trying to arrange his features into an expression composed in equal parts of contrition, cheerfulness and sexual allurement when the door opened and in walked Michael Wenton-Weakes.

Everything stopped.

Outside, the wind ceased. Owls halted in mid-flight. Well, maybe they did, maybe they didn't, certainly the central heating chose that moment to shut down, unable perhaps to cope with the supernatural chill that suddenly whipped through the room.

'What are you doing here, Wednesday?' demanded Richard. He rose from the sofa as if levitated with anger.

Michael Wenton-Weakes was a large sad-faced man known by some people as Michael Wednesday-Week, because that was when he usually promised to have things done by. He was dressed in a suit that had been superbly well tailored when his father, the late Lord Magna, had bought it forty years previously.

Michael Wenton-Weakes came very high on the small but select list of people whom Richard thoroughly disliked.

He disliked him because he found the idea of someone who was not only privileged, but was also sorry for himself because he thought the world didn't really understand the problems of privileged people, deeply obnoxious. Michael, on the other hand, disliked Richard for the fairly simple reason that Richard disliked him and made no secret of it.

Michael gave a slow and lugubrious look back out into the hallway as Susan walked through. She stopped when she saw Richard. She put down her handbag, unwound her scarf, unbuttoned her coat, slipped it off, handed it to Michael, walked over to Richard and smacked him in the face.

'I've been saving that up all evening,' she said furiously. 'And don't try and pretend that's a bunch of flowers you've forgotten to bring which you're hiding behind your back. You tried that gag last time.' She turned and stalked off.

'It's a box of chocolates I forgot this time,' said Richard glumly and held out his empty hand to her retreating back. 'I climbed up the entire outside wall without them. Did I feel a fool when I got in.'

'Not very funny,' said Susan. She swept into the kitchen and sounded as if she was grinding coffee with her bare hands. For someone who always looked so neat and sweet and delicate, she packed a hell of a temper.

'It's true,' said Richard, ignoring Michael completely. 'I nearly killed myself.'

'I'm not going to rise to that,' said Susan from within the kitchen. 'If you want something big and sharp thrown at you, why don't you come in here and be funny?'

'I suppose it would be pointless saying I'm sorry at this point,' Richard called out.

'You bet,' said Susan, sweeping back out of the kitchen again. She looked at him with her eyes flashing, and actually stamped her foot.

'Honestly, Richard,' she said, 'you're just going to say

you forgot again. How can you have the gall to stand there with two arms, two legs and a head as if you're a human being? This is behaviour that a bout of amoebic dysentery would be ashamed of. I bet that even the very lowest form of dysentery amoeba shows up to take its girlfriend out for a quick trot around the stomach lining once in a while. Well, I hope you had a lousy evening.'

'I did,' said Richard. 'You wouldn't have liked it. There was a horse in the bathroom, and you know how you hate that sort of thing.'

'Oh, Michael,' said Susan brusquely, 'don't just stand there like a sinking pudding. Thank you very much for dinner and the concert, you were very sweet and I did enjoy listening to your troubles all evening because they were such a nice change from mine. But I think it would be best if I just found your book and pushed you out. I've got some serious jumping up and down and ranting to do, and I know how it upsets your delicate sensibilities.'

She retrieved her coat from him and hung it up. While he had been holding it he had seemed entirely taken up with this task and oblivious to anything else. Without it he seemed a little lost and naked and was forced to stir himself back into life. He turned his big heavy eyes back on Richard.

'Richard,' he said, 'I, er, read your piece in ... in *Fathom*. On Music and, er ...'

'Fractal Landscapes,' said Richard shortly. He didn't want to talk to Michael, and he certainly didn't want to get drawn into a conversation about Michael's wretched magazine. Or rather, the magazine that *used* to be Michael's.

That was the precise aspect of the conversation that Richard didn't want to get drawn into.

'Er, yes. Very interesting, of course,' said Michael in

his silky, over-rounded voice. 'Mountain shapes and tree shapes and all sorts of things. Recycled algae.'

'Recursive algorithms.'

'Yes, of course. Very interesting. But so wrong, so terribly wrong. For the magazine, I mean. It is, after all, an *arts* review. I would never have allowed such a thing, of course. Ross has utterly ruined it. Utterly. He'll have to go. *Have* to. He has no sensibilities and he's a thief.'

'He's not a thief, Wednesday, that's absolutely absurd,' snapped Richard, instantly getting drawn into it in spite of his resolution not to. 'He had nothing to do with your getting the push whatsoever. That was your own silly fault, and you . . .'

There was a sharp intake of breath.

'Richard,' said Michael in his softest, quietest voice – arguing with him was like getting tangled in parachute silk – 'I think you do not understand how important . . .'

'Michael,' said Susan gently but firmly, holding open the door. Michael Wenton-Weakes nodded faintly and seemed to deflate.

'Your book,' Susan added, holding out to him a small and elderly volume on the ecclesiastical architecture of Kent. He took it, murmured some slight thanks, looked about him for a moment as if he'd suddenly realised something rather odd, then gathered himself together, nodded farewell and left.

Richard didn't appreciate quite how tense he had become till Michael left and he was suddenly able to relax. He'd always resented the indulgent soft spot that Susan had for Michael even if she did try to disguise it by being terribly rude to him all the time. Perhaps even because of that.

'Susan, what can I say . . . ?' he started lamely.

'You could say "Ouch" for a start. You didn't even give me that satisfaction when I hit you, and I thought I did it rather hard. God, it's freezing in here. What's that window doing wide open?'

She went over to shut it.

'I told you. That's how I got in,' said Richard.

He sounded sufficiently as if he meant it to make her look round at him in surprise.

'Really,' he said. 'Like in the chocolate ads, only I forgot the box of chocolates . . .' He shrugged sheepishly.

She stared at him in amazement.

'What on earth possessed you to do that?' she said. She stuck her head out of the window and looked down. 'You could have got killed,' she said, turning back to him.

'Well, er, yes . . .' he said. 'It just seemed the only way to . . . I don't know.' He rallied himself. 'You took your key back, remember?'

'Yes. I got fed up with you coming and raiding my larder when you couldn't be bothered to do your own shopping. Richard, you really climbed up this wall?'

'Well, I wanted to be here when you got in.'

She shook her head in bewilderment. 'It would have been a great deal better if you'd been here when I went out. Is that why you're wearing those filthy old clothes?'

'Yes. You don't think I went to dinner at St Cedd's like this?'

'Well, I no longer know what you consider to be rational behaviour.' She sighed and fished about in a small drawer. 'Here,' she said, 'if it's going to save your life,' and handed him a couple of keys on a ring. 'I'm too tired to be angry anymore. An evening of being lobbied by Michael has taken it out of me.'

'Well, I'll never understand why you put up with him,' said Richard, going to fetch the coffee.

'I know you don't like him, but he's very sweet and

can be charming in his sad kind of way. Usually it's very relaxing to be with someone who's so self-absorbed, because it doesn't make any demands on you. But he's obsessed with the idea that I can do something about his magazine. I can't, of course. Life doesn't work like that. I do feel sorry for him, though.'

'I don't. He's had it very, very easy all his life. He still has it very, very easy. He's just had his toy taken away from him, that's all. It's hardly unjust, is it?'

'It's not a matter of whether it's just or not. I feel sorry for him because he's unhappy.'

'Well, of course he's unhappy. Al Ross has turned *Fathom* into a really sharp, intelligent magazine that everyone suddenly wants to read. It was just a bumbling shambles before. Its only real function was to let Michael have lunch and toady about with whoever he liked on the pretext that maybe they might like to write a little something. He hardly ever got an actual issue out. The whole thing was a sham. He pampered himself with it. I really don't find that charming or engaging. I'm sorry, I'm going on about it and I didn't mean to.'

Susan shrugged uneasily.

'I think you overreact,' she said, 'though I think I will have to steer clear of him if he's going to keep on at me to do something I simply can't do. It's too exhausting. Anyway, listen, I'm glad you had a lousy evening. I want to talk about what we were going to do this weekend.'

'Ah,' said Richard, 'well . . .'

'Oh, I'd better just check the messages first.'

She walked past him to the telephone-answering machine, played the first few seconds of Gordon's message and then suddenly ejected the cassette.

'I can't be bothered,' she said, giving it to him. 'Could

you just give this straight to Susan at the office tomorrow? Save her a trip. If there's anything important on it she can tell me.'

Richard blinked, said, 'Er, yes,' and pocketed the tape, tingling with the shock of the reprieve.

'Anyway, the weekend' said Susan, sitting down on the sofa.

Richard wiped his hand over his brow. 'Susan, I . . .'

'I'm afraid I've got to work. Nicola's sick and I'm going to have to dep for her at the Wigmore on Friday week. There's some Vivaldi and some Mozart I don't know too well, so that means a lot of extra practice this weekend, I'm afraid. Sorry.'

'Well, in fact,' said Richard, 'I have to work as well.' He sat down by her.

'I know. Gordon keeps on at me to nag you. I wish he wouldn't. It's none of my business and it puts me in an invidious position. I'm tired of being pressurised by people, Richard. At least you don't do that.'

She took a sip of her coffee.

'But I'm sure,' she added, 'that there's some kind of grey area between being pressurised and being completely forgotten about that I'd quite like to explore. Give me a hug.'

He hugged her, feeling that he was monstrously and unworthily lucky. An hour later he let himself out and discovered that the Pizza Express was closed.

Meanwhile, Michael Wenton-Weakes made his way back to his home in Chelsea. As he sat in the back of the taxi he watched the streets with a blank stare and tapped his fingers lightly against the window in a slow thoughtful rhythm.

Rap tap tap a rap tap a rap a tap.

He was one of those dangerous people who are soft,

squidgy and cowlike provided they have what they want. And because he had always had what he wanted, and had seemed easily pleased with it, it had never occurred to anybody that he was anything other than soft, squidgy and cowlike. You would have to push through a lot of soft squidgy bits in order to find a bit that didn't give when you pushed it. That was the bit that all the soft squidgy bits were there to protect.

Michael Wenton-Weakes was the younger son of Lord Magna, publisher, newspaper owner and over-indulgent father, under whose protective umbrella it had pleased Michael to run his own little magazine at a magnificent loss. Lord Magna had presided over the gradual but dignified and well-respected decline of the publishing empire originally founded by his father, the first Lord Magna.

Michael continued to tap his knuckles lightly on the glass.

A rap tap a rap a tap.

He remembered the appalling, terrible day when his father had electrocuted himself changing a plug, and his mother, his *mother*, took over the business. Not only took it over but started running it with completely unexpected verve and determination. She examined the company with a very sharp eye as to how it was being run, or walked, as she put it, and eventually even got around to looking at the accounts of Michael's magazine.

Tap tap tap.

Now Michael knew just enough about the business side of things to know what the figures ought to be, and he had simply assured his father that that was indeed what they were.

'Can't allow this job just to be a sinecure, you must see that, old fellow, you have to pay your way or how would it look, how would it be?' his father used to say, and Michael would nod seriously, and start thinking up the figures for next month, or whenever it was he would next manage to get an issue out.

His mother, on the other hand, was not so indulgent. Not by a lorryload.

Michael usually referred to his mother as an old battleaxe, but if she was fairly to be compared to a battleaxe it would only be to an exquisitely crafted, beautifully balanced battleaxe, with an elegant minimum of fine engraving which stopped just short of its gleaming razored edge. One swipe from such an instrument and you wouldn't even know you'd been hit until you tried to look at your watch a bit later and discovered that your arm wasn't on.

She had been waiting patiently – or at least with the appearance of patience – in the wings all this time, being the devoted wife, the doting but strict mother. Now someone had taken her – to switch metaphors for a moment – out of her scabbard and everyone was running for cover.

Including Michael.

It was her firm belief that Michael, whom she quietly adored, had been spoiled in the fullest and worst sense of the word, and she was determined, at this late stage, to stop it.

It didn't take her more than a few minutes to see that he had been simply making up the figures every month, and that the magazine was haemorrhaging money as Michael toyed with it, all the time running up huge lunch bills, taxi accounts and staff costs that he would playfully set against fictitious taxes. The whole thing had simply got lost somewhere in the gargantuan accounts of Magna House.

She had then summoned Michael to see her.

Tap tap a rap a tappa.

'How do you want me to treat you,' she said, 'as my son or as the editor of one of my magazines? I'm happy to do either.'

'Your magazines? Well, I am your son, but I don't see . . .'

'Right. Michael, I want you to look at these figures,' she said briskly, handing over a sheet of computer printout. 'The ones on the left show the actual incomings and outgoings of *Fathom*, the ones on the right are your own figures. Does anything strike you about them?'

'Mother, I can explain, I—'

'Good,' said Lady Magna sweetly, 'I'm very glad of that.'

She took the piece of paper back. 'Now. Do you have any views on how the magazine should best be run in the future?'

'Yes, absolutely. Very strong ones. I—'

'Good,' said Lady Magna, with a bright smile. 'Well, that's all perfectly satisfactory, then.'

'Don't you want to hear—?'

'No, that's all right, dear. I'm just happy to know that you do have something to say on the matter to clear it all up. I'm sure the new owner of *Fathom* will be glad to listen to whatever it is.'

'What?' said a stunned Michael. 'You mean you're actually selling *Fathom*?'

'No. I mean I've already sold it. Didn't get much for it, I'm afraid. One pound plus a promise that you would be retained as editor for the next three issues, and after that it's at the new owner's discretion.'

Michael stared, pop-eyed.

'Well, come now,' said his mother reasonably, 'we could hardly continue under the present arrangement, could we? You always agreed with your father that the job should not be a sinecure for you. And since I would have a great deal of difficulty in either believing or resisting your stories, I thought I would hand the problem on to someone with whom you could have a more objective relationship. Now, I have another appointment, Michael.'

'Well, but ... who have you sold it to?' spluttered Michael.

'Gordon Way.'

'Gordon Way! But for heaven's sake, Mother, he's—'

'He's very anxious to be seen to patronise the arts. And I think I do mean patronise. I'm sure you'll get on splendidly, dear. Now, if you don't mind—'

Michael stood his ground.

'I've never heard of anything so outrageous! I—'

'Do you know, that's exactly what Mr Way said when I showed him these figures and then demanded that you be kept on as editor for three issues.'

Michael huffed and puffed and went red and wagged his finger, but could think of nothing more to say. Except, 'What difference would it have made to all this if I'd said treat me as the editor of one of your magazines?'

'Why, dear,' said Lady Magna with her sweetest smile, 'I would have called you Mr Wenton-Weakes, of course. And I wouldn't now be telling you straighten your tie,' she added, with a tiny little gesture under her chin.

Rap tap tap rap tap tap.

'Number seventeen, was it, guv?'

'Er ... what?' said Michael, shaking his head.

'It was seventeen you said, was it?' said the cab driver, ''Cause we're 'ere.'

'Oh. Oh, yes, thank you,' said Michael. He climbed out and fumbled in his pocket for some money.

'Tap tap tap, eh?'

'What?' said Michael handing over the fare.

114

'Tap tap tap,' said the cab driver, 'all the bloody way here. Got something on your mind, eh, mate?'

'Mind your own bloody business,' snapped Michael savagely.

'If you say so, mate. Just thought you might be going mad or something,' said the cabbie and drove off.

Michael let himself into his house and walked through the cold hall to the dining room, turned on the overhead light and poured himself a brandy from the decanter. He took off his coat, threw it across the large mahogany dining table and pulled a chair over to the window where he sat nursing his drink and his grievances.

Tap tap tap, he went on the window.

He had sullenly remained as editor for the stipulated three issues and was then, with little ceremony, let go. A new editor was found, a certain A. K. Ross, who was young, hungry and ambitious, and he quickly turned the magazine into a resounding success. Michael, in the meantime, had been lost and naked. There was nothing else for him.

He tapped on the window again and looked, as he frequently did, at the small table lamp that stood on the sill. It was a rather ugly, ordinary little lamp, and the only thing about it that regularly transfixed his attention was that this was the lamp that had electrocuted his father, and this was where he had been sitting.

The old boy was such a fool with anything technical. Michael could just see him peering with profound concentration through his half-moons and sucking his moustache as he tried to unravel the arcane complexities of a thirteen-amp plug. He had, it seemed, plugged it back in the wall without first screwing the cover back on and then tried to change the fuse *in situ*. From this he received the shock which had stilled his already dicky heart.

Such a simple, simple error, thought Michael, such as anyone could have made, anyone, but the consequences of it were catastrophic. Utterly catastrophic. His father's death, his own loss, the rise of the appalling Ross and his disastrously successful magazine and . . .

Tap tap tap.

He looked at the window, at his own reflection, and at the dark shadows of the bushes on the other side of it. He looked again at the lamp. This was the very object, this the very place, and the error was such a simple one. Simple to make, simple to prevent.

The only thing that separated him from that simple moment was the invisible barrier of the months that had passed in between.

A sudden, odd calm descended on him as if something inside him had suddenly been resolved.

Tap tap tap.

Fathom was his. It wasn't *meant* to be a success, it was his life. His life had been taken from him, and that demanded a response.

Tap tap tap crack.

He surprised himself by suddenly punching his hand through the window and cutting himself quite badly.

15

Some of the less pleasant aspects of being dead were beginning to creep up on Gordon Way as he stood in front of his 'cottage'.

It was in fact a rather large house by anybody else's standards, but he had always wanted to have a cottage in the country and so when the time came for him finally to buy one and he discovered that he had rather more money available than he had ever seriously believed he might own, he bought a large old rectory and called it a cottage in spite of its seven bedrooms and its four acres of dank Cambridgeshire land. This did little to endear him to people who only had cottages, but then if Gordon Way had allowed his actions to be governed by what endeared him to people he wouldn't have been Gordon Way.

He wasn't, of course, Gordon Way any longer. He was the ghost of Gordon Way.

In his pocket he had the ghosts of Gordon Way's keys.

It was this realisation that had stopped him for a moment in his invisible tracks. The idea of walking through walls frankly revolted him. It was something he had been trying strenuously to avoid all night. He had instead been fighting to grip and grapple with every object he touched in order to render it, and thereby himself, substantial. To enter his house, his own house, by any means other than that of opening the front door and striding in in a proprietorial manner filled him with a hurtling sense of loss.

He wished, as he stared at it, that the house was not such an extreme example of Victorian Gothic, and that the moonlight didn't play so coldly on its narrow gabled windows and its forbidding turrets. He had joked, stupidly, when he bought it that it looked as if it ought to be haunted, not realising that one day it would be – or by whom.

A chill of the spirit gripped him as he made his way silently up the driveway, lined by the looming shapes of yew trees that were far older than the rectory itself. It was a disturbing thought that anybody else might be scared walking up such a driveway on such a night for fear of meeting something such as him.

Behind a screen of yew trees off to his left stood the gloomy bulk of the old church, decaying now, only used in rotation with others in neighbouring villages and presided over by a vicar who was always breathless from bicycling there and dispirited by the few who were waiting for him when he arrived. Behind the steeple of the church hung the cold eye of the moon.

A glimpse of movement seemed suddenly to catch his eye, as if a figure had moved in the bushes near the house, but it was, he told himself, only his imagination, overwrought by the strain of being dead. What was there here that he could possibly be afraid of?

He continued onwards, around the angle of the wing of the rectory, towards the front door set deep within its gloomy porch wreathed in ivy. He was suddenly startled to realise that there was light coming from within the house. Electric light and also the dim flicker of firelight.

It was a moment or two before he realised that he was, of course, expected that night, though hardly in his present form. Mrs Bennett, the elderly housekeeper, would have been in to make the bed, light the fire and leave out a light supper for him.

The television, too, would be on, especially so that he could turn it off impatiently upon entering.

His footsteps failed to crunch on the gravel as he approached. Though he knew that he must fail at the door, he nevertheless could not but go there first, to try if he could open it, and only then, hidden within the shadows of the porch, would he close his eyes and let himself slip ashamedly through it. He stepped up to the door and stopped.

It was open.

Just half an inch, but it was open. His spirit fluttered in fearful surprise. How could it be open? Mrs Bennett was always so conscientious about such things. He stood uncertainly for a moment and then with difficulty exerted himself against the door. Under the little pressure he could bring to bear on it, it swung slowly and unwillingly open, its hinges groaning in protest. He stepped through and slipped along the stone-flagged hallway. A wide staircase led up into the darkness, but the doors that led off from the hallway all stood closed.

The nearest door led into the drawing room, in which the fire was burning, and from which he could hear the muted car chases of the late movie. He struggled futilely for a minute or two with its shiny brass doorknob, but was forced in the end to admit a humiliating defeat, and with a sudden rage flung himself straight at the door – and through it.

The room inside was a picture of pleasant domestic warmth. He staggered violently into it, and was unable to stop himself floating on through a small occasional table set with thick sandwiches and a Thermos flask of hot coffee, through a large overstuffed armchair, into the fire, through the thick hot brickwork and into the cold dark dining room beyond.

The connecting door back into the sitting room was

also closed. Gordon fingered it numbly and then, submitting himself to the inevitable, braced himself, and slid back through it, calmly, gently, noticing for the first time the rich internal grain of the wood.

The coziness of the room was almost too much for Gordon, and he wandered distractedly around it, unable to settle, letting the warm liveliness of the firelight play through him. Him it couldn't warm.

What, he wondered, were ghosts supposed to do all night?

He sat, uneasily, and watched the television. Soon, however, the car chases drifted peacefully to a close and there was nothing left but grey snow and white noise, which he was unable to turn off.

He found he'd sunk too far into the chair and confused himself with bits of it as he pushed and pulled himself up. He tried to amuse himself by standing in the middle of a table, but it did little to alleviate a mood that was sliding inexorably from despondency downwards.

Perhaps he would sleep.

Perhaps.

He felt no tiredness or drowsiness, but just a deadly craving for oblivion. He passed back through the closed door and into the dark hallway, from which the wide heavy stairs led to the large gloomy bedrooms above.

Up these, emptily, he trod.

It was for nothing, he knew. If you cannot open the door to a bedroom you cannot sleep in its bed. He slid himself through the door and lifted himself on to the bed which he knew to be cold though he could not feel it. The moon seemed unable to leave him alone and shone full on him as he lay there wide-eyed and empty, unable now to remember what sleep was or how to do it.

The horror of hollowness lay on him, the horror of

lying ceaselessly and forever awake at four o'clock in the morning.

He had nowhere to go, nothing to do when he got there, and no one he could go and wake up who wouldn't be utterly horrified to see him.

The worst moment had been when he had seen Richard on the road, Richard's face frozen white in the windscreen. He saw again his face, and that of the pale figure next to him.

That had been the thing which had shaken out of him the lingering shred of warmth at the back of his mind which said that this was just a temporary problem. It seemed terrible in the night hours, but would be all right in the morning when he could see people and sort things out. He fingered the memory of the moment in his mind and could not let it go.

He had seen Richard and Richard, he knew, had seen him.

It was not going to be all right.

Usually when he felt this bad at night he popped downstairs to see what was in the fridge, so he went now. It would be more cheerful than this moonlit bedroom. He would hang around the kitchen going bump in the night.

He slid down – and partially through – the banisters, wafted through the kitchen door without a second thought and then devoted all his concentration and energy for about five minutes to getting the light switch on.

That gave him a real sense of achievement and he determined to celebrate with a beer.

After a minute or two of repeatedly juggling and dropping a can of Fosters he gave it up. He had not the slightest conception of how he could manage to open a ring pull, and besides, the stuff was all shaken up by now – and what was he going to do with the stuff even if he did get it open?

He didn't have a body to keep it in. He hurled the can away from him and it scuttled off under a cupboard.

He began to notice something about himself, which was the way in which his ability to grasp things seemed to grow and fade in a slow rhythm, as did his visibility.

There was an irregularity in the rhythm, though, or perhaps it was just that sometimes the effects of it would be much more pronounced than at others. That, too, seemed to vary according to a slower rhythm. Just at that moment it seemed to him that his strength was on the increase.

In a sudden fever of activity he tried to see how many things in the kitchen he could move or use or somehow get to work.

He pulled open cupboards, he yanked out drawers, scattering cutlery on the floor. He got a brief whirr out of the food processor, he knocked over the electric coffee grinder without getting it to work, he turned on the gas on the cooker hob but then couldn't light it, he savaged a loaf of bread with a carving knife. He tried stuffing lumps of bread into his mouth, but they simply fell through his mouth to the floor. A mouse appeared, but scurried from the room, its coat electric with fear.

Eventually he stopped and sat at the kitchen table, emotionally exhausted but physically numb.

How, he wondered, would people react to his death?

Who would be most sorry to know that he had gone?

For a while there would be shock, then sadness, then they would adjust, and he would be a fading memory as people got on with their own lives without him, thinking that he had gone on to wherever people go. That was a thought that filled him with the most icy dread.

He had not gone. He was still here.

He sat facing one cupboard that he hadn't managed to open yet because its handle was too stiff, and that annoyed him. He grappled awkwardly with a tin of tomatoes, then went over again to the large cupboard and attacked the handle with the tin. The door flew open and his own missing bloodstained body fell horribly forward out of it.

Gordon hadn't realised up till this point that it was possible for a ghost to faint.

He realised it now and did it.

He was woken a couple of hours later by the sound of his gas cooker exploding.

16

The following morning Richard woke up twice.

The first time he assumed he had made a mistake and turned over for a fitful few minutes more. The second time he sat up with a jolt as the events of the previous night insisted themselves upon him.

He went downstairs and had a moody and unsettled breakfast, during which nothing went right. He burned the toast, spilled the coffee, and realised that though he'd meant to buy some more marmalade yesterday, he hadn't. He surveyed his feeble attempt at feeding himself and thought that maybe he could at least allow himself the time to take Susan out for an amazing meal tonight, to make up for last night.

If he could persuade her to come.

There was a restaurant that Gordon had been enthusing about at great length and recommending that they try. Gordon was pretty good on restaurants – he certainly seemed to spend enough time in them. He sat and tapped his teeth with a pencil for a couple of minutes, and then went up to his workroom and lugged a telephone directory out from under a pile of computer magazines.

L'Esprit d'Escalier.

He phoned the restaurant and tried to book a table, but when he said when he wanted it for this seemed to cause a little amusement.

'Ah, non, m'sieur,' said the maître d', 'I regret that it is impossible. At this moment it is necessary to make reservations at least three weeks in advance. Pardon, m'sieur.'

Richard marvelled at the idea that there were people who actually knew what they wanted to do three weeks in advance, thanked the maître d' and rang off. Well, maybe a pizza again instead. This thought connected back to the appointment he had failed to keep last night, and after a moment curiosity overcame him and he reached for the phone book again.

Gentleman . . .

Gentles . . .

Gentry.

There was no Gently at all. Not a single one. He found the other directories, except for the S–Z book which his cleaning lady continually threw away for reasons he had never yet fathomed.

There was certainly no Cjelli, or anything like it. There was no Jently, no Dgently, no Djently, no Dzently, nor anything remotely similar. He wondered about Tjently, Tsentli or Tzentli and tried Directory Enquiries, but they were out. He sat and tapped his teeth with a pencil again and watched his sofa slowly revolving on the screen of his computer.

How very peculiar it had been that it had only been hours earlier that Reg had asked after Dirk with such urgency.

If you really wanted to find someone, how would you set about it, what would you do?

He tried phoning the police, but they were out too. Well, that was that. He had done all he could do for the moment short of hiring a private detective, and he had better ways of wasting his time and money. He would run into Dirk again, as he did every few years or so.

He found it hard to believe there were really such people, anyway, as private detectives.

What sort of people were they? What did they look like, where did they work?

What sort of tie would you wear if you were a private detective? Presumably it would have to be exactly the sort of tie that people wouldn't expect private detectives to wear. Imagine having to sort out a problem like that when you'd just got up.

Just out of curiosity as much as anything else, and because the only alternative was settling down to *Anthem* coding, he found himself leafing through the Yellow Pages.

Private Detectives – see Detective Agencies.

The words looked almost odd in such a solid and businesslike context. He flipped back through the book. Dry Cleaners, Dog Breeders, Dental Technicians, Detective Agencies . . .

At that moment the phone rang and he answered it, a little curtly. He didn't like being interrupted.

'Something wrong, Richard?'

'Oh, hi, Kate, sorry, no. I was . . . my mind was elsewhere.'

Kate Anselm was another star programmer at Way-Forward Technologies. She was working on a long-term Artificial Intelligence project, the sort of thing that sounded like an absurd pipe dream until you heard her talking about it. Gordon needed to hear her talking about it quite regularly, partly because he was nervous about the money it was costing and partly because, well, there was little doubt that Gordon liked to hear Kate talking anyway.

'I didn't want to disturb you,' she said. 'It's just I was trying to contact Gordon and can't. There's no reply from London or the cottage, or his car or his bleeper. It's just that for someone as obsessively in contact as Gordon it's a bit odd. You heard he's had a phone put in his isolation tank? True.'

'I haven't spoken to him since yesterday,' said Richard. He suddenly remembered the tape he had taken from Susan's answering machine, and hoped to God there wasn't anything more important in Gordon's message than ravings about rabbits. He said. 'I know he was going to the cottage. Er, I don't know where he is. Have you tried—' Richard couldn't think of anywhere else to try – '. . . er. Good God.'

'Richard?'

'How extraordinary . . .'

'Richard, what's the matter?'

'Nothing, Kate. Er, I've just read the most astounding thing.'

'Really, what are you reading?'

'Well, the telephone directory, in fact . . .'

'Really? I must rush out and buy one. Have the film rights gone?'

'Look, sorry, Kate, can I get back to you? I don't know where Gordon is at the moment and—'

'Don't worry. I know how it is when you can't wait to turn the next page. They always keep you guessing till the end, don't they? It must have been Zbigniew that did it. Have a good weekend.' She hung up.

Richard hung up too, and sat staring at the box advertisement lying open in front of him in the Yellow Pages.

DIRK GENTLY'S
HOLISTIC DETECTIVE AGENCY
We solve the *whole* crime
We find the *whole* person
Phone today for the *whole* solution to your problem
(Missing cats and messy divorces a speciality)
33a Peckender St., London N1 01-354 9112

Peckender Street was only a few minutes' walk away. Richard scribbled down the address, pulled on his coat and trotted downstairs, stopping to make another quick inspection of the sofa. There must, he thought, be something terribly obvious that he was overlooking. The sofa was jammed on a slight turn in the long narrow stairway. At this point the stairs were interrupted for a couple of yards of flat landing, which corresponded with the position of the flat directly beneath Richard's. However, his inspection produced no new insights, and he eventually clambered on over it and out of the front door.

In Islington you can hardly hurl a brick without hitting three antique shops, an estate agent and a bookshop.

Even if you didn't actually hit them you would certainly set off their burglar alarms, which wouldn't be turned off again till after the weekend. A police car played its regular game of dodgems down Upper Street and squealed to a halt just past him. Richard crossed the road behind it.

The day was cold and bright, which he liked. He walked across the top of Islington Green, where winos get beaten up, past the site of the old Collins Music Hall which had got burnt down, and through Camden Passage where American tourists get ripped off. He browsed among the antiques for a while and looked at a pair of earrings that he thought Susan would like, but he wasn't sure. Then he wasn't sure that he liked them, got confused and gave up. He looked in at a bookshop, and on an impulse bought an anthology of Coleridge's poems since it was just lying there.

From here he threaded his way through the winding backstreets, over the canal, past the council estates that lined the canal, through a number of smaller and smaller squares, till finally he reached Peckender Street, which had turned out to be a good deal farther than he'd thought.

It was the sort of street where property developers in large Jaguars drive around at the weekend salivating. It was full of end-of-lease shops, Victorian industrial architecture and a short, decaying late-Georgian terrace, all just itching to be pulled down so that sturdy young concrete boxes could sprout in their places. Estate agents roamed the area in hungry packs, eyeing each other warily, their clipboards on a hair trigger.

Number 33, when he eventually found it neatly sandwiched between 37 and 45, was in a poorish state of repair, but no worse than most of the rest.

The ground floor was a dusty travel agent's whose window was cracked and whose faded BOAC posters were probably now quite valuable. The doorway next to the shop had been painted bright red, not well, but at least recently. A push button next to the door said, in neatly pencilled lettering, 'Dominique, French lessons, 3me Floor'.

The most striking feature of the door, however, was the bold and shiny brass plaque fixed in the dead centre of it, on which was engraved the legend 'Dirk Gently's Holistic Detective Agency'.

Nothing else. It looked brand new – even the screws that held it in place were still shiny.

The door opened to Richard's push and he peered inside.

He saw a short and musty hallway which contained little but the stairway that led up from it. A door at the back of the hall showed little sign of having been opened in recent years, and had stacks of old metal shelving, a fish tank and the carcass of a bike piled up against it. Everything else, the walls, the floor, the stairs themselves, and as much of the rear door as could be got at, had been painted grey in an attempt to smarten it up cheaply, but it was all now badly scuffed, and little cups of fungus were peeking from a damp stain near the ceiling.

The sounds of angry voices reached him, and as he started up the stairs he was able to disentangle the noises of two entirely separate but heated arguments that were going on somewhere above him.

One ended abruptly – or at least half of it did – as an angry overweight man came clattering down the stairs pulling his raincoat collar straight. The other half of the argument continued in a torrent of aggrieved French from high above them. The man pushed past Richard, said, 'Save your money, mate, it's a complete washout,' and disappeared out into the chilly morning.

The other argument was more muffled. As Richard reached the first corridor a door slammed somewhere and brought that too to an end. He looked into the nearest open doorway.

It led into a small ante-office. The other, inner door leading from it was firmly closed. A youngish plump-faced girl in a cheap blue coat was pulling sticks of make-up and boxes of Kleenex out of her desk drawer and thrusting them into her bag.

'Is this the detective agency?' Richard asked her tentatively.

The girl nodded, biting her lip and keeping her head down.

'And is Mr Gently in?'

'He may be,' she said, throwing back her hair, which was too curly for throwing back properly, 'and then again he may not be, I am not in a position to tell. It is not my business to know of his whereabouts. His whereabouts are, as of now, entirely his own business.'

She retrieved her last pot of nail varnish and tried to slam the drawer shut. A fat book sitting upright in the drawer prevented it from closing. She tried to slam the drawer again, without success. She picked up the book, ripped out a clump of pages and replaced it. This time she was able to slam the drawer with ease.

'Are you his secretary?' asked Richard.

'I am his ex-secretary and I intend to stay that way,' she said, firmly snapping her bag shut. 'If he intends to spend his money on stupid expensive brass plaques rather than on paying me, then let him. But I won't stay to stand for it, thank you very much. Good for business, my foot. Answering the phones properly is good for business and I'd like to see his fancy brass plaque do that. If you'll excuse me I'd like to storm out, please.'

Richard stood aside, and out she stormed.

'And good riddance!' shouted a voice from the inner office. A phone rang and was picked up immediately.

'Yes?' answered the voice from the inner office, testily. The girl popped back for her scarf, but quietly, so her ex-employer wouldn't hear. Then she was finally gone.

'Yes, Dirk Gently's Holistic Detective Agency. How can we be of help to you?'

The torrent of French from upstairs had ceased. A kind of tense calm descended.

Inside, the voice said, 'That's right, Mrs Sunderland, messy divorces are our particular speciality.'

There was a pause.

'Yes, thank you, Mrs Sunderland, not quite that messy.' Down went the phone again, to be replaced instantly by the ringing of another one.

Richard looked around the grim little office. There was very little in it. A battered chipboard veneer desk, an old grey filing cabinet and a dark green tin wastepaper bin. On the wall was a Duran Duran poster on which someone had scrawled in fat red felt tip, 'Take this down please'.

Beneath that another hand had scrawled, 'No'.

Beneath that again the first hand had written, 'I insist that you take it down'.

Beneath that the second hand had written, 'Won't!'

Beneath that – 'You're fired'.

Beneath that – 'Good!'

And there the matter appeared to have rested.

He knocked on the inner door, but was not answered. Instead the voice continued, 'I'm very glad you asked me that, Mrs Rawlinson. The term "holistic" refers to my conviction that what we are concerned with here is the fundamental interconnectedness of all things. I do not concern myself with such petty things as fingerprint powder, telltale pieces of pocket fluff and inane foot-prints, I see the solution to each problem as being detectable in the pattern and web of the whole. The connections between causes and effects are often much more subtle and complex than we with our rough and ready understanding of the physical world might nat-urally suppose, Mrs Rawlinson.

'Let me give you an example. If you go to an acu-puncturist with toothache he sticks a needle instead into your thigh. Do you know why he does that, Mrs Rawlinson?

'No, neither do I, Mrs Rawlinson, but we intend to find out. A pleasure talking to you, Mrs Rawlinson. Goodbye.'

Another phone was ringing as he put this one down.

Richard eased the door open and looked in.

It was the same Svlad, or Dirk, Cjelli. Looking a little rounder about the middle, a little looser and redder about the eyes and the neck, but it was still essentially the same face that he remembered most vividly smiling a grim smile as its owner climbed into the back of one of the Black Marias of the Cambridgeshire constabulary, eight years previously.

He wore a heavy old light-brown suit which looked as if it has been worn extensively for bramble-hacking expeditions in some distant and better past, a red checked shirt which failed entirely to harmonise with the suit, and a green striped tie which refused to speak to either of them. He also wore thick metal-rimmed spectacles, which probably accounted at least in part for his dress sense.

'Ah, Mrs Bluthall, how thoroughly uplifting to hear from you,' he was saying. 'I was so distressed to learn that Miss Tiddles has passed over. This is desperate news indeed. And yet, and yet ... Should we allow black despair to hide from us the fairer light in which your blessed moggy now forever dwells?

'I think not. Hark. I think I hear Miss Tiddles miaowing e'en now. She calls to you, Mrs Bluthall. She says she is content, she is at peace. She says she'll be even more at peace when you've paid some bill or other. Does that ring a bell with you at all, Mrs Bluthall? Come to think of it I think I sent you one myself not three months ago. I wonder if it can be that which is disturbing her eternal rest.'

Dirk beckoned Richard in with a brisk wave and then motioned him to pass the crumpled pack of French cigarettes that was sitting just out of his reach.

'Sunday night, then, Mrs Bluthall, Sunday night at eight-thirty. You know the address. Yes, I'm sure Miss Tiddles will appear, as I'm sure will your chequebook. Till then, Mrs Bluthall, till then.'

Another phone was already ringing as he got rid of Mrs Bluthall. He grabbed at it, lighting his crumpled cigarette at the same time.

'Ah, Mrs Sauskind,' he said in answer to the caller, 'my oldest and may I say most valued client. Good day to you, Mrs Sauskind, good day. Sadly, no sign as yet of young Roderick, I'm afraid, but the search is intensifying as it moves into what I am confident are its closing stages, and I am sanguine that within mere days from today's date we will have the young rascal permanently restored to your arms and mewing prettily, ah yes the bill, I was wondering if you had received it.'

Dirk's crumpled cigarette turned out to be too crumpled to smoke, so he hooked the phone on his shoulder and poked around in the packet for another, but it was empty.

He rummaged on his desk for a piece of paper and a stub of pencil and wrote a note which he passed to Richard.

'Yes, Mrs Sauskind,' he assured the telephone, 'I am listening with the utmost attention.'

The note said 'Tell secretary get cigs'.

'Yes,' continued Dirk into the phone, 'but as I have endeavoured to explain to you, Mrs Sauskind, over the seven years of our acquaintance, I incline to the quantum mechanical view in this matter. My theory is that your cat is not lost, but that his waveform has temporarily collapsed and must be restored. Schrödinger. Planck. And so on.'

Richard wrote on the note 'You haven't got secretary' and pushed it back.

Dirk considered this for a while, then wrote 'Damn and blast' on the paper and pushed it to Richard again.

'I grant you, Mrs Sauskind,' continued Dirk blithely, 'that nineteen years is, shall we say, a distinguished age for a cat to reach, yet can we allow ourselves to believe that a cat such as Roderick has not reached it?

'And should we now in the autumn of h
abandon him to his fate? This surely is the time th
most needs the support of our continuing investigatio.
This is the time that we should redouble our efforts, and
with your permission, Mrs Sauskind, that is what I
intend to do. Imagine, Mrs Sauskind, how you would
face him if you had not done this simple thing for him.'

Richard fidgeted with the note, shrugged to himself,
and wrote 'I'll get them' on it and passed it back once
more.

Dirk shook his head in admonition, then wrote 'I
couldn't possibly that would be most kind'. As soon as
Richard had read this, Dirk took the note back and
added 'Get money from secretary' to it.

Richard looked at the paper thoughtfully, took the
pencil and put a tick next to where he had previously
written 'You haven't got secretary'. He pushed the paper
back across the table to Dirk, who merely glanced at it
and ticked 'I couldn't possibly that would be most kind'.

'Well, perhaps,' continued Dirk to Mrs Sauskind, 'you
could just run over any of the areas in the bill that cause
you difficulty. Just the broader areas.'

Richard let himself out.

Running down the stairs, he passed a young hopeful
in a denim jacket and close-cropped hair peering anxiously up the stairwell.

'Any good, mate?' he said to Richard.

'Amazing,' murmured Richard, 'just amazing.'

He found a nearby newsagent's and picked up a
couple of packets of Disque Bleu for Dirk, and a copy of
the new edition of *Personal Computer World*, which had a
picture of Gordon Way on the front.

'Pity about him, isn't it?' said the newsagent.

'What? Oh, er . . . yes,' said Richard. He often thought

the same himself, but was surprised to find his feelings so widely echoed. He picked up a *Guardian* as well, paid and left.

Dirk was still on the phone with his feet on the table when Richard returned, and it was clear that he was relaxing into his negotiations.

'Yes, expenses were, well, expensive in the Bahamas, Mrs Sauskind, it is in the nature of expenses to be so. Hence the name.' He took the proffered packets of cigarettes, seemed disappointed there were only two, but briefly raised his eyebrows to Richard in acknowledgement of the favour he had done him, and then waved him to a chair.

The sounds of an argument conducted partly in French drifted down from the floor above.

'Of course I will explain to you again why the trip to the Bahamas was so vitally necessary,' said Dirk Gently soothingly. 'Nothing could give me greater pleasure. I believe, as you know, Mrs Sauskind, in the fundamental interconnectedness of all things. Furthermore, I have plotted and triangulated the vectors of the interconnectedness of all things and traced them to a beach in Bermuda which it is therefore necessary for me to visit from time to time in the course of my investigations. I wish it were not the case, since, sadly, I am allergic to both the sun and rum punches, but then we all have our crosses to bear, do we not, Mrs Sauskind?'

A babble seemed to break out from the telephone.

'You sadden me, Mrs Sauskind. I wish I could find it in my heart to tell you that I find your scepticism rewarding and invigorating, but with the best will in the world I cannot. I am drained by it, Mrs Sauskind, drained. I think you will find an item in the bill to that 'fect. Let me see.'

He picked up a flimsy carbon copy lying near him.

'"Detecting and triangulating the vectors of interconnectedness of all things, one hundred and fifty pounds." We've dealt with that.

'"Tracing same to beach on Bahamas, fare and accommodation". A mere fifteen hundred. The accommodation was, of course, distressingly modest.

'Ah yes, here we are, "Struggling on in the face of draining scepticism from client, drinks – three hundred and twenty-seven pounds fifty."

'Would that I did not have to make such charges, my dear Mrs Sauskind, would that the occasion did not continually arise. Not believing in my methods only makes my job more difficult, Mrs Sauskind, and hence, regrettably, more expensive.'

Upstairs, the sounds of argument were becoming more heated by the moment. The French voice seemed to be verging on hysteria.

'I do appreciate, Mrs Sauskind,' continued Dirk, 'that the cost of the investigation has strayed somewhat from the original estimate, but I am sure that you will in your turn appreciate that a job which takes seven years to do must clearly be more difficult than one that can be pulled off in an afternoon and must therefore be charged at a higher rate. I have continually to revise my estimate of how difficult the task is in the light of how difficult it has so far proved to be.'

The babble from the phone became more frantic.

'My dear Mrs Sauskind – or may I call you Joyce? Very well then. My dear Mrs Sauskind, let me say this. Do not worry yourself about this bill, do not let it alarm or discomfit you. Do not, I beg you, let it become a source of anxiety to you. Just grit your teeth and pay it.'

He pulled his feet down off the table and leaned forward over the desk, inching the telephone receiver inexorably back towards its cradle.

'As always, the very greatest pleasure to speak with you, Mrs Sauskind. For now, goodbye.'

He at last put down the receiver, picked it up again, and dropped it for the moment into the waste basket.

'My dear Richard MacDuff,' he said, producing a large flat box from under his desk and pushing it across the table at him, 'your pizza.'

Richard started back in astonishment.

'Er, no thanks,' he said, 'I had breakfast. Please. You have it.'

Dirk shrugged. 'I told them you'd pop in and settle up over the weekend,' he said. 'Welcome, by the way, to my offices.'

He waved a vague hand around the tatty surroundings.

'The light works,' he said, indicating the window, 'the gravity works,' he said, dropping a pencil on the floor. 'Anything else we have to take our chances with.'

Richard cleared his throat. 'What,' he said, 'is this?'

'What is what?'

'This,' exclaimed Richard, 'all this. You appear to have a Holistic Detective Agency and I don't even know what one is.'

'I provide a service that is unique in this world,' said Dirk. 'The term "holistic" refers to my conviction that what we are concerned with here is the fundamental interconnectedness of all—'

'Yes, I got that bit earlier,' said Richard. 'I have to say that it sounded a bit like an excuse for exploiting gullible old ladies.'

'Exploiting?' asked Dirk. 'Well, I suppose it would be if anybody ever paid me, but I do assure you, my dear

Richard, that there never seems to be the remotest danger of that. I live in what are known as hopes. I hope for fascinating and remunerative cases, my secretary hopes that I will pay her, her landlord hopes that she will produce some rent, the Electricity Board hopes that he will settle their bill, and so on. I find it a wonderfully optimistic way of life.

'Meanwhile, I give a lot of charming and silly old ladies something to be happily cross about and virtually guarantee the freedom of their cats. Is there, you ask – and I put the question for you because I know you know I hate to be interrupted – is there a single case that exercises the tiniest part of my intellect, which, as you hardly need me to tell you, is prodigious? No. But do I despair? Am I downcast? Yes. Until,' he added, 'today.'

'Oh, well, I'm glad of that,' said Richard, 'but what was all that rubbish about cats and quantum mechanics?'

With a sigh Dirk flipped up the lid of the pizza with a single flick of practised fingers. He surveyed the cold round thing with a kind of sadness and then tore off a hunk of it. Pieces of pepperoni and anchovy scattered over his desk.

'I am sure, Richard,' he said, 'that you are familiar with the notion of Schrödinger's Cat,' and he stuffed the larger part of the hunk into his mouth.

'Of course,' said Richard. 'Well, reasonably familiar.'

'What is it?' said Dirk through a mouthful.

Richard shifted irritably in his seat. 'It's an illustration,' he said, 'of the principle that at a quantum level all events are governed by probabilities . . .'

'At a quantum level, and therefore at all levels,' interrupted Dirk. 'Though at any level higher than the subatomic the cumulative effect of those probabilities is, in the normal course of events, indistinguishable from the effect of hard and fast physical laws. Continue.'

He put some more cold pizza into his face.

Richard reflected that Dirk's was a face into which too much had already been put. What with that and the amount he talked, the traffic through his mouth was almost incessant. His ears, on the other hand, remained almost totally unused in normal conversation.

It occurred to Richard that if Lamarck had been right and you were to take a line through this behaviour for several generations, the chances were that some radical replumbing of the interior of the skull would eventually take place.

Richard continued, 'Not only are quantum level events governed by probabilities, but those probabilities aren't even resolved into actual events until they are measured. Or to use a phrase that I just heard you use in a rather bizarre context, the act of measurement collapses the probability waveform. Up until that point all the possible courses of action open to, say, an electron, coexist as probability waveforms. Nothing is decided. Until it's measured.'

Dirk nodded. 'More or less,' he said, taking another mouthful. 'But what of the cat?'

Richard decided that there was only one way to avoid having to watch Dirk eat his way through all the rest of the pizza, and that was to eat the rest himself. He rolled it up and took a token nibble off the end. It was rather good. He took another bite.

Dirk watched this with startled dismay.

'So,' said Richard, 'the idea behind Schrödinger's Cat was to try and imagine a way in which the effects of probabilistic behaviour at a quantum level could be considered at a macroscopic level. Or let's say an every-day level.'

'Yes, let's,' said Dirk, regarding the rest of the pizza

with a stricken look. Richard took another bite and continued cheerfully.

'So you imagine that you take a cat and put it in a box that you can seal completely. Also in the box you put a small lump of radioactive material, and a phial of poison gas. You arrange it so that within a given period of time there is an exactly fifty-fifty chance that an atom in the radioactive lump will decay and emit an electron. If it does decay then it triggers the release of the gas and kills the cat. If it doesn't, the cat lives. Fifty-fifty. Depending on the fifty-fifty chance that a single atom does or does not decay.

'The point as I understand it is this: since the decay of a single atom is a quantum-level event that wouldn't be resolved either way until it was observed, and since you don't make the observation until you open the box and see whether the cat is alive or dead, then there's a rather extraordinary consequence.

'Until you do open the box the cat itself exists in an indeterminate state. The possibility that it is alive, and the possibility that it is dead, are two different waveforms superimposed on each other inside the box. Schrödinger put forward this idea to illustrate what he thought was absurd about quantum theory.'

Dirk got up and padded over to the window, probably not so much for the meagre view it afforded over an old warehouse on which an alternative comedian was lavishing his vast lager-commercial fees developing it into luxury apartments, as for the lack of view it afforded of the last piece of pizza disappearing.

'Exactly,' said Dirk, 'bravo!'

'But what's all that got to do with this – this Detective Agency?'

'Oh, that. Well, some researchers were once conducting

such an experiment, but when they opened up the box, the cat was neither alive nor dead but was in fact completely missing, and they called me in to investigate. I was able to deduce that nothing very dramatic had happened. The cat had merely got fed up with being repeatedly locked up in a box and occasionally gassed and had taken the first opportunity to hoof it through the window. It was for me the work of a moment to set a saucer of milk by the window and call "Bernice" in an enticing voice – the cat's name was Bernice, you understand—'

'Now, wait a minute—' said Richard.

'—and the cat was soon restored. A simple enough matter, but it seemed to create quite an impression in certain circles, and soon one thing led to another as they do and it all culminated in the thriving career you see before you.'

'Wait a minute, wait a minute,' insisted Richard, slapping the table.

'Yes?' enquired Dirk innocently.

'Now, what are you talking about, Dirk?'

'You have a problem with what I have told you?'

'Well, I hardly know where to begin,' protested Richard. 'All right. You said that some people were performing the experiment. That's nonsense. Schrödinger's Cat isn't a real experiment. It's just an illustration for arguing about the idea. It's not something you'd actually do.'

Dirk was watching him with odd attention.

'Oh, really?' he said at last. 'And why not?'

'Well, there's nothing you can test. The whole point of the idea is to think about what happens before you make your observation. You can't know what's going on inside the box without looking, and the very instant you look the wave packet collapses and the probabilities resolve. It's self-defeating. It's completely purposeless.'

'You are, of course, perfectly correct as far as you go,' replied Dirk, returning to his seat. He drew a cigarette out of the packet, tapped it several times on the desk, and leant across the desk and pointed the filter at Richard.

'But think about this,' he continued. 'Supposing you were to introduce a psychic, someone with clairvoyant powers, into the experiment – someone who is able to divine what state of health the cat is in without opening the box. Someone who has, perhaps, a certain eerie sympathy with cats. What then? Might that furnish us with an additional insight into the problem of quantum physics?'

'Is that what they wanted to do?'

'It's what they did.'

'Dirk, this is *complete nonsense.*'

Dirk raised his eyebrows challengingly.

'All right, all right,' said Richard, holding up his palms, 'let's just follow it through. Even if I accepted – which I don't for one second – that there was any basis at all for clairvoyance, it wouldn't alter the fundamental undoableness of the experiment. As I said, the whole thing turns on what happens inside the box before it's observed. It doesn't matter how you observe it, whether you look into the box with your eyes or – well, with your mind, if you insist. If clairvoyance works, then it's just another way of looking into the box, and if it doesn't then of course it's irrelevant.'

'It might depend, of course, on the view you take of clairvoyance . . .'

'Oh yes? And what view do you take of clairvoyance? I should be very interested to know, given your history.'

Dirk tapped the cigarette on the desk again and looked narrowly at Richard.

There was a deep and prolonged silence, disturbed only by the sound of distant crying in French.

'I take the view I have always taken,' said Dirk eventually.

'Which is?'

'That I am not clairvoyant.'

'Really,' said Richard. 'Then what about the exam papers?'

The eyes of Dirk Gently darkened at the mention of this subject.

'A coincidence,' he said, in a low, savage voice, 'a strange and chilling coincidence, but none the less a coincidence. One, I might add, which caused me to spend a considerable time in prison. Coincidences can be frightening and dangerous things.'

Dirk gave Richard another of his long appraising looks.

'I have been watching you carefully,' he said. 'You seem to be extremely relaxed for a man in your position.'

This seemed to Richard to be an odd remark, and he tried to make sense of it for a moment. Then the light dawned, and it was an aggravating light.

'Good heavens,' he said, 'he hasn't got to you as well, has he?'

This remark seemed to puzzle Dirk in return.

'Who hasn't got to me?' he said.

'Gordon. No, obviously not. Gordon Way. He has this habit of trying to get other people to bring pressure on me to get on with what he sees as important work. I thought for a moment – oh, never mind. What did you mean, then?'

'Ah. Gordon Way *has* this habit, has he?'

'Yes. I don't like it. Why?'

Dirk looked long and hard at Richard, tapping a pencil lightly on the desk.

Then he leaned back in his chair and said as follows:

'The body of Gordon Way was discovered before dawn

this morning. He had been shot, strangled, and then his house was set on fire. Police are working on the theory that he was not actually shot in the house because no shotgun pellets were discovered there other than those in the body.

'However, pellets were found near to Mr Way's Mercedes 500 SEC, which was found abandoned about three miles from his house. This suggests that the body was moved after the murder. Furthermore, the doctor who examined the body is of the opinion that Mr Way was in fact strangled after he was shot, which seems to suggest a certain confusion in the mind of the killer.

'By a startling coincidence it appears that the police last night had occasion to interview a very confused-seeming gentleman who said that he was suffering from some kind of guilt complex about having just run over his employer.

'That man was a Mr Richard MacDuff, and his employer was the deceased, Mr Gordon Way. It has further been suggested that Mr Richard MacDuff is one of the two people most likely to benefit from Mr Way's death, since WayForward Technologies would almost certainly pass at least partly into his hands. The other person is his only living relative, Miss Susan Way, into whose flat Mr Richard MacDuff was observed to break last night. The police don't know that bit, of course. Nor, if we can help it, will they. However, any relationship between the two of them will naturally come under close scrutiny. The news reports on the radio say that they are urgently seeking Mr MacDuff, who they believe will be able to help them with their enquiries, but the tone of voice says that he's clearly guilty as hell.

'My scale of charges is as follows: two hundred pounds a day, plus expenses. Expenses are not negotiable and will sometimes strike those who do not understand these matters as somewhat tangential. They are all necessary and are, as I say, not negotiable. Am I hired?'

'Sorry,' said Richard, nodding slightly. 'Would you start that again?'

17

The Electric Monk hardly knew what to believe any more.

He had been through a bewildering number of belief systems in the previous few hours, most of which had failed to provide him with the long-term spiritual solace that it was his bounden programming eternally to seek.

He was fed up. Frankly. And tired. And dispirited.

And furthermore, which caught him by surprise, he rather missed his horse. A dull and menial creature, to be sure, and as such hardly worthy of the preoccupation of one whose mind was destined forever to concern itself with higher things beyond the understanding of a simple horse, but nevertheless he missed it.

He wanted to sit on it. He wanted to pat it. He wanted to feel that it didn't understand.

He wondered where it was.

He dangled his feet disconsolately from the branch of the tree in which he had spent the night. He had climbed it in pursuit of some wild fantastic dream and then had got stuck and had to stay there till the morning.

Even now, by daylight, he wasn't certain how he was going to get down. He came for a moment perilously close to believing that he could fly, but a quick-thinking error-checking protocol cut in and told him not to be so silly.

It was a problem though.

Whatever burning fire of faith had borne him, inspired

on wings of hope, upwards through the branches of the tree in the magic hours of night, had not also provided him with instructions on how to get back down again when, like altogether too many of these burning fiery night-time faiths, it had deserted him in the morning.

And speaking – or rather thinking – of burning fiery things, there had been a major burning fiery thing a little distance from here in the early pre-dawn hours.

It lay, he thought, in the direction from which he himself had come when he had been drawn by a deep spiritual compulsion towards this inconveniently high but otherwise embarrassingly ordinary tree. He had longed to go and worship at the fire, to pledge himself eternally to its holy glare, but while he had been struggling hopelessly to find a way downwards through the branches, fire engines had arrived and put the divine radiance out, and that had been another creed out of the window.

The sun had been up for some hours now, and though he had occupied the time as best as he could, believing in clouds, believing in twigs, believing in a peculiar form of flying beetle, he believed now that he was fed up, and was utterly convinced, furthermore, that he was getting hungry.

He wished he'd taken the precaution of providing himself with some food from the dwelling place he had visited in the night, to which he had carried his sacred burden for entombment in the holy broom cupboard, but he had left in the grip of a white passion, believing that such mundane matters as food were of no consequence, that the tree would provide.

Well, it had provided.

It had provided twigs.

Monks did not eat twigs.

In fact, now he came to think of it, he felt a little

uncomfortable about some of the things he had believed last night and had found some of the results a little confusing. He had been quite clearly instructed to 'shoot off' and had felt strangely compelled to obey, but perhaps he had made a mistake in acting so precipitately on an instruction given in a language he had learned only two minutes before. Certainly the reaction of the person he had shot off at had seemed a little extreme.

In his own world when people were shot at like that they came back next week for another episode, but he didn't think this person would be doing that.

A gust of wind blew through the tree, making it sway giddily. He climbed down a little way. The first part was reasonably easy, since the branches were all fairly close together. It was the last bit that appeared to be an insuperable obstacle – a sheer drop which could cause him severe internal damage or rupture and might in turn cause him to start believing things that were seriously strange.

The sound of voices over in a distant corner of the field suddenly caught his attention. A lorry had pulled up by the side of the road. He watched carefully for a moment, but couldn't see anything particular to believe in and so returned to his introspection.

There was, he remembered, an odd function call he had had last night, which he hadn't encountered before, but he had a feeling that it might be something he'd heard of called remorse. He hadn't felt at all comfortable about the way the person he had shot at had just lain there, and after initially walking away the Monk had returned to have another look. There was definitely an expression on the person's face which seemed to suggest that something was up, that this didn't fit in with the scheme of things. The Monk worried that he might have badly spoiled his evening.

Still, he reflected, so long as you did what you believed to be right, that was the main thing.

The next thing he had believed to be right was that having spoiled this person's evening he should at least convey him to his home, and a quick search of his pockets had produced an address, some maps and some keys. The trip had been an arduous one, but he had been sustained on the way by his faith.

The word 'bathroom' floated unexpectedly across the field.

He looked up again at the lorry in the distant corner. There was a man in a dark blue uniform explaining something to a man in rough working clothes, who seemed a little disgruntled about whatever it was. The words 'until we trace the owner' and 'completely batty, of course' were gusted over on the wind. The man in the working clothes clearly agreed to accept the situation, but with bad grace.

A few moments later, a horse was led out of the back of the lorry and into the field. The Monk blinked. His circuits thrilled and surged with astonishment. Now here at last was something he could believe in, a truly miraculous event, a reward at last for his unstinting if rather promiscuous devotion.

The horse walked with a patient, uncomplaining gait. It had long grown used to being wherever it was put, but for once it felt it didn't mind this. Here, it thought, was a pleasant field. Here was grass. Here was a hedge it could look at. There was enough space that it could go for a trot later on if it felt the urge. The humans drove off and left it to its own devices, to which it was quite content to be left. It went for a little amble, and then, just for the hell of it, stopped ambling. It could do what it liked.

What pleasure.

What very great and unaccustomed pleasure.

It slowly surveyed the whole field, and then decided to plan out a nice relaxed day for itself. A little trot later on, it thought, maybe around threeish. After that a bit of a lie down over on the east side of the field where the grass was thicker. It looked like a suitable spot to think about supper in.

Lunch, it rather fancied, could be taken at the south end of the field where a small stream ran. Lunch by a stream, for heaven's sake. This was bliss.

It also quite liked the notion of spending half an hour walking alternately a little bit to the left and then a little bit to the right, for no apparent reason. It didn't know whether the time between two and three would be best spent swishing its tail or mulling things over.

Of course, it could always do both, if it so wished, and go for its trot a little later. And it had just spotted what looked like a fine piece of hedge for watching things over, and that would easily while away a pleasant pre-prandial hour or two.

Good.

An excellent plan.

And the best thing about it was that having made it the horse could now completely and utterly ignore it. It went instead for a leisurely stand under the only tree in the field.

From out of its branches the Electric Monk dropped on to the horse's back, with a cry which sounded suspiciously like 'Geronimo'.

18

Dirk Gently briefly ran over the salient facts once more while Richard MacDuff's world crashed slowly and silently into a dark, freezing sea which he hadn't even known was there, waiting, inches beneath his feet. When Dirk had finished for the second time the room fell quiet while Richard stared fixedly at his face.

'Where did you hear this?' said Richard at last.

'The radio,' said Dirk, with a slight shrug, 'at least the main points. It's all over the news of course. The details? Well, discreet enquiries among contacts here and there. There are one or two people I got to know at Cambridge police station, for reasons which may occur to you.'

'I don't even know whether to believe you,' said Richard quietly. 'May I use the phone?'

Dirk courteously picked a telephone receiver out of the wastepaper bin and handed it to him. Richard dialled Susan's number.

The phone was answered almost immediately and a frightened voice said, 'Hello?'

'Susan, it's Ri—'

'*Richard!* Where are you? For God's sake, where are you? Are you all right?'

'Don't tell her where you are,' said Dirk.

'Susan, what's happened?'

'Don't you—?'

'Somebody told me that something's happened to Gordon, but . . .'

'Something's *happened*—? He's *dead*, Richard, he's been *murdered*—'

'Hang up,' said Dirk.

'Susan, listen. I—'

'Hang up,' repeated Dirk, and then leaned forward to the phone and cut him off.

'The police will probably have a trace on the line,' he explained. He took the receiver and chucked it back in the bin.

'But I have to go to the police,' Richard exclaimed.

'*Go* to the police?'

'What else can I do? I have to go to the police and tell them that it wasn't me.'

'Tell them that it wasn't you?' said Dirk incredulously. 'Well, I expect that will probably make it all right, then. Pity Dr Crippen didn't think of that. Would have saved him a lot of bother.'

'Yes, but he was guilty!'

'Yes, so it would appear. And so it would appear, at the moment, are you.'

'But I didn't do it, for God's sake!'

'You are talking to someone who has spent time in prison for something he didn't do, remember. I told you that coincidences are strange and dangerous things. Believe me, it is a great deal better to find cast-iron proof that you're innocent, than to languish in a cell hoping that the police – who already think you're guilty – will find it for you.'

'I can't think straight,' said Richard, with his hand to his forehead. 'Just stop for a moment and let me think this out—'

'If I may—'

'Let me think—!'

Dirk shrugged and turned his attention back to his cigarette, which seemed to be bothering him.

'It's no good,' said Richard shaking his head after a few moments, 'I can't take it in. It's like trying to do trigonometry when someone's kicking your head. OK, tell me what you think I should do.'

'Hypnotism.'

'What?'

'It is hardly surprising in the circumstances that you should be unable to gather your thoughts clearly. However, it is vital that somebody gathers them. It will be much simpler for both of us if you will allow me to hypnotise you. I strongly suspect that there is a very great deal of information jumbled up in your head that will not emerge while you are shaking it up so – that might not emerge at all because you do not realise its significance. With your permission we can short-cut all that.'

'Well, that's decided then,' said Richard, standing up, 'I'm going to the police.'

'Very well,' said Dirk, leaning back and spreading his palms on the desk, 'I wish you the very best of luck. Perhaps on your way out you would be kind enough to ask my secretary to get me some matches.'

'You haven't got a secretary,' said Richard, and left.

Dirk sat and brooded for a few seconds, made a valiant but vain attempt to fold the sadly empty pizza box into the wastepaper bin, and then went to look in the cupboard for a metronome.

Richard emerged blinking into the daylight. He stood on the top step rocking slightly, then plunged off down the street with an odd kind of dancing walk which reflected the whirling dance of his mind. On the one hand he simply couldn't believe that the evidence wouldn't show perfectly clearly that he couldn't have committed the murder; on the other hand he had to admit that it all looked remarkably odd.

He found it impossible to think clearly or rationally about it. The idea that Gordon had been murdered kept blowing up in his mind and throwing all other thoughts into total confusion and disruption.

It occurred to him for a moment that whoever did it must have been a damn fast shot to get the trigger pulled before being totally overwhelmed by waves of guilt, but instantly he regretted the thought. In fact he was a little appalled by the general quality of the thoughts that sprang into his mind. They seemed inappropriate and unworthy and mostly had to do with how it would affect his projects in the company.

He looked about inside himself for any feeling of great sorrow or regret, and assumed that it must be there somewhere, probably hiding behind the huge wall of shock.

He arrived back within sight of Islington Green, hardly noticing the distance he had walked. The sudden sight of the police squad car parked outside his house hit him like a hammer and he swung on his heel and stared with furious concentration at the menu displayed in the window of a Greek restaurant.

'Dolmades,' he thought, frantically.

'Souvlaki,' he thought.

'A small spicy Greek sausage,' passed hectically through his mind. He tried to reconstruct the scene in his mind's eye without turning round. There had been a policeman standing watching the street, and as far as he could recall from the brief glance he had, it looked as if the side door of the building which led up to his flat was standing open.

The police were in his flat. *In* his flat. Fassolia Plaki!

A filling bowl of haricot beans cooked in a tomato and vegetable sauce!

He tried to shift his eyes sideways and back over his shoulder. The policeman was looking at him. He yanked his eyes back to the menu and tried to fill his mind with finely ground meat mixed with potato, breadcrumbs, onions and herbs rolled into small balls and fried. The policeman must have recognised him and was at that very moment dashing across the road to grab him and lug him off in a Black Maria just as they had done to Dirk all those years ago in Cambridge.

He braced his shoulders against the shock, but no hand came to grab him. He glanced back again, but the policeman was looking unconcernedly in another direction. Stifado.

It was very apparent to him that his behaviour was not that of one who was about to go and hand himself in to the police.

So what else was he to do?

Trying in a stiff, awkward way to walk naturally, he yanked himself away from the window, strolled tensely down the road a few yards, and then ducked back down Camden Passage again, walking fast and breathing hard. Where could he go? To Susan? No – the police would be there or watching. To the WFT offices in Primrose Hill? No – same reason. What on earth, he screamed silently at himself, was he doing suddenly as a fugitive?

He insisted to himself, as he had insisted to Dirk, that he should not be running away from the police. The police, he told himself, as he had been taught when he was a boy, were there to help and protect the innocent. This thought caused him instantly to break into a run and he nearly collided with the proud new owner of an ugly Edwardian floor lamp.

'Sorry,' he said, 'sorry.' He was startled that anyone

should want such a thing, and slowed his pace to a walk, glancing with sharp hunted looks around him. The very familiar shop fronts full of old polished brass, old polished wood and pictures of Japanese fish suddenly seemed very threatening and aggressive.

Who could possibly have wanted to kill Gordon? This was the thought that suddenly hammered at him as he turned down Charlton Place. All that had concerned him so far was that he hadn't.

But who had?

This was a new thought.

Plenty of people didn't care for him much, but there is a huge difference between disliking somebody – maybe even disliking them a lot – and actually shooting them, strangling them, dragging them through the fields and setting their house on fire. It was a difference which kept the vast majority of the population alive from day to day.

Was it just theft? Dirk hadn't mentioned anything being missing but then he hadn't asked him.

Dirk. The image of his absurd but oddly commanding figure sitting like a large toad, brooding in his shabby office, kept insisting itself upon Richard's mind. He realised that he was retracing the way he had come, and deliberately made himself turn right instead of left.

That way madness lay.

He just needed a space, a bit of time to think and collect his thoughts together.

All right – so where was he going? He stopped for a moment, turned around and then stopped again. The idea of dolmades suddenly seemed very attractive and it occurred to him that the cool, calm and collected course of action would have been simply to walk in and have some. That would have shown Fate who was boss.

Instead, Fate was engaged on exactly the same course

of action. It wasn't actually sitting in a Greek restaurant eating dolmades, but it might as well have been, because it was clearly in charge. Richard's footsteps drew him inexorably back through the winding streets, over the canal.

He stopped, briefly, at a corner shop, and then hurried on past the council estates, and into developer territory again until he was standing once more outside 33, Peckender Street. At about the same time as Fate would have been pouring itself the last of the retsina, wiping its mouth and wondering if it had any room left for baklavas, Richard gazed up at the tall ruddy Victorian building with its soot-darkened brickwork and its heavy, forbidding windows. A gust of wind whipped along the street and a small boy bounded up to him.

'Fuck off,' chirped the little boy, then paused and looked at him again.

''Ere, mister,' he added, 'can I have your jacket?'

'No,' said Richard.

'Why not?' said the boy.

'Er, because I like it,' said Richard.

'Can't see why,' muttered the boy. 'Fuck off.' He slouched off moodily down the street, kicking a stone at a cat.

Richard entered the building once more, mounted the stairs uneasily and looked again into the office.

Dirk's secretary was sitting at her desk, head down, arms folded.

'I'm not here,' she said.

'I see,' said Richard.

'I only came back,' she said, without looking up from the spot on her desk at which she was staring angrily, 'to make sure he notices that I've gone. Otherwise he might just forget.'

'Is he in?' asked Richard.

'Who knows? Who cares? Better ask someone who works for him, because I don't.'

'Show him in!' boomed Dirk's voice.

She glowered for a moment, stood up, went to the inner door, wrenched it open, said 'Show him in yourself,' slammed the door once more and returned to her seat.

'Er, why don't I just show myself in?' said Richard.

'I can't even hear you,' said Dirk's ex-secretary, staring resolutely at her desk. 'How do you expect me to hear you if I'm not even here?'

Richard made a placatory gesture, which was ignored, and walked through and opened the door to Dirk's office himself. He was startled to find the room in semi-darkness. A blind was drawn down over the window, and Dirk was lounging back in his seat, his face bizarrely lit by the strange arrangement of objects sitting on the desk. At the forward edge of the desk sat an old grey bicycle lamp, facing backwards and shining a feeble light on a metronome which was ticking softly back and forth, with a highly polished silver teaspoon strapped to its metal rod.

Richard tossed a couple of boxes of matches on to the desk.

'Sit down, relax, and keep looking at the spoon,' said Dirk, 'you are already feeling sleepy . . .'

Another police car pulled itself up to a screeching halt outside Richard's flat, and a grim-faced man climbed out and strode over to one of the constables on duty outside, flashing an identity card.

'Detective Inspector Mason, Cambridgeshire CID,' he said. 'This the MacDuff place?'

The constable nodded and showed him to the side-door entrance which opened on to the long narrow staircase leading up to the top flat. Mason bustled in and then bustled straight out again.

'There's a sofa halfway up the stairs,' he told the constable. 'Get it moved.'

'Some of the lads have already tried, sir,' the constable replied anxiously. 'It seems to be stuck. Everyone's having to climb over it for the moment, sir. Sorry, sir.'

Mason gave him another grim look from a vast repertoire he had developed which ranged from very, very blackly grim indeed at the bottom of the scale, all the way up to tiredly resigned and only faintly grim, which he reserved for his children's birthdays.

'Get it moved,' he repeated grimly, and bustled grimly back through the door, grimly hauling up his trousers and coat in preparation for the grim ascent ahead.

'No sign of him yet?' asked the driver of the car, coming over himself. 'Sergeant Gilks,' he introduced himself. He looked tired.

'Not as far as I know,' said the constable, 'but no one tells me anything.'

'Know how you feel,' agreed Gilks. 'Once the CID gets involved you just get relegated to driving them about. And I'm the only one who knows what he looked like. Stopped him in the road last night. We just came from Way's house. Right mess.'

'Bad night, eh?'

'Varied. Everything from murder to hauling horses out of bathrooms. No, don't even ask. Do you have the same cars as these?' he added, pointing at his own. 'This one's been driving me crazy all the way up. Cold even with the heater on full blast, and the radio keeps turning itself on and off.'

19

The same morning found Michael Wenton-Weakes in something of an odd mood.

You would need to know him fairly well to know that it was an especially odd mood, because most people regarded him as being a little odd to start with. Few people knew him that well. His mother, perhaps, but there existed between them a state of cold war and neither had spoken to the other now in weeks.

He also had an elder brother, Peter, who was now tremendously senior in the Marines. Apart from at their father's funeral, Michael had not seen Peter since he came back from the Falklands, covered in glory, promotion, and contempt for his younger brother.

Peter had been delighted that their mother had taken over Magna, and had sent Michael a regimental Christmas card to that effect. His own greatest satisfaction still remained that of throwing himself into a muddy ditch and firing a machine gun for at least a minute, and he didn't think that the British newspaper and publishing industry, even in its current state of unrest, was likely to afford him that pleasure, at least until some more Australians moved into it.

Michael had risen very late after a night of cold savagery and then of troubled dreams which still disturbed him now in the late morning daylight.

His dreams had been filled with the familiar sensations of loss, isolation, guilt and so forth, but had also been inexplicably involved with large quantities of mud. By the telescopic power of the night, the nightmare of mud and loneliness had seemed to stretch on for terrifying, unimaginable lengths of time, and had only concluded with the appearance of slimy things with legs that had crawled on the slimy sea. This had been altogether too much and he had woken with a start in a cold sweat.

Though all the business with the mud had seemed strange to him, the sense of loss, of isolation, and above all the aggrievement, the need to undo what had been done, these had all found an easy home in his spirit.

Even the slimy things with legs seemed oddly familiar and ticked away irritably at the back of his mind while he made himself a late breakfast, a piece of grapefruit and some China tea, allowed his eyes to rest lightly on the arts pages of the *Daily Telegraph* for a while, and then rather clumsily changed the dressing on the cuts on his hand.

These small tasks accomplished, he was then in two minds as to what to do next.

He was able to view the events of the previous night with a cool detachment that he would not have expected. It had been right, it had been proper, it had been correctly done. But it resolved nothing. All that mattered was yet to be done.

All what? He frowned at the odd way his thoughts ebbed and flowed.

Normally he would pop along to his club at about this time. It used to be that he would do this with a luxurious sense of the fact that there were many other things that he should be doing. Now there was nothing else to do, which made time spent there, as anywhere else, hang somewhat heavy on his hands.

When he went he would do as he always did – indulge

in a gin and tonic and a little light conversation, and then allow his eyes to rest gently on the pages of the *Times Literary Supplement*, *Opera*, *The New Yorker* or whatever else fell easily to hand, but there was no doubt that he did it these days with less verve and relish than previously.

Then there would be lunch. Today, he had no lunch date planned – again – and would probably therefore have stayed at his club, and eaten a lightly grilled Dover sole, with potatoes garnished with parsley and boiled to bits, followed by a large heap of trifle. A glass or two of Sancerre. And coffee. And then the afternoon, with whatever that might bring.

But today he felt oddly impelled not to do that. He flexed the muscles in his cut hand, poured himself another cup of tea, looked with curious dispassion at the large kitchen knife that still lay by the fine bone china teapot, and waited for a moment to see what he would do next. What he did next, in fact, was to walk upstairs.

His house was rather chill in its formal perfection, and looked much as people who buy reproduction furniture would like their houses to look. Except of course that everything here was genuine – crystal, mahogany and Wilton – and only looked as if it might be fake because there was no life to any of it.

He walked up into his workroom, which was the only room in the house that was not sterile with order, but here the disorder of books and papers was instead sterile with neglect. A thin film of dust had settled over everything. Michael had not been into it in weeks, and the cleaner was under strict instructions to leave it well alone. He had not worked here since he edited the last edition of *Fathom*. Not, of course, the actual last edition, but the last proper edition. The last edition as far as *he* was concerned.

He set his china cup down in the fine dust and went to inspect his elderly record player. On it he found an elderly recording of some Vivaldi wind concertos, set it to play and sat down.

He waited again to see what he would do next and suddenly found to his surprise that he was already doing it, and it was this: he was *listening* to the music.

A bewildered look crept slowly across his face as he realised that he had never done this before. He had *heard* it many, many times and thought that it made a very pleasant noise. Indeed, he found that it made a pleasant background against which to discuss the concert season, but it had never before occurred to him that there was anything actually to *listen* to.

He sat thunderstruck by the interplay of melody and counterpoint which suddenly stood revealed to him with a clarity that owed nothing to the dust-ridden surface of the record or the fourteen-year-old stylus.

But with this revelation came an almost immediate sense of disappointment, which confused him all the more. The music suddenly revealed to him was oddly unfulfilling. It was as if his capacity to understand the music had suddenly increased up to and far beyond the music's ability to satisfy it, all in one dramatic moment.

He strained to listen for what was missing, and felt that the music was like a flightless bird that didn't even know what capacity it had lost. It walked very well, but it walked where it should soar, it walked where it should swoop, it walked where it should climb and bank and dive, it walked where it should thrill with the giddiness of flight. It never even looked up.

He looked up.

After a while he became aware that all he was doing was simply staring stupidly at the ceiling. He shook his head, and discovered that the perception had faded, leaving him feeling slightly sick and dizzy. It had not vanished entirely, but had dropped deep inside him, deeper than he could reach.

The music continued. It was an agreeable enough assortment of pleasant sounds in the background, but it no longer stirred him.

He needed some clues as to what it was he had just experienced, and a thought flicked momentarily at the back of his mind as to where he might find them. He let go of the thought in anger, but it flicked at him again, and kept on flicking at him until at last he acted upon it.

From under his desk he pulled out the large tin wastepaper bin. Since he had barred his cleaning lady from even coming in here for the moment, the bin had remained unemptied and he found in it the tattered shreds of what he was looking for with the contents of an ashtray emptied over them.

He overcame his distaste with grim determination and slowly jiggled around the bits of the hated object on his desk, clumsily sticking them together with bits of sticky tape that curled around and stuck the wrong bit to the wrong bit and stuck the right bit to his pudgy fingers and then to the desk, until at last there lay before him, crudely reassembled, a copy of *Fathom*. As edited by the execrable creature A. K. Ross.

Appalling.

He turned the sticky lumpish pages as if he was picking over chicken giblets. Not a single line drawing of Joan Sutherland or Marilyn Horne anywhere. No profiles of any of the major Cork Street art dealers, not a one.

His series on the Rossettis: discontinued.

'Green Room Gossip': discontinued.

He shook his head in incredulity and then he found the article he was after.

'Music and Fractal Landscapes' by Richard MacDuff.

He skipped over the first couple of paragraphs of introduction and picked it up further on:

Mathematical analysis and computer modelling are revealing to us that the shapes and processes we encounter in nature – the way that plants grow, the way that mountains erode or rivers flow, the way that snowflakes or islands achieve their shapes, the way that light plays on a surface, the way the milk folds and spins into your coffee as you stir it, the way that laughter sweeps through a crowd of people – all these things in their seemingly magical complexity can be described by the interaction of mathematical processes that are, if anything, even more magical in their simplicity.

Shapes that we think of as random are in fact the products of complex shifting webs of numbers obeying simple rules. The very word 'natural' that we have often taken to mean 'unstructured' in fact describes shapes and processes that appear so unfathomably complex that we cannot consciously perceive the simple natural laws at work.

They can all be described by numbers.

Oddly, this idea seemed less revolting now to Michael than it had done on his first, scant reading.

He read on with increasing concentration.

We know, however, that the mind is capable of understanding these matters in all their complexity and in all their simplicity. A ball flying through the air is responding to the force and direction with which it was thrown, the action of gravity, the friction of the air which it must expend its energy

166

on overcoming, the turbulence of the air around its surface, and the rate and direction of the ball's spin.

And yet, someone who might have difficulty consciously trying to work out what $3 \times 4 \times 5$ comes to would have no trouble in doing differential calculus and a whole host of related calculations so astoundingly fast that they can *actually catch a flying ball*.

People who call this 'instinct' are merely giving the phenomenon a name, not explaining anything.

I think that the closest that human beings come to expressing our understanding of these natural complexities is in music. It is the most abstract of the arts – it has no meaning or purpose other than to be itself.

Every single aspect of a piece of music can be represented by numbers. From the organisation of movements in a whole symphony, down through the patterns of pitch and rhythm that make up the melodies and harmonies, the dynamics that shape the performance, all the way down to the timbres of the notes themselves, their harmonics, the way they change over time, in short, all the elements of a noise that distinguish between the sound of one person piping on a piccolo and another one thumping a drum – all of these things can be expressed by patterns and hierarchies of numbers.

And in my experience the more internal relationships there are between the patterns of numbers at different levels of the hierarchy, however complex and subtle those relationships may be, the more satisfying and, well, whole, the music will seem to be.

In fact the more subtle and complex those relationships, and the further they are beyond the grasp of the conscious mind, the more the instinctive part of your mind – by which I mean that part of your mind that can do differential calculus so astoundingly fast that it will put your hand in the right place to catch a flying ball – the more that part of your brain revels in it.

Music of any complexity (and even 'Three Blind Mice' is complex in its way by the time someone has actually performed it on an instrument with its own individual timbre and articulation) passes beyond your conscious mind into the arms of your own private mathematical genius who dwells in your unconscious responding to all the inner complexities and relationships and proportions that we think we know nothing about.

Some people object to such a view of music, saying that if you reduce music to mathematics, where does the emotion come into it? I would say that it's never been out of it.

The things by which our emotions can be moved – the shape of a flower or a Grecian urn, the way a baby grows, the way the wind brushes across your face, the way clouds move, their shapes, the way light dances on the water, or daffodils flutter in the breeze, the way in which the person you love moves their head, the way their hair follows that movement, the curve described by the dying fall of the last chord of a piece of music – all these things can be described by the complex flow of numbers.

That's not a reduction of it, that's the beauty of it.

Ask Newton.

Ask Einstein.

Ask the poet (Keats) who said that what the imagination seizes as beauty must be truth.

He might also have said that what the hand seizes

as a ball must be truth, but he didn't, because he was a poet and preferred loafing about under trees with a bottle of laudanum and a notebook to playing cricket, but it would have been equally true.

This jogged a thought at the back of Michael's memory, but he couldn't immediately place it.

Because that is at the heart of the relationship between on the one hand our 'instinctive' understanding of shape, form, movement, light, and on the other hand our emotional responses to them.

And that is why I believe that there must be a form of music inherent in nature, in natural objects, in the patterns of natural processes. A music that would be as deeply satisfying as any naturally occurring beauty – and our own deepest emotions are, after all, a form of naturally occurring beauty . . .

Michael stopped reading and let his gaze gradually drift from the page.

He wondered if he knew what such a music would be and tried to grope in the dark recesses of his mind for it. Each part of his mind that he visited seemed as if that music had been playing there only seconds before and all that was left was the last dying echo of something he was unable to catch at and hear. He laid the magazine limply aside.

Then he remembered what it was that the mention of Keats had jogged in his memory.

The slimy things with legs from his dream.

A cold calm came over him as he felt himself coming very close to something.

Coleridge. That man.

Yea, slimy things did crawl with legs
Upon the slimy sea.

'The Rime of the Ancient Mariner.'

Dazed, Michael walked over to the bookshelf and pulled down his Coleridge anthology. He took it back to his seat and with a certain apprehension he riffled through the pages until he found the opening lines.

> It is an ancient Mariner,
> And he stoppeth one of three.

The words were very familiar to him, and yet as he read on through them they awoke in him strange sensations and fearful memories that he knew were not his. There reared up inside him a sense of loss and desolation of terrifying intensity which, while he knew it was not his own, resonated so perfectly now with his own aggrievements that he could not but surrender to it absolutely.

> And a thousand thousand slimy things
> Lived on; and so did I.

20

The blind rolled up with a sharp rattle and Richard blinked.

'A fascinating evening you appear to have spent,' said Dirk Gently, 'even though the most interesting aspects of it seem to have escaped your curiosity entirely.'

He returned to his seat and lounged back in it pressing his fingertips together.

'Please,' he said, 'do not disappoint me by saying "where am I?" A glance will suffice.'

Richard looked around him in slow puzzlement and felt as if he were returning unexpectedly from a long sojourn on another planet where all was peace and light and music that went on for ever and ever. He felt so relaxed he could hardly be bothered to breathe.

The wooden toggle on the end of the blind cord knocked a few times against the window, but otherwise all was now silent. The metronome was still. He glanced at his watch. It was just after one o'clock.

'You have been under hypnosis for a little less than an hour,' said Dirk, 'during which I have learned many interesting things and been puzzled by some others which I would now like to discuss with you. A little fresh air will probably help revive you and I suggest a bracing stroll along the canal. No one will be looking for you there. Janice!'

Silence.

A lot of things were still not clear to Richard, and he

frowned to himself. When his immediate memory returned a moment later, it was like an elephant suddenly barging through the door and he sat up with a startled jolt.

'Janice!' shouted Dirk again. 'Miss Pearce! Damn the girl.'

He yanked the telephone receivers out of the wastepaper basket and replaced them. An old and battered leather briefcase stood by the desk, and he picked this up, retrieved his hat from the floor and stood up, screwing his hat absurdly on his head.

'Come,' he said, sweeping through the door to where Miss Janice Pearce sat glaring at a pencil, 'let us go. Let us leave this festering hellhole. Let us think the unthinkable, let us do the undoable. Let us prepare to grapple with the ineffable itself, and see if we may not eff it after all. Now, Janice—'

'Shut up.'

Dirk shrugged, and then picked off her desk the book which earlier she had mutilated when trying to slam her drawer. He leafed through it, frowning, and then replaced it with a sigh. Janice returned to what she had clearly been doing a moment or two earlier, which was writing a long note with the pencil.

Richard regarded all this in silence, still feeling only semipresent. He shook his head.

Dirk said to him, 'Events may seem to you to be a tangled mass of confusion at the moment. And yet we have some interesting threads to pull on. For of all the things you have told me that have happened, only two are actually physically impossible.'

Richard spoke at last. 'Impossible?' he said with a frown.

'Yes,' said Dirk, 'completely and utterly impossible.'

He smiled.

'Luckily,' he went on, 'you have come to exactly the right place with your interesting problem, for there is no such word as "impossible" in my dictionary. In fact,' he added, brandishing the abused book, 'everything between "herring" and "marmalade" appears to be missing. Thank you, Miss Pearce, you have once again rendered me sterling service, for which I thank you and will, in the event of a successful outcome to this endeavour, even attempt to pay you. In the meantime we have much to think on, and I leave the office in your very capable hands.'

The phone rang and Janice answered it.

'Good afternoon,' she said, 'Wainwright's Fruit Emporium. Mr Wainwright is not able to take calls at this time since he is not right in the head and thinks he is a cucumber. Thank you for calling.'

She slammed the phone down. She looked up again to see the door closing softly behind her ex-employer and his befuddled client.

'Impossible?' said Richard again, in surprise.

'Everything about it,' insisted Dirk, 'completely and utterly – well, let us say inexplicable. There is no point in using the word "impossible" to describe something that has clearly happened. But it cannot be explained by anything we know.'

The briskness of the air along the Grand Union Canal got in among Richard's senses and sharpened them up again. He was restored to his normal faculties, and though the fact of Gordon's death kept jumping at him all over again every few seconds, he was at least now able to think more clearly about it. Oddly enough, though, that seemed for the moment to be the last thing on Dirk's mind. Dirk was instead picking on the most trivial of the night's sequence of bizarre incidents on which to cross-examine him.

A jogger going one way and a cyclist going the other both shouted at each other to get out of the way, and narrowly avoided hurling each other into the murky, slow-moving waters of the canal. They were watched carefully by a very slow-moving old lady who was dragging an even slower-moving old dog.

On the other bank, large empty warehouses stood startled, every window shattered and glinting. A burned-out barge lolled brokenly in the water. Within it a couple of detergent bottles floated on the brackish water. Over the nearest bridge heavy-goods lorries thundered, shaking the foundations of the houses, belching petrol fumes into the air and frightening a mother trying to cross the road with her pram.

Dirk and Richard were walking along from the fringes of South Hackney, a mile from Dirk's office, back towards the heart of Islington, where Dirk knew the nearest lifebelts were positioned.

'But it was only a conjuring trick, for heaven's sake,' said Richard. 'He does them all the time. It's just sleight of hand. Looks impossible but I'm sure if you asked any conjurer he'd say it's easy once you know how these things are done. I once saw a man on the street in New York doing—'

'I know how these things are done,' said Dirk, pulling two lighted cigarettes and a large glazed fig out of his nose. He tossed the fig up in to the air, but it somehow failed to land anywhere. 'Dexterity, misdirection, suggestion. All things you can learn if you have a little time to waste. Excuse me, dear lady,' he said to the elderly, slow-moving dog-owner as they passed her. He bent down to the dog and pulled a long string of brightly coloured flags from its bottom. 'I think he will move more comfortably now,' he said, tipped his hat courteously to her and moved on.

'These things, you see,' he said to a flummoxed Richard, 'are easy. Sawing a lady in half is easy. Sawing a lady in half and then joining her up together again is less easy, but can be done with practice. The trick you described to me with the two-hundred-year-old vase and the college salt cellar is – ' he paused for emphasis – 'completely and utterly inexplicable.'

'Well there was probably some detail of it I missed, but . . .'

'Oh, without question. But the benefit of questioning somebody under hypnosis is that it allows the questioner to see the scene in much greater detail than the subject was even aware of at the time. The girl Sarah, for instance. Do you recall what she was wearing?'

'Er, no,' said Richard, vaguely, 'a dress of some kind, I suppose—'

'Colour? Fabric?'

'Well, I can't remember, it was dark. She was sitting several places away from me. I hardly glimpsed her.'

'She was wearing a dark blue cotton velvet dress gathered to a dropped waist. It had raglan sleeves gathered to the cuffs, a white Peter Pan collar and six small pearl buttons down the front – the third one down had a small thread hanging off it. She had long dark hair pulled back with a red butterfly hairgrip.'

'If you're going to tell me you know all that from looking at a scuff mark on my shoes, like Sherlock Holmes, then I'm afraid I don't believe you.'

'No, no,' said Dirk, 'it's much simpler than that. You told me yourself under hypnosis.'

Richard shook his head.

'Not true,' he said, 'I don't even know what a Peter Pan collar is.'

'But I do and you described it to me perfectly accurately. As you did the conjuring trick. And that trick was not possible in the form in which it occurred. Believe me. I know whereof I speak. There are some other things I would like to discover about the Professor, like for instance who wrote the note you discovered on the table and how many questions George III actually asked, but—'

'What?'

'—but I think I would do better to question the fellow directly. Except . . .' He frowned deeply in concentration. 'Except,' he added, 'that being rather vain in these matters I would prefer to know the answers before I asked the questions. And I do not. I absolutely do not.' He gazed abstractedly into the distance, and made a rough calculation of the remaining distance to the nearest lifebelt.

'And the second impossible thing,' he added, just as Richard was about to get a word in edgeways, 'or at least, the next completely inexplicable thing, is of course the matter of your sofa.'

'Dirk,' exclaimed Richard in exasperation, 'may I remind you that Gordon Way is dead, and that I appear to be under suspicion of his murder! None of these things have the remotest connection with that, and I—'

'But I am extremely inclined to believe that they are connected.'

'That's absurd!'

'I believe in the fundamental inter—'

'Oh, yeah, yeah,' said Richard, 'the fundamental interconnectedness of all things. Listen, Dirk, I am not a gullible old lady and you won't be getting any trips to Bermuda out of me. If you're going to help me then let's stick to the point.'

Dirk bridled at this. 'I believe that all things are fundamentally interconnected, as anyone who follows the principles of quantum mechanics to their logical extremes cannot, if they are honest, help but accept. But I also believe that some things are a great deal more interconnected than others. And when two apparently impossible events and a sequence of highly peculiar ones all occur to the same person, and when that person suddenly becomes the suspect of a highly peculiar murder, then it seems to me that we should look for the solution in the connection between these events. You are the connection, and you yourself have been behaving in a highly peculiar and eccentric way.'

'I have not,' said Richard. 'Yes, some odd things have happened to me, but I—'

'You were last night observed, by me, to climb the outside of a building and break into the flat of your girlfriend, Susan Way.'

'It may have been unusual,' said Richard, 'it may not even have been wise. But it was perfectly logical and rational. I just wanted to undo something I had done before it caused any damage.'

Dirk thought for a moment, and slightly quickened his pace.

'And what you did was a perfectly reasonable and normal response to the problem of the message you had left on the tape – yes, you told me all about that in our little session – it's what anyone would have done?'

Richard frowned as if to say that he couldn't see what all the fuss was about. 'I don't say anyone would have done it,' he said, 'I probably have a slightly more logical and literal turn of mind than many people, which is why I can write computer software. It was a logical and literal solution to the problem.'

'Not a little disproportionate, perhaps?'

'It was very important to me not to disappoint Susan yet again.'

'So you are absolutely satisfied with your own reasons for doing what you did?'

'Yes,' insisted Richard angrily.

'Do you know,' said Dirk, 'what my old maiden aunt who lived in Winnipeg used to tell me?'

'No,' said Richard. He quickly took off all his clothes and dived into the canal. Dirk leapt for the lifebelt, with which they had just drawn level, yanked it out of its holder and flung it to Richard, who was floundering in the middle of the canal looking completely lost and disoriented.

'Grab hold of this,' shouted Dirk, 'and I'll haul you in.'

'It's all right,' spluttered Richard, 'I can swim—'

'No, you can't,' yelled Dirk, 'now grab it.'

Richard tried to strike out for the bank, but quickly gave up in consternation and grabbed hold of the lifebelt. Dirk pulled on the rope till Richard reached the edge, and then bent down to give him a hand out. Richard came up out of the water puffing and spitting, then turned and sat shivering on the edge with his hands in his lap.

'God, it's foul in there!' he exclaimed and spat again. 'It's absolutely disgusting. Yeuchh. Whew. God. I'm usually a pretty good swimmer. Must have got some kind of cramp. Lucky coincidence we were so close to the lifebelt. Oh thanks.' This last he said in response to the large towel which Dirk handed him.

He rubbed himself down briskly, almost scraping himself with the towel to get the filthy canal water off him. He stood up and looked about. 'Can you find my pants?'

'Young man,' said the old lady with the dog, who had just reached them. She stood looking at them sternly, and was about to rebuke them when Dirk interrupted.

'A thousand apologies, dear lady,' he said, 'for any offence my friend may inadvertently have caused you. Please,' he added, drawing a slim bunch of anemones from Richard's bottom, 'accept these with my compliments.'

The lady dashed them out of Dirk's hand with her stick, and hurried off, horror-struck, yanking her dog after her.

'That wasn't very nice of you,' said Richard, pulling on his clothes underneath the towel that was now draped strategically around him.

'I don't think she's a very nice woman,' replied Dirk, 'she's always down here, yanking her poor dog around and telling people off. Enjoy your swim?'

'Not much, no,' said Richard, giving his hair a quick rub. 'I hadn't realised how filthy it would be in there. And cold. Here,' he said, handing the towel back to Dirk, 'thanks. Do you always carry a towel around in your briefcase?'

'Do you always go swimming in the afternoons?'

'No, I usually go in the mornings, to the swimming pool on Highbury Fields, just to wake myself up, get the brain going. It just occurred to me I hadn't been this morning.'

'And, er – that was why you just dived into the canal?'

'Well, yes. I just thought that getting a bit of exercise would probably help me deal with all this.'

'Not a little disproportionate, then, to strip off and jump into the canal.'

'No,' he said, 'it may not have been wise given the state of the water, but it was perfectly—'

'You were perfectly satisfied with your own reasons for doing what you did.'

'Yes—'

'And it was nothing to do with my aunt, then?'

Richard's eyes narrowed suspiciously. 'What on earth are you talking about?' he said.

'I'll tell you,' said Dirk. He went and sat on a nearby bench and opened his case again. He folded the towel away into it and took out instead a small Sony tape recorder. He beckoned Richard over and then pushed the Play button. Dirk's own voice floated from the tiny speaker in a lilting sing-song voice. It said, 'In a minute I will click my fingers and you will wake and forget all of this except for the instructions I shall now give you.

'In a little while we will go for a walk along the canal, and when you hear me say the words "my old maiden aunt who lived in Winnipeg"—'

Dirk suddenly grabbed Richard's arm to restrain him.

The tape continued, 'You will take off all your clothes and dive into the canal. You will find that you are unable to swim, but you will not panic or sink, you will simply tread water until I throw you the lifebelt . . .'

Dirk stopped the tape and looked round at Richard's face, which for the second time that day was pale with shock.

'I would be interested to know exactly what it was that possessed you to climb into Miss Way's flat last night,' said Dirk, 'and why.'

Richard didn't respond – he was continuing to stare at the tape recorder in some confusion. Then he said in a shaking voice, 'There was a message from Gordon on Susan's tape. He phoned from the car. The tape's in my flat. Dirk, I'm suddenly very frightened by all this.'

21

Dirk watched the police officer on duty outside Richard's house from behind a van parked a few yards away. He had been stopping and questioning everyone who tried to enter the small side alley down which Richard's door was situated, including, Dirk was pleased to note, other policemen if he didn't immediately recognise them. Another police car pulled up and Dirk started to move.

A police officer climbed out of the car carrying a saw and walked towards the doorway. Dirk briskly matched his pace with him, a step or two behind, striding authoritatively.

'It's all right, he's with me,' said Dirk, sweeping past at the exact moment that the one police officer stopped the other.

And he was inside and climbing the stairs.

The officer with the saw followed him in.

'Er, excuse me, sir,' he called up after Dirk.

Dirk had just reached the point where the sofa obstructed the stairway. He stopped and twisted round.

'Stay here,' he said, 'guard this sofa. Do not let anyone touch it, and I mean anyone. Understood?'

The officer seemed flummoxed for a moment.

'I've had orders to saw it up,' he said.

'Countermanded,' barked Dirk. 'Watch it like a hawk. I shall want a full report.'

He turned back and climbed up over the thing. A moment or two later he emerged into a large open area.

This was the lower of the two floors that comprised Richard's flat.

'Have you searched that?' snapped Dirk at another officer, who was sitting at Richard's dining table looking through some notes. The officer looked up in surprise and started to stand up. Dirk was pointing at the wastepaper basket.

'Er, yes—'

'Search it again. Keep searching it. Who's here?'

'Er, well—'

'I haven't got all day.'

'Detective Inspector Mason just left, with—'

'Good, I'm having him pulled off. I'll be upstairs if I'm needed, but I don't want any interruptions unless it's very important. Understood?'

'Er, who—'

'I don't see you searching the wastepaper basket.'

'Er, right, sir. I'll—'

'I want it deep-searched. You understand?'

'Er—'

'Get cracking.' Dirk swept on upstairs and into Richard's workroom.

The tape was lying exactly where Richard had told him it would be, on the long desk on which the six Macintoshes sat. Dirk was about to pocket it when his curiosity was caught by the image of Richard's sofa slowly twisting and turning on the big Macintosh screen, and he sat down at the keyboard.

He explored the program Richard had written for a short while, but quickly realised that in its present form it was less than self-explanatory and he learned little. He managed at last to get the sofa unstuck and move it back down the stairs, but he realised that he had had to turn part of the wall off in order to do it. With a grunt of irritation he gave up.

Another computer he looked at was displaying a steady sine wave. Around the edges of the screen were the small images of other waveforms which could be selected and added to the main one or used to modify it in other ways. He quickly discovered that this enabled you to build up very complex waveforms from simple ones and he played with this for a while. He added a simple sine wave to itself, which had the effect of doubling the height of the peaks and troughs of the wave. Then he slid one of the waves half a step back with respect to the other, and the peaks and troughs of one simply cancelled out the peaks and troughs of the other, leaving a completely flat line. Then he changed the frequency of one of the sine waves by a small extent.

The result of this was that at some positions along the combined waveform the two waves reinforced each other, and at others they cancelled each other out. Adding a third simple wave of yet another frequency resulted in a combined wave in which it was hard to see any pattern at all. The line danced up and down seemingly at random, staying quite low for some periods and then suddenly building into very large peaks and troughs as all three waves came briefly into phase with each other.

Dirk assumed that there must be amongst this array of equipment a means for translating the waveform dancing on the Macintosh screen into an actual musical tone and hunted among the menus available in the program. He found one menu item which invited him to transfer the wave sample into an Emu.

This puzzled him. He glanced around the room in search of a large flightless bird, but was unable to locate any such thing. He activated the process anyway, and then traced the cable which led from the back of the Macintosh, down behind the desk, along the floor, behind a cupboard, under a rug until it fetched up plugged into the back of a large grey keyboard called an Emulator II.

This, he assumed, was where his experimental waveform had just arrived. Tentatively he pushed a key.

The nasty farting noise that surged instantly out of the speakers was so loud that for a moment he didn't hear the words 'Svlad Cjelli!' that were barked simultaneously from the doorway.

Richard sat in Dirk's office and threw tiny screwed-up balls of paper at the wastepaper bin which was already full of telephones. He broke pencils. He played major extracts from an old Ginger Baker solo on his knees.

In a word, he fretted.

He had been trying to write down on a piece of Dirk's notepaper all that he could remember of the events of the previous evening and, as far as he could pinpoint them, the times at which each had occurred. He was astonished at how difficult it was, and how feeble his conscious memory seemed to be in comparison with his unconscious memory, as Dirk had demonstrated it to him.

'Damn Dirk,' he thought. He wanted to talk to Susan.

Dirk had told him he must not do so on any account as there would be a trace on the phone lines.

'Damn Dirk,' he said suddenly, and sprang to his feet.

'Have you got any ten-pence pieces?' he said to the resolutely glum Janice.

Dirk turned.

Framed in the doorway stood a tall dark figure.

The tall dark figure appeared to be not at all happy with what it saw, to be rather cross about it, in fact. To be more than cross. It appeared to be a tall dark figure who could very easily yank the heads off half a dozen chickens and still be cross at the end of it.

It stepped forward into the light and revealed itself to be Sergeant Gilks of the Cambridgeshire Constabulary.

'Do you know,' said Sergeant Gilks of the Cambridgeshire Constabulary, blinking with suppressed emotion, 'that when I arrive back here to discover one police officer guarding a sofa with a saw and another dismembering an innocent wastepaper basket I have to ask myself certain questions? And I have to ask them with the disquieting sense that I am not going to like the answers when I find them.

'I then find myself mounting the stairs with a horrible premonition, Svlad Cjelli, a very horrible premonition indeed. A premonition, I might add, that I now find horribly justified. I suppose you can't shed any light on a horse discovered in a bathroom as well? That seemed to have an air of you about it.'

'I cannot,' said Dirk, 'as yet. Though it interests me strangely.'

'I should think it bloody did. It would have interested you strangely if you'd had to get the bloody thing down a bloody winding staircase at one o'clock in the morning as well. What the hell are you doing here?' said Sergeant Gilks, wearily.

'I am here,' said Dirk, 'in pursuit of justice.'

'Well, I wouldn't mix with me then,' said Gilks, 'and I certainly wouldn't mix with the Met. What do you know of MacDuff and Way?'

'Of Way? Nothing beyond what is common knowledge. MacDuff I knew at Cambridge.'

'Oh, you did, did you? Describe him.'

'Tall. Tall and absurdly thin. And good-natured. A bit

like a preying mantis that doesn't prey – a non-preying mantis if you like. A sort of pleasant genial mantis that's given up preying and taken up tennis instead.'

'Hmm,' said Gilks gruffly, turning away and looking about the room. Dirk pocketed the tape.

'Sounds like the same one,' said Gilks.

'And of course,' said Dirk, 'completely incapable of murder.'

'That's for us to decide.'

'And of course a jury.'

'Tchah! Juries!'

'Though, of course, it will not come to that, since the facts will speak for themselves long before it comes to a court of law for my client.'

'Your bleeding client, eh? All right, Cjelli, where is he?'

'I haven't the faintest idea.'

'I'll bet you've got a billing address.'

Dirk shrugged.

'Look, Cjelli, this is a perfectly normal, harmless murder enquiry, and I don't want you mucking it up. So consider yourself warned off as of now. If I see a single piece of evidence being levitated I'll hit you so hard you won't know if it's tomorrow or Thursday. Now get out, and give me that tape on the way.' He held out his hand.

Dirk blinked, genuinely surprised. 'What tape?'

Gilks sighed. 'You're a clever man, Cjelli, I grant you that,' he said, 'but you make the same mistake a lot of clever people do of thinking everyone else is stupid. If I turn away it's for a reason, and the reason was to see what you picked up. I didn't need to see you pick it up, I just had to see what was missing afterwards. We are trained you know. We used to get half an hour Observation Training on Tuesday afternoons. Just as a break after four hours solid of Senseless Brutality.'

Dirk hid his anger with himself behind a light smile. He fished in the pocket of his leather overcoat and handed over the tape.

'Play it,' said Gilks, 'let's see what you didn't want us to hear.'

'It wasn't that I didn't want you to hear it,' said Dirk, with a shrug. 'I just wanted to hear it first.' He went over to the shelf which carried Richard's hi-fi equipment and slipped the tape into the cassette player.

'So do you want to give me a little introduction?'

'It's a tape,' said Dirk, 'from Susan Way's telephone-answering machine. Way apparently had this habit of leaving long . . .'

'Yeah, I know about that. And his secretary goes round picking up his prattlings in the morning, poor devil.'

'Well, I believe there may be a message on the tape from Gordon Way's car last night.'

'I see. OK. Play it.'

With a gracious bow Dirk pressed the Play button.

'Oh, Susan, hi, it's Gordon,' said the tape once again. 'Just on my way to the cottage—'

'Cottage!' exclaimed Gilks, satirically.

'It's, er, Thursday night, and it's, er . . . 8.47. Bit misty on the roads. Listen, I have those people from the States coming over this weekend . . .'

Gilks raised his eyebrows, looked at his watch, and made a note on his pad.

Both Dirk and the police sergeant experienced a chill as the dead man's voice filled the room.

'—it's a wonder I don't end up dead in the ditch, that would be something wouldn't it, leaving your famous last words on somebody's answering machine, there's no reason—'

They listened in a tense silence as the tape played on through the entire message.

'That's the problem with crunch-heads – they have one great idea that actually works and then they expect you to carry on funding them for years while they sit and calculate the topographies of their navels. I'm sorry, I'm going to have to stop and close the boot properly. Won't be a moment.'

Next came the muffled bump of the telephone receiver being dropped on the passenger seat, and a few seconds later the sound of the car door being opened. In the meantime, the music from the car's sound system could be heard burbling away in the background.

A few seconds later still came the distant, muffled, but unmistakable double blam of a shotgun.

'Stop the tape,' said Gilks sharply and glanced at his watch. 'Three minutes and twenty-five seconds since he said it was 8.47.' He glanced up at Dirk again. 'Stay here. Don't move. Don't touch anything. I've made a note of the position of every particle of air in this room, so I shall know if you've been breathing.'

He turned smartly and left. Dirk heard him saying as he went down the stairs, 'Tuckett, get on to Way-Forward's office, get the details of Way's earphone, what number, which network . . .' The voice faded away downstairs.

Quickly Dirk twisted down the volume control on the hi-fi, and resumed playing the tape.

The music continued for a while. Dirk drummed his fingers in frustration. Still the music continued.

He flicked the Fast Forward button for just a moment. Still music. It occurred to him that he was looking for something, but that he didn't know what. That thought stopped him in his tracks.

He was very definitely looking for something.

He very definitely didn't know what.

The realisation that he didn't know exactly why he was doing what he was doing suddenly chilled and electrified him. He turned slowly like a fridge door opening.

There was no one there, at least no one that he could see. But he knew the chill prickling through his skin and detested it above all things.

He said in a low savage whisper, 'If anyone can hear me, hear this. My mind is my centre and everything that happens there is my responsibility. Other people may believe what it pleases them to believe, but I will do nothing without knowing the reason why and knowing it clearly. If you want something then let me know, but do not you dare touch my mind.'

He was trembling with a deep and old rage. The chill dropped slowly and almost pathetically from him and seemed to move off into the room. He tried to follow it with his senses, but was instantly distracted by a sudden voice that seemed to come at him on the edge of his hearing, on a distant howl of wind.

It was a hollow, terrified, bewildered voice, no more than an insubstantial whisper, but it was there, audible, on the telephone-answering-machine tape.

It said, 'Susan! Susan, help me! Help me for God's sake. Susan, I'm dead—'

Dirk whirled round and stopped the tape.

'I'm sorry,' he said under his breath, 'but I have the welfare of my client to consider.'

He wound the tape back a very short distance, to just before where the voice began, twisted the Record Level knob to zero and pressed Record. He left the tape to run, wiping off the voice and anything that might follow it. If the tape was going to establish the time of Gordon Way's death, then Dirk didn't want any embarrassing examples of Gordon speaking to turn up on the tape after that point, even if it was only to confirm that he was, in fact, dead.

There seemed to be a great eruption of emotion in the air near to him. A wave of something surged through the room, causing the furniture to flutter in its wake. Dirk watched where it seemed to go, towards a shelf near the door on which, he suddenly realised, stood Richard's own telephone-answering machine. The machine started to jiggle fitfully where it sat, but then sat still as Dirk approached it. Dirk reached out slowly and calmly and pushed the button which set the machine to Answer.

The disturbance in the air then passed back through the room to Richard's long desk where two old-fashioned rotary-dial telephones nestled among the piles of paper and micro floppy disks. Dirk guessed what would happen, but elected to watch rather than to intervene.

One of the telephone receivers toppled off its cradle. Dirk could hear the dialling tone. Then, slowly and with obvious difficulty, the dial began to turn. It moved unevenly round, further round, slower and slower, and then suddenly slipped back.

There was a moment's pause. Then the receiver rests went down and up again to get a new dialling tone. The dial began to turn again, but creaking even more fitfully than the last time.

Again it slipped back.

There was a longer pause this time, and then the entire process was repeated once more.

When the dial slipped back a third time there was a sudden explosion of fury – the whole phone leapt into the air and hurtled across the room. The receiver cord wrapped itself round an Anglepoise lamp on the way and brought it crashing down in a tangle of cables, coffee cups and floppy disks. A pile of books erupted off the desk and on to the floor.

The figure of Sergeant Gilks stood stony-faced in the doorway.

'I'm going to come in again,' he said, 'and when I do, I don't want to see anything of that kind going on whatsoever. Is that understood?' He turned and disappeared.

Dirk leapt for the cassette player and hit the Rewind button. Then he turned and hissed at the empty air, 'I don't know who you are, but I can guess. If you want my help, don't you ever embarrass me like that again!'

A few moments later, Gilks walked in again. 'Ah, there you are,' he said.

He surveyed the wreckage with an even gaze. 'I'll pretend I can't see any of this, so that I won't have to ask any questions the answers to which would, I know, only irritate me.'

Dirk glowered.

In the moment or two of silence that followed, a slight ticking whirr could be heard which caused the sergeant to look sharply at the cassette player.

'What's that tape doing?'

'Rewinding.'

'Give it to me.'

The tape reached the beginning and stopped as Dirk reached it. He took it out and handed it to Gilks.

'Irritatingly, this seems to put your client completely in the clear,' said the sergeant. 'Cellnet have confirmed that the last call made from the car was at 8.46 p.m. last night, at which point your client was lightly dozing in front of several hundred witnesses. I say witnesses, in fact they were mostly students, but we will probably be forced to assume that they can't all be lying.'

'Good,' said Dirk, 'well, I'm glad that's all cleared up.'

'We never thought he had actually done it, of course. Simply didn't fit. But you know us – we like to get results. Tell him we still want to ask him some questions, though.'

'I shall be sure to mention it if I happen to run into him.'

'You just do that little thing.'

'Well, I shan't detain you any longer, Sergeant,' said Dirk, airily waving at the door.

'No, but I shall bloody detain you if you're not out of here in thirty seconds, Cjelli. I don't know what you're up to, but if I can possibly avoid finding out I shall sleep easier in my office. Out.'

'Then I shall bid you good day, Sergeant. I won't say it's been a pleasure because it hasn't.'

Dirk swept out of the room, and made his way out of the flat, noting with sorrow that where there had been a large chesterfield sofa wedged magnificently in the staircase, there was now just a small, sad pile of sawdust.

With a jerk Michael Wenton-Weakes looked up from his book.

His mind suddenly was alive with purpose. Thoughts, images, memories, intentions, all crowded in upon him, and the more they seemed to contradict each other the more they seemed to fit together, to pair and settle.

The match at last was perfect, the teeth of one slowly aligned with the teeth of another.

A pull and they were zipped.

Though the waiting had seemed an eternity of eternities when it was filled with failure, with fading waves of weakness, with feeble groping and lonely impotence, the match once made cancelled it all. Would cancel it all. Would undo what had been so disastrously done.

Who thought that? It did not matter, the match was made, the match was perfect.

Michael gazed out of the window across the well-manicured Chelsea street and did not care whether what he saw were slimy things with legs or whether they were all Mr A. K. Ross. What mattered was what they had stolen and what they would be compelled to return. Ross now lay in the past. What he was now concerned with lay still further in it.

His large soft cowlike eyes returned to the last few lines of 'Kubla Khan', which he had just been reading. The match was made, the zip was pulled.

He closed the book and put it in his pocket.

His path back now was clear. He knew what he must do. It only remained to do a little shopping and then do it.

22

'You? Wanted for murder? Richard, what are you talking about?'

The telephone wavered in Richard's hand. He was holding it about half an inch away from his ear anyway because it seemed that somebody had dipped the earpiece in some chow mein recently, but that wasn't so bad. This was a public telephone so it was clearly an oversight that it was working at all. But Richard was beginning to feel as if the whole world had shifted about half an inch away from him, like someone in a deodorant commercial.

'Gordon,' said Richard, hesitantly, 'Gordon's been murdered – hasn't he?'

Susan paused before she answered.

'Yes, Richard' she said in a distressed voice, 'but no one thinks you did it. They want to question you of course, but—'

'So there are no police with you now?'

'No, Richard,' insisted Susan, 'Look, why don't you come here?'

'And they're not out searching for me?'

'No! Where on earth did you get the idea that you were wanted for – that they thought you had done it?'

'Er – well, this friend of mine told me.'

'Who?'

'Well, his name is Dirk Gently.'

'You've never mentioned him. Who is he? Did he say anything else?'

'He hypnotised me and, er, made me jump in the canal, and, er, well, that was it really—'

There was a terribly long pause at the other end.

'Richard,' said Susan at last with the sort of calmness that comes over people when they realise that however bad things may seem to be, there is absolutely no reason why they shouldn't simply get worse and worse, 'come over here. I was going to say I need to see you, but I think you need to see me.'

'I should probably go to the police.'

'Go to the police later. Richard, please. A few hours won't make any difference. I . . . I can hardly even think. Richard, it's so awful. It would just help if you were here. Where are you?'

'OK,' said Richard, 'I'll be with you in about twenty minutes.'

'Shall I leave the window open or would you like to try the door?' she said with a sniff.

23

'No, please,' said Dirk, restraining Miss Pearce's hand from opening a letter from the Inland Revenue, 'there are wilder skies than these.'

He had emerged from a spell of tense brooding in his darkened office, and there was an air of excited concentration about him. It had taken his actual signature on an actual salary cheque to persuade Miss Pearce to forgive him for the latest unwarrantable extravagance with which he had returned to the office and he felt that just to sit there blatantly opening letters from the taxman was to take his magnanimous gesture in entirely the wrong spirit.

She put the envelope aside.

'Come!' he said. 'I have something I wish you to see. I shall observe your reactions with the very greatest of interest.'

He bustled back into his own office and sat at his desk.

She followed him in patiently and sat opposite, pointedly ignoring the new unwarrantable extravagance sitting on the desk.

The flashy brass plaque for the door had stirred her up pretty badly but the silly phone with big red push buttons she regarded as being beneath contempt. And she certainly wasn't going to do anything rash like smile until she knew for certain that the cheque wouldn't bounce. The last time he signed a cheque for her he cancelled it before the end of the day, to prevent it, as he explained, 'falling into the wrong hands'. The wrong hands, presumably, being those of her bank manager.

He thrust a piece of paper across the desk.

She picked it up and looked at it. Then she turned it round and looked at it again. She looked at the other side and then she put it down.

'Well?' demanded Dirk. 'What do you make of it? Tell me!'

Miss Pearce sighed.

'It's a lot of meaningless squiggles done in blue felt tip on a piece of typing paper,' she said. 'It looks like you did them yourself.'

'No!' barked Dirk, 'Well, yes,' he admitted, 'but only because I believe that it is the answer to the problem!'

'What problem?'

'The problem,' insisted Dirk, slapping the table, 'of the conjuring trick! I told you!'

'Yes, Mr Gently, several times. I think it was just a conjuring trick. You see them on the telly.'

'With this difference – that this one was completely impossible!'

'Couldn't have been impossible or he wouldn't have done it. Stands to reason.'

'Exactly!' said Dirk excitedly. 'Exactly! Miss Pearce, you are a lady of rare perception and insight.'

'Thank you, sir, can I go now?'

'Wait! I haven't finished yet! Not by a long way, not by a bucketful! You have demonstrated to me the depth of your perception and insight, allow me to demonstrate mine!'

Miss Pearce slumped patiently in her seat.

'I think,' said Dirk, 'you will be impressed. Consider this. An intractable problem. In trying to find the solution to it I was going round and round in little circles in my mind, over and over the same maddening things. Clearly I wasn't going to be able to think of anything else until I had the answer, but equally clearly I would have to think of something else if I was ever going to *get* the answer. How to break this circle? Ask me how.'

'How?' said Miss Pearce obediently, but without enthusiasm.

'By writing down what the answer is!' exclaimed Dirk. 'And here it is!' He slapped the piece of paper triumphantly and sat back with a satisfied smile.

Miss Pearce looked at it dumbly.

'With the result,' continued Dirk, 'that I am now able to turn my mind to fresh and intriguing problems, like, for instance . . .'

He took the piece of paper, covered with its aimless squiggles and doodlings, and held it up to her.

'What language,' he said in a low, dark voice, 'is this written in?'

Miss Pearce continued to look at it dumbly.

Dirk flung the piece of paper down, put his feet up on the table, and threw his head back with his hands behind it.

'You see what I have done?' he asked the ceiling, which seemed to flinch slightly at being yanked so suddenly into the conversation. 'I have transformed the problem from an intractably difficult and possibly quite insoluble conundrum into a mere linguistic puzzle. Albeit,' he muttered, after a long moment of silent pondering, 'an intractably difficult and possibly insoluble one.'

He swung back to gaze intently at Janice Pearce.

'Go on,' he urged, 'say that it's insane – but it might just work!'

Janice Pearce cleared her throat.

'It's insane,' she said, 'trust me.'

Dirk turned away and sagged sideways off his chair, much as the sitter for The Thinker probably did when Rodin went off to be excused.

He suddenly looked profoundly tired and depressed.

'I know,' he said in a low, dispirited voice, 'that there is something profoundly wrong somewhere. And I know that I must go to Cambridge to put it right. But I would feel less fearful if I knew what it was . . .'

'Can I get on now, please, then?' said Miss Pearce.

Dirk looked up at her glumly.

'Yes,' he said with a sigh, 'but just – just tell me he flicked at the piece of paper with his fingertips – 'what do you think of this, then?'

'Well, I think it's childish,' said Janice Pearce, frankly.

'But – but – but!' said Dirk thumping the table in frustration. 'Don't you understand that we need to be childish in order to understand? Only a child sees things with perfect clarity, because it hasn't developed all those filters which prevent us from seeing things that we don't expect to see?'

'Then why don't you go and ask one?'

'Thank you, Miss Pearce,' said Dirk reaching for his hat, 'once again you have rendered me an inestimable service for which I am profoundly grateful.'

He swept out.

24

The weather began to bleaken as Richard made his way to Susan's flat. The sky which had started out with such verve and spirit in the morning was beginning to lose its concentration and slip back into its normal English condition, that of a damp and rancid dish cloth. Richard took a taxi, which got him there in a few minutes.

'They should all be deported,' said the taxi driver as they drew to a halt.

'Er, who should?' said Richard, who realised he hadn't been listening to a word the driver said.

'Er—' said the driver, who suddenly realised he hadn't been listening either, 'er, the whole lot of them. Get rid of the whole bloody lot, that's what I say. And their bloody newts,' he added for good measure.

'Expect you're right,' said Richard, and hurried into the house.

Arriving at the front door of her flat he could hear from within the sounds of Susan's cello playing a slow, stately melody. He was glad of that, that she was playing. She had an amazing emotional self-sufficiency and control provided she could play her cello. He had noticed an odd and extraordinary thing about her relationship with the music she played. If ever she was feeling emotional or upset she could sit and play some music with utter concentration and emerge seeming fresh and calm.

The next time she played the same music, however, it

would all burst from her and she would go completely to pieces.

He let himself in as quietly as possible so as not to disturb her concentration.

He tiptoed past the small room she practised in, but the door was open so he paused and looked at her, with the slightest of signals that she shouldn't stop. She was looking pale and drawn, but gave him a flicker of a smile and continued bowing with a sudden intensity.

With an impeccable timing of which it is very rarely capable the sun chose that moment to burst briefly through the gathering rainclouds, and as she played her cello a stormy light played on her and on the deep old brown of the wood of the instrument. Richard stood transfixed. The turmoil of the day stood still for a moment and kept a respectful distance.

He didn't know the music, but it sounded like Mozart and he remembered her saying she had some Mozart to learn. He walked quietly on and sat down to wait and listen.

Eventually she finished the piece, and there was about a minute of silence before she came through. She blinked and smiled and gave him a long, trembling hug, then released herself and put the phone back on the hook. It usually got taken off when she was practising.

'Sorry,' she said, 'I didn't want to stop.' She briskly brushed away a tear as if it was a slight irritation. 'How are you, Richard?'

He shrugged and gave her a bewildered look. That seemed about to cover it.

'And I'm going to have to carry on, I'm afraid,' said Susan with a sigh. 'I'm sorry. I've just been . . .' She shook her head. 'Who would do it?'

'I don't know. Some madman. I'm not sure that it matters who.'

'No,' she said. 'Look, er, have you had any lunch?'

'No. Susan, you keep playing and I'll see what's in the fridge. We can talk about it all over some lunch.'

Susan nodded.

'All right,' she said, 'except . . .'

'Yes?'

'Well, just for the moment I don't really want to talk about Gordon. Just till it sinks in. I feel sort of caught out. It would be easier if I'd been closer to him, but I wasn't and I'm sort of embarrassed by not having a reaction ready. Talking about it would be all right except that you have to use the past tense and that's what's . . .'

She clung to him for a moment and then quieted herself with a sigh.

'There's not much in the fridge at the moment,' she said, 'some yoghurt, I think, and a jar of roll-mop herrings you could open. I'm sure you'll be able to muck it up if you try, but it's actually quite straightforward. The main trick is not to throw them all over the floor or get jam on them.'

She gave him a hug, a kiss and a glum smile and then retreated back to her music room.

The phone rang and Richard answered it.

'Hello?' he said. There was nothing, just a faint sort of windy noise on the line.

'Hello?' he said again, waited, shrugged and put the phone back down.

'Was there anybody there?' called Susan.

'No, no one,' said Richard.

'That's happened a couple of times,' said Susan. 'I think it's a sort of minimalist heavy breather.' She resumed playing.

Richard went into the kitchen and opened the fridge. He was less of a health-conscious eater than Susan and was therefore less than thrilled by what he found there, but he managed to put some roll-mop herrings, some yoghurt, some rice and some oranges on a tray without difficulty and tried not to think that a couple of fat hamburgers and fries would round it off nicely.

He found a bottle of white wine and carried it all through to the small dining table.

After a minute or two Susan joined him there. She was at her most calm and composed, and after a few mouthsful she asked him about the canal.

Richard shook his head in bemusement and tried to explain about it, and about Dirk.

'*What* did you say his name was?' said Susan with a frown when he had come, rather lamely, to a conclusion.

'It's, er, Dirk Gently,' said Richard, 'in a way.'

'In a way?'

'Er, yes,' said Richard with a difficult sigh. He reflected that just about anything you could say about Dirk was subject to these kind of vague and shifty qualifications. There was even, on his letter heading, a string of vague and shifty-looking qualifications after his name. He pulled out the piece of paper on which he had vainly been trying to organise his thoughts earlier in the day.

'I . . . ,' he started, but the doorbell rang. They looked at each other.

'If it's the police,' said Richard, 'I'd better see them. Let's get it over with.'

Susan pushed back her chair, went to the front door and picked up the Entryphone.

'Hello?' she said.

'Who?' she said after a moment. She frowned as she listened, then swung round and frowned at Richard.

'You'd better come up,' she said in a less than friendly

tone of voice and then pressed the button. She came back and sat down.

'Your friend,' she said evenly, 'Mr Gently.'

The Electric Monk's day was going tremendously well and he broke into an excited gallop. That is to say that, excitedly, he spurred his horse to a gallop and, unexcitedly, his horse broke into it.

This world, the Monk thought, was a good one. He loved it. He didn't know whose it was or where it had come from, but it was certainly a deeply fulfilling place for someone with his unique and extraordinary gifts.

He was appreciated. All day he had gone up to people, fallen into conversation with them, listened to their troubles, and then quietly uttered those three magic words, 'I believe you.'

The effect had invariably been electrifying. It wasn't that people on this world didn't occasionally say it to each other, but they rarely, it seemed, managed to achieve that deep timbre of sincerity which the Monk had been so superbly programmed to reproduce.

On his own world, after all, he was taken for granted. People would just expect him to get on and believe things for them without bothering them. Someone would come to the door with some great new idea or proposal or even a new religion, and the answer would be, 'Oh, go and tell that to the Monk.' And the Monk would sit and listen and patiently believe it all, but no one would take any further interest.

Only one problem seemed to arise on this otherwise excellent world. Often, after he had uttered the magic words, the subject would rapidly change to that of money, and the Monk of course didn't have any – a shortcoming that had quickly blighted a number of otherwise very promising encounters.

Perhaps he should acquire some – but where?

He reined his horse in for a moment, and the horse jerked gratefully to a halt and started in on the grass on the roadside verge. The horse had no idea what all this galloping up and down was in aid of, and didn't care. All it did care about was that it was being made to gallop up and down past a seemingly perpetual roadside buffet. It made the best of its moment while it had it.

The Monk peered keenly up and down the road. It seemed vaguely familiar. He trotted a little further up it for another look. The horse resumed its meal a few yards further along.

Yes. The Monk had been here last night.

He remembered it clearly, well, sort of clearly. He believed that he remembered it clearly, and that, after all, was the main thing. Here was where he had walked to in a more than usually confused state of mind, and just around the very next corner, if he was not very much mistaken, again, lay the small roadside establishment at which he had jumped into the back of that nice man's car – the nice man who had subsequently reacted so oddly to being shot at.

Perhaps they would have some money there and would let him have it. He wondered. Well, he would find out. He yanked the horse from its feast once again and galloped towards it.

As he approached the petrol station he noticed a car parked there at an arrogant angle. The angle made it quite clear that the car was not there for anything so mundane as to have petrol put into it, and was much too important to park itself neatly out of the way. Any other car that arrived for petrol would just have to manoeuvre around it as best it could. The car was white with stripes and badges and important-looking lights.

Arriving at the forecourt the Monk dismounted and

tethered his horse to a pump. He walked towards the small shop building and saw that inside it there was a man with his back to him wearing a dark blue uniform and a peaked cap. The man was dancing up and down and twisting his fingers in his ears, and this was clearly making a deep impression on the man behind the till.

The Monk watched in transfixed awe. The man, he believed with an instant effortlessness which would have impressed even a Scientologist, must be a God of some kind to arouse such fervour. He waited with bated breath to worship him. In a moment the man turned around and walked out of the shop, saw the Monk and stopped dead.

The Monk realised that the God must be waiting for him to make an act of worship, so he reverently danced up and down twisting his fingers in his ears.

His God stared at him for a moment, caught hold of him, twisted him round, slammed him forward spread-eagled over the car and frisked him for weapons.

Dirk burst into the flat like a small podgy tornado.

'Miss Way,' he said, grasping her slightly unwilling hand and doffing his absurd hat, 'it is the most inexpressible pleasure to meet you, but also the matter of the deepest regret that the occasion of our meeting should be one of such great sorrow and one which bids me extend to you my most profound sympathy and commiseration. I ask you to believe me that I would not intrude upon your private grief for all the world if it were not on a matter of the gravest moment and magnitude. Richard – I have solved the problem of the conjuring trick and it's extraordinary.'

He swept through the room and deposited himself on a spare chair at the small dining table, on which he put his hat.

'You will have to excuse us, Dirk—' said Richard, coldly.

'No, I am afraid you will have to excuse me,' returned Dirk. 'The puzzle is solved, and the solution is so astounding that it took a seven-year-old child on the street to give it to me. But it is undoubtedly the correct one, absolutely undoubtedly. "What, then, is the solution?" you ask me, or rather would ask me if you could get a word in edgeways, which you can't, so I will save you the bother and ask the question for you, and answer it as well by saying that I will not tell you, because you won't believe me. I shall instead show you, this very afternoon.

'Rest assured, however, that it explains everything. It explains the trick. It explains the note you found – that should have made it perfectly clear to me but I was a fool. And it explains what the missing third question was, or rather – and this is the significant point – it explains what the missing *first* question was!'

'What missing question?' exclaimed Richard, confused by the sudden pause, and leaping in with the first phrase he could grab.

Dirk blinked as if at an idiot. 'The missing question that George III asked, of course,' he said.

'Asked who?'

'Well, the Professor,' said Dirk impatiently. 'Don't you listen to anything you say? The whole thing was obvious!' he exclaimed, thumping the table. 'So obvious that the only thing which prevented me from seeing the solution was the trifling fact that it was *completely impossible*. Sherlock Holmes observed that once you have eliminated the impossible, then whatever remains, however improbable, must be the answer. I, however, do not like to eliminate the impossible. Now. Let us go.'

'No.'

'What?' Dirk glanced up at Susan, from whom this unexpected – or at least, unexpected to him – opposition had come.

'Mr Gently,' said Susan in a voice you could notch a stick with, 'why did you deliberately mislead Richard into thinking that he was wanted by the police?'

Dirk frowned.

'But he was wanted by the police,' he said, 'and still is.'

'Yes, but just to answer questions! Not because he's a suspected murderer.'

Dirk looked down.

'Miss Way,' he said, 'the police are interested in knowing who murdered your brother. I, with the very greatest respect, am not. It may, I concede, turn out to have a bearing on the case, but it may just as likely turn out to be a casual madman. I wanted to know, still need desperately to know, *why Richard climbed into this flat last night.*'

'I told you,' protested Richard.

'What you told me is immaterial – it only reveals the crucial fact that you do not know the reason yourself! For heaven's sake, I thought I had demonstrated that to you clearly enough at the canal!'

Richard simmered.

'It was perfectly clear to me watching you,' pursued Dirk, 'that you had very little idea what you were doing, and had absolutely no concern about the physical danger you were in. At first I thought, watching, that it was just a brainless thug out on his first and quite possibly last burgle. But then the figure looked back and I realised it was you – and I know you to be an intelligent, rational, and moderate man. Richard MacDuff? Risking his neck carelessly climbing up drainpipes at night? It seemed to me that you would only behave in such a reckless and extreme way if you were desperately worried about something of terrible importance. Is that not true, Miss Way?'

He looked sharply up at Susan, who slowly sat down, looking at him with an alarm in her eyes which said that he had struck home.

'And yet, when you came to see me this morning you seemed perfectly calm and collected. You argued with me perfectly rationally when I talked a lot of nonsense about Schrödinger's Cat. This was not the behaviour of someone who had the previous night been driven to extremes by some desperate purpose. I confess that it was at that moment that I stooped to, well, exaggerating your predicament, simply in order to keep hold of you.'

'You didn't. I left.'

'With certain ideas in your head. I knew you would be back. I apologise most humbly for having misled you, er, somewhat, but I knew that what *I* had to find out lay far beyond what the police would concern themselves with. And it was this – if you were not quite yourself when you climbed the wall last night . . . then *who were you – and why*?'

Richard shivered. A silence lengthened.

'What has it got to do with conjuring tricks?' he said at last.

'That is what we must go to Cambridge to find out.'

'But what makes you so sure—?'

'It disturbs me,' said Dirk, and a dark and heavy look came into his face.

For one so garrulous he seemed suddenly oddly reluctant to speak.

He continued, 'It disturbs me very greatly when I find that I know things and do not know why I know them. Maybe it is the same instinctive processing of data that allows you to catch a ball almost before you've seen it.

Maybe it is the deeper and less explicable instinct that tells you when someone is watching you. It is a very great offence to my intellect that the very things that I despise other people for being credulous of actually occur to me. You will remember the . . . unhappiness surrounding certain exam questions.'

He seemed suddenly distressed and haggard. He had to dig deep inside himself to continue speaking.

He said, 'The ability to put two and two together and come up instantly with four is one thing. The ability to put the square root of five hundred and thirty-nine point seven together with the cosine of twenty-six point four three two and come up with . . . with whatever the answer to that is, is quite another. And I . . . well, let me give you an example.'

He leant forward intently. 'Last night I saw you climbing into this flat. I *knew* that something was wrong. Today I got you to tell me every last detail you knew about what happened last night, and already, as a result, using my intellect alone, I have uncovered possibly the greatest secret lying hidden on this planet. I swear to you that this is true and that I can prove it. Now you must believe me when I tell you that I know, I *know* that there is something terribly, desperately, appallingly wrong and that we must find it. Will you go with me now, to Cambridge?'

Richard nodded dumbly.

'Good,' said Dirk. 'What is this?' he added, pointing at Richard's plate.

'A pickled herring. Do you want one?'

'Thank you, no,' said Dirk, rising and buckling his coat. 'There is,' he added as he headed towards the door, steering Richard with him, 'no such word as "herring" in my dictionary. Good afternoon, Miss Way, wish us God speed.'

25

There was a rumble of thunder, and the onset of that interminable light drizzle from the north-east by which so many of the world's most momentous events seem to be accompanied.

Dirk turned up the collar of his leather overcoat against the weather, but nothing could dampen his demonic exuberance as he and Richard approached the great twelfth-century gates.

'St Cedd's College, Cambridge,' he exclaimed, looking at them for the first time in eight years. 'Founded in the year something or other, by someone I forget in honour of someone whose name for the moment escapes me.'

'St Cedd?' suggested Richard.

'Do you know, I think it very probably was? One of the duller Northumbrian saints. His brother Chad was even duller. Has a cathedral in Birmingham if that gives you some idea. Ah, Bill, how good to see you again,' he added, accosting the porter who was just walking into the college as well. The porter looked round.

'Mr Cjelli, nice to see you back, sir. Sorry you had a spot of bother, hope that's all behind you now.'

'Indeed, Bill, it is. You find me thriving. And Mrs Roberts? How is she? Foot still troubling her?'

'Not since she had it off, thanks for asking, sir. Between you and me, sir, I would've been just as happy to have had her amputated and kept the foot. I had a little spot reserved on the mantelpiece, but there we are, we have to take things as we find them.

'Mr MacDuff, sir,' he added, nodding curtly at Richard. 'Oh, that horse you mentioned, sir, when you were here last night. I'm afraid we had to have it removed. It was bothering Professor Chronotis.'

'I was only curious, er, Bill,' said Richard. 'I hope it didn't disturb you.'

'Nothing ever disturbs me, sir, so long as it isn't wearing a dress. Can't abide it when the young fellers wear dresses, sir.'

'If the horse bothers you again, Bill,' interrupted Dirk, patting him on the shoulder, 'send it up to me and I shall speak with it. Now, you mention the good Professor Chronotis. Is he in at the moment? We've come on an errand.'

'Far as I know, sir. Can't check for you because his phone's out of order. Suggest you go and look yourself. Far left corner of Second Court.'

'I know it well, Bill, thank you, and my best to what remains of Mrs Roberts.'

They swept on through into First Court, or at least Dirk swept, and Richard walked in his normal heron-like gait, wrinkling up his face against the measly drizzle.

Dirk had obviously mistaken himself for a tour guide.

'St Cedd's,' he pronounced, 'the college of Coleridge, and the college of Sir Isaac Newton, renowned inventor of the milled-edge coin and the catflap!'

'The what?' said Richard.

'The catflap! A device of the utmost cunning, perspicuity and invention. It is a door within a door, you see, a . . .'

'Yes,' said Richard, 'there was also the small matter of gravity.'

'Gravity,' said Dirk with a slightly dismissive shrug, 'yes, there was that as well, I suppose. Though that, of course, was merely a discovery. It was there to be discovered.'

He took a penny out of his pocket and tossed it casually on to the pebbles that ran alongside the paved pathway.

'You see?' he said. 'They even keep it on at weekends. Someone was bound to notice sooner or later. But the catflap . . . ah, there is a very different matter. Invention, pure creative invention.'

'I would have thought it was quite obvious. Anyone could have thought of it.'

'Ah,' said Dirk, 'it is a rare mind indeed that can render the hitherto non-existent blindingly obvious. The cry "I could have thought of that" is a very popular and misleading one, for the fact is that they didn't, and a very significant and revealing fact it is too. This, if I am not mistaken, is the staircase we seek. Shall we ascend?'

Without waiting for an answer he plunged on up the stairs. Richard, following uncertainly, found him already knocking on the inner door. The outer one stood open.

'Come in!' called a voice from within. Dirk pushed the door open, and they were just in time to see the back of Reg's white head as he disappeared into the kitchen.

'Just making some tea,' he called out. 'Like some? Sit down, sit down, whoever you are.'

'That would be most kind,' returned Dirk. 'We are two.' Dirk sat, and Richard followed his lead.

'Indian or China?' called Reg.

'Indian, please.'

There was a rattle of cups and saucers.

Richard looked around the room. It seemed suddenly humdrum. The fire was burning quietly away to itself, but the light was that of the grey afternoon. Though everything about it was the same, the old sofa, the table burdened with books, there seemed nothing to connect it with the hectic strangeness of the previous night. The room seemed to sit there with raised eyebrows, innocently saying 'Yes?'

'Milk?' called out Reg from the kitchen.

'Please,' replied Dirk. He gave Richard a smile which seemed to him to be half-mad with suppressed excitement.

'One lump or two?' called Reg again.

'One, please,' said Dirk, '. . . and two spoons of sugar if you would.'

There was a suspension of activity in the kitchen. A moment or two passed and Reg stuck his head round the door.

'Svlad Cjelli!' he exclaimed. 'Good heavens! Well, that was quick work, young MacDuff, well done. My dear fellow, how very excellent to see you, how good of you to come.'

He wiped his hands on a tea towel he was carrying and hurried over to shake hands.

'My dear Svlad.'

'Dirk, please, if you would,' said Dirk, grasping his hand warmly, 'I prefer it. It has more of a sort of Scottish dagger feel to it, I think. Dirk Gently is the name under which I now trade. There are certain events in the past, I'm afraid, from which I would wish to disassociate myself.'

'Absolutely, I know how you feel. Most of the fourteenth century, for instance, was pretty grim,' agreed Reg earnestly.

Dirk was about to correct the misapprehension, but thought that it might be somewhat of a long trek and left it.

'So how have you been, then, my dear Professor?' he

said instead, decorously placing his hat and scarf upon the arm of the sofa.

'Well,' said Reg, 'it's been an interesting time recently, or rather, a dull time. But dull for interesting reasons. Now, sit down again, warm yourselves by the fire, and I will get the tea and endeavour to explain.' He bustled out again, humming busily, and left them to settle themselves in front of the fire.

Richard leant over to Dirk. 'I had no idea you knew him so well,' he said with a nod in the direction of the kitchen.

'I don't,' said Dirk instantly. 'We met once by chance at some dinner, but there was an immediate sympathy and rapport.'

'So how come you never met again?'

'He studiously avoided me, of course. Close rapports with people are dangerous if you have a secret to hide. And as secrets go, I fancy that this is somewhat of a biggie. If there is a bigger secret anywhere in the world I would very much care,' he said quietly, 'to know what it is.'

He gave Richard a significant look and held his hands out to the fire. Since Richard had tried before without success to draw him out on exactly what the secret was, he refused to rise to the bait on this occasion, but sat back in his armchair and looked about him.

'Did I ask you,' said Reg, returning at that moment, 'if you wanted any tea?'

'Er, yes,' said Richard, 'we spoke about it at length. I think we agreed in the end that we would, didn't we?'

'Good,' said Reg, vaguely, 'by a happy chance there seems to be some ready in the kitchen. You'll have to forgive me. I have a memory like a . . . like a . . . what are those things you drain rice in? What am I talking about?'

With a puzzled look he turned smartly round and disappeared once more into the kitchen.

'Very interesting,' said Dirk quietly, 'I wondered if his memory might be poor.'

He stood, suddenly, and prowled around the room. His eyes fell on the abacus which stood on the only clear space on the large mahogany table.

'Is this the table,' he asked Richard in a low voice, 'where you found the note about the salt cellar?'

'Yes,' said Richard, standing, and coming over, 'tucked into this book.' He picked up the guide to the Greek islands and flipped through it.

'Yes, yes, of course,' said Dirk, impatiently. 'We know about all that. I'm just interested that this was the table.' He ran his fingers along its edge, curiously.

'If you think it was some sort of prior collaboration between Reg and the girl,' Richard said, 'then I must say that I don't think it possibly can have been.'

'Of course it wasn't,' said Dirk testily, 'I would have thought that was perfectly clear.'

Richard shrugged in an effort not to get angry and put the book back down again.

'Well, it's an odd coincidence that the book should have been . . .'

'Odd coincidence!' snorted Dirk. 'Ha! We shall see how much of a coincidence. We shall see exactly how odd it was. I would like you, Richard, to ask our friend how he performed the trick.'

'I thought you said you knew already.'

'I do,' said Dirk airily. 'I would like to hear it confirmed.'

'Oh, I see,' said Richard, 'yes, that's rather easy, isn't it? Get him to explain it, and then say, "Yes, that's exactly what I thought it was!" Very good, Dirk. Have we come all the way up here in order to have him explain how he did a conjuring trick? I think I must be mad.'

Dirk bridled at this.

'Please do as I ask,' he snapped angrily. 'You saw him do the trick, you must ask how he did it. Believe me, there is an astounding secret hidden within it. I know it, but I want you to hear it from him.'

He spun round as Reg re-entered, bearing a tray, which he carried round the sofa and put on to the low coffee table that sat in front of the fire.

'Professor Chronotis . . .' said Dirk.

'Reg,' said Reg, 'please.'

'Very, well,' said Dirk, 'Reg . . .'

'Sieve!' exclaimed Reg.

'What?'

'Thing you drain rice in. A sieve. I was trying to remember the word, though I forget now the reason why. No matter. Dirk, dear fellow, you look as if you are about to explode about something. Why don't you sit down and make yourself comfortable?'

'Thank you, no, I would rather feel free to pace up and down fretfully if I may. Reg . . .'

He turned to face him square on, and raised a single finger.

'I must tell you,' he said, 'that I know your secret.'

'Ah, yes, er – do you indeed?' mumbled Reg, looking down awkwardly and fiddling with the cups and teapot. 'I see.'

The cups rattled violently as he moved them. 'Yes, I was afraid of that.'

'And there are some questions that we would like to ask you. I must tell you that I await the answers with the very greatest apprehension.'

'Indeed, indeed,' Reg muttered. 'Well, perhaps it is at

last time. I hardly know myself what to make of recent events and am ... fearful myself. Very well. Ask what you will.' He looked up sharply, his eyes glittering.

Dirk nodded curtly at Richard, turned, and started to pace, glaring at the floor.

'Er,' said Richard, 'well, I'd be ... interested to know how you did the conjuring trick with the salt cellar last night.'

Reg seemed surprised and rather confused by the question. 'The *conjuring* trick?' he said.

'Er, yes,' said Richard, 'the conjuring trick.'

'Oh,' said Reg, taken aback, 'well, the conjuring part of it, I'm not sure I should – Magic Circle rules, you know, very strict about revealing these secrets. Very strict. Impressive trick, though, don't you think?' he added slyly.

'Well, yes,' said Richard, 'it seemed very natural at the time, but now that I ... think about it, I have to admit that it was a bit dumbfounding.'

'Ah, well,' said Reg, 'it's skill, you see. Practice. Make it look natural.'

'It did look very natural,' continued Richard, feeling his way, 'I was quite taken in.'

'You liked it?'

'It was very impressive.'

Dirk was getting a little impatient. He shot a look to that effect at Richard.

'And I can quite see,' said Richard firmly, 'why it's impossible for you to tell me. I was just interested, that's all. Sorry I asked.'

'Well,' said Reg in a sudden seizure of doubt, 'I suppose ... well, so long as you absolutely promise not to tell anyone else,' he carried on, 'I suppose you can probably work out for yourself that I used two of the salt cellars on the table. No one was going to notice the difference between one and another. The quickness of the hand, you know, deceives the eye, particularly some of the eyes around that table. While I was fiddling with my woolly hat, giving, though I say so myself, a very cunning simulation of clumsiness and muddle, I simply slipped the salt cellar down my sleeve. You see?'

His earlier agitation had been swept away completely by his pleasure in showing off his craft.

'It's the oldest trick in the world, in fact,' he continued, 'but nevertheless takes a great deal of skill and deftness. Then a little later, of course, I returned it to the table with the appearance of simply passing it to someone else. Takes years of practice, of course, to make it look natural, but I much prefer it to simply slipping the thing down to the floor. Amateur stuff that. You can't pick it up, and the cleaners never notice it for at least a fort-night. I once had a dead thrush under my seat for a month. No trick involved there, of course. Cat killed it.'

Reg beamed.

Richard felt he had done his bit, but hadn't the faintest idea where it was supposed to have got them. He glanced at Dirk, who gave him no help whatsoever, so he plunged on blindly.

'Yes,' he said, 'yes, I understand that that can be done by sleight of hand. What I don't understand is how the salt cellar got embedded in the pot.'

Reg looked puzzled once again, as if they were all talking at cross purposes. He looked at Dirk, who stopped pacing and stared at him with bright, expectant eyes.

'Well, that's ... perfectly straightforward,' said Reg, 'didn't take any conjuring skill at all. I nipped out for my hat, you remember?'

'Yes,' said Richard, doubtfully.

'Well,' said Reg, 'while I was out of the room I went

to find the man who made the pot. Took some time, of course. About three weeks of detective work to track him down and another couple of days to sober him up, and then with a little difficulty I persuaded him to bake the salt cellar into the pot for me. After that I briefly stopped off somewhere to find some, er, powder to disguise the suntan, and of course I had to time the return a little carefully so as to make it all look natural. I bumped into myself in the ante-room, which I always find embarrassing, I never know where to look, but, er . . . well, there you have it.'

He smiled a rather bleak and nervous smile.

Richard tried to nod, but eventually gave up.

'What on earth are you talking about?' he said.

Reg looked at him in surprise.

'I thought you said you knew my secret,' he said.

'I do,' said Dirk, with a beam of triumph. 'He, as yet, does not, though he furnished all the information I needed to discover it. Let me,' he added, 'fill in a couple of little blanks. In order to help disguise the fact that you had in fact been away for weeks when as far as anyone sitting at the table was concerned you had only popped out of the door for a couple of seconds, you had to write down for your own reference the last thing you said, in order that you could pick up the thread of conversation again as naturally as possible. An important detail if your memory is not what it once was. Yes?'

'What it once was,' said Reg, slowly shaking his white head, 'I can hardly remember what it once was. But yes, you are very sharp to pick up such a detail.'

'And then there is the little matter,' continued Dirk, 'of the questions that George III asked. Asked you.'

This seemed to catch Reg quite by surprise.

'He asked you,' continued Dirk, consulting a small notebook he had pulled from his pocket,'if there was any particular reason why one thing happened after another and if there was any way of stopping it. Did he not also ask you, and ask you *first*, if it was possible to move backwards in time, or something of that kind?'

Reg gave Dirk a long and appraising look.

'I was right about you,' he said, 'you have a very remarkable mind, young man.' He walked slowly over to the window that looked out on to Second Court. He watched the odd figures scuttling through it hugging themselves in the drizzle or pointing at things.

'Yes,' said Reg at last in a subdued voice, 'that is precisely what he said.'

'Good,' said Dirk, snapping shut his notebook with a tight little smile which said that he lived for such praise, 'then that explains why the answers were "yes, no and maybe" – in that order. Now. Where is it?'

'Where is what?'

'The time machine.'

'You're standing in it,' said Reg.

26

A party of noisy people spilled into the train at Bishop's Stortford. Some were wearing morning suits with carnations looking a little battered by a day's festivity. The women of the party were in smart dresses and hats, chattering excitedly about how pretty Julia had looked in all that silk taffeta, how Ralph still looked like a smug oaf even done up in all his finery, and generally giving the whole thing about two weeks.

One of the men stuck his head out of the window and hailed a passing railway employee just to check that this was the right train and was stopping at Cambridge. The porter confirmed that of course it bloody was. The young man said that they didn't all want to find they were going off in the wrong direction, did they, and made a sound a little like that of a fish barking, as if to indicate that this was a pricelessly funny remark, and then pulled his head back in, banging it on the way.

The alcohol content of the atmosphere in the carriage rose sharply.

There seemed to be a general feeling in the air that the best way of getting themselves in the right mood for the post-wedding reception party that evening was to make a foray to the bar so that any members of the party who were not already completely drunk could finish the task. Rowdy shouts of acclamation greeted this notion, the train restarted with a jolt and a lot of those still standing fell over.

Three young men dropped into the three empty seats round one table, of which the fourth was already taken by a sleekly overweight man in an old-fashioned suit. He had a lugubrious face and his large, wet, cowlike eyes gazed into some unknown distance.

Very slowly his eyes began to refocus all the way from infinity and gradually to home in on his more immediate surroundings, his new and intrusive companions. There was a need he felt, as he had felt before.

The three men were discussing loudly whether they would all go to the bar, whether some of them would go to the bar and bring back drinks for the others, whether the ones who went to the bar would get so excited by all the drinks there that they would stay put and forget to bring any back for the others who would be sitting here anxiously awaiting their return, and whether even if they did remember to come back immediately with the drinks they would actually be capable of carrying them and wouldn't simply throw them all over the carriage on the way back, incommoding other passengers.

Some sort of consensus seemed to be reached, but almost immediately none of them could remember what it was. Two of them got up, then sat down again as the third one got up. Then he sat down. The two other ones stood up again, expressing the idea that it might be simpler if they just bought the entire bar.

The third was about to get up again and follow them, when slowly, but with unstoppable purpose, the cow-eyed man sitting opposite him leant across, and gripped him firmly by the forearm.

The young man in his morning suit looked up as sharply as his somewhat bubbly brain would allow and, startled, said, 'What do you want?'

Michael Wenton-Weakes gazed into his eyes with

terrible intensity, and said, in a low voice, 'I was on a ship . . .'

'What?'

'A ship . . .' said Michael.

'What ship, what are you talking about? Get off me. Let go!'

'We came,' continued Michael, in a quiet, almost inaudible, but compelling voice, 'a monstrous distance. We came to build a paradise. A paradise. Here.'

His eyes swam briefly round the carriage, and then gazed briefly out through the spattered windows at the gathering gloom of a drizzly East Anglian evening. He gazed with evident loathing. His grip on the other's forearm tightened.

'Look, I'm going for a drink,' said the wedding guest, though feebly, because he clearly wasn't.

'We left behind those who would destroy themselves with war,' murmured Michael. 'Ours was to be a world of peace, of music, of art, of enlightenment. All that was petty, all that was mundane, all that was contemptible would have no place in our world . . .'

The stilled reveller looked at Michael wonderingly. He didn't look like an old hippy. Of course, you never could tell. His own elder brother had once spent a couple of years living in a Druidic commune, eating LSD doughnuts and thinking he was a tree, since when he had gone on to become a director of a merchant bank. The difference, of course, was that he hardly ever still thought he was a tree, except just occasionally, and he had long ago learnt to avoid the particular claret which sometimes triggered off that flashback.

'There were those who said we would fail,' continued Michael in his low tone that carried clearly under the boisterous noise that filled the carriage, 'who prophesied that we too carried in us the seed of war, but it was our high resolve and purpose that only art and beauty should flourish, the highest art, the highest beauty – music. We took with us only those who believed, who wished it to be true.'

'But what are you talking about?' asked the wedding guest, though not challengingly, for he had fallen under Michael's mesmeric spell. 'When was this? Where was this?'

Michael breathed hard. 'Before you were born,' he said at last. 'Be still, and I will tell you.'

27

There was a long startled silence during which the evening gloom outside seemed to darken appreciably and gather the room into its grip. A trick of the light wreathed Reg in shadows.

Dirk was, for one of the few times in a life of exuberantly prolific loquacity, wordless. His eyes shone with a child's wonder as they passed anew over the dull and shabby furniture of the room, the panelled walls, the threadbare carpets. His hands were trembling.

Richard frowned faintly to himself for a moment as if he was trying to work out the square root of something in his head, and then looked back directly at Reg.

'Who are you?' he asked.

'I have absolutely no idea,' said Reg brightly, 'much of my memory's gone completely. I am very old, you see. Startlingly old. Yes, I think if I were to tell you how old I was it would be fair to say that you would be startled. Odds are that so would I, because I can't remember. I've seen an awful lot, you know. Forgotten most of it, thank God. Trouble is, when you start getting to my age, which, as I think I mentioned earlier, is a somewhat startling one – did I say that?'

'Yes, you did mention it.'

'Good. I'd forgotten whether I had or not. The thing is that your memory doesn't actually get any bigger, and a lot of stuff just falls out. So you see, the major difference between someone of my age and someone of yours is not how much I know, but how much I've forgotten. And after a while you even forget what it is you've forgotten, and after that you even forget that there was something to remember. Then you tend to forget, er, what it was you were talking about.'

He stared helplessly at the teapot.

'Things you remember . . .' prompted Richard gently.

'Smells and earrings.'

'I beg your pardon?'

'Those are things that linger for some reason,' said Reg, shaking his head in a puzzled way. He sat down suddenly. 'The earrings that Queen Victoria wore on her Silver Jubilee. Quite startling objects. Toned down in the pictures of the period, of course. The smell of the streets before there were cars in them. Hard to say which was worse. That's why Cleopatra remains so vividly in the memory, of course. A quite devastating combination of earrings and smell. I think that will probably be the last thing that remains when all else has finally fled. I shall sit alone in a darkened room, *sans* teeth, *sans* eyes, *sans* taste, *sans* everything but a little grey old head, and in that little grey old head a peculiar vision of hideous blue and gold dangling things flashing in the light, and the smell of sweat, catfood and death. I wonder what I shall make of it . . .'

Dirk was scarcely breathing as he began to move slowly round the room, gently brushing his fingertips over the walls, the sofa, the table.

'How long,' he said, 'has this been—'

'Here?' said Reg. 'Just about two hundred years. Ever since I retired.'

'Retired from what?'

'Search me. Must have been something pretty good, though, what do you think?'

'You mean you've been in this same set of rooms here

227

for ... two hundred years?' murmured Richard. 'You'd think someone would notice, or think it was odd.'

'Oh, that's one of the delights of the older Cambridge colleges,' said Reg, 'everyone is so discreet. If we all went around mentioning what was odd about each other we'd be here till Christmas. Svlad, er – Dirk, my dear fellow, please don't touch that just at the moment.'

Dirk's hand was reaching out to touch the abacus standing on its own on the only clear spot on the big table.

'What is it?' said Dirk sharply.

'It's just what it looks like, an old wooden abacus,' said Reg. 'I'll show you in a moment, but first I must congratulate you on your powers of perception. May I ask how you arrived at the solution?'

'I have to admit,' said Dirk with rare humility, 'that I did not. In the end I asked a child. I told him the story of the trick and asked him how he thought it had been done, and he said, and I quote, "It's bleedin' obvious, innit, he must've 'ad a bleedin' time machine." I thanked the little fellow and gave him a shilling for his trouble. He kicked me rather sharply on the shin and went about his business. But he was the one who solved it. My only contribution to the matter was to see that he *must* be right. He had even saved me the bother of kicking myself.'

'But you had the perception to think of asking a child,' said Reg. 'Well then, I congratulate you on that instead.'

Dirk was still eyeing the abacus suspiciously.

'How ... does it work?' he said, trying to make it sound like a casual enquiry.

'Well, it's really terribly simple.' said Reg, 'it works any way you want it to. You see, the computer that runs it is a rather advanced one. In fact it is more powerful than the sum total of all the computers on this planet including – and this is the tricky part – including itself. Never really understood that bit myself, to be honest with you. But over ninety-five per cent of that power is used in simply understanding what it is you want it to do. I simply plonk my abacus down there and it understands the way I use it. I think I must have been brought up to use an abacus when I was a . . . well, a child, I suppose.

'Richard, for instance, would probably want to use his own personal computer. If you put it down there, where the abacus is, the machine's computer would simply take charge of it and offer you lots of nice user-friendly time-travel applications complete with pull-down menus and desk accessories if you like. Except that you point to 1066 on the screen and you've got the Battle of Hastings going on outside your door, er, if that's the sort of thing you're interested in.'

Reg's tone of voice suggested that his own interests lay in other areas.

'It's, er, really quite fun in its way,' he concluded. 'Certainly better than television and a great deal easier to use than a video recorder. If I miss a programme I just pop back in time and watch it. I'm hopeless fiddling with all those buttons.'

Dirk reacted to this revelation with horror.

'You have a time machine and you use it for . . . watching television?'

'Well, I wouldn't use it at all if I could get the hang of the video recorder. It's a very delicate business, time travel, you know. Full of appalling traps and dangers, if you should change the wrong thing in the past, you could entirely disrupt the course of history.

'Plus, of course, it mucks up the telephone. I'm sorry,' he said to Richard a little sheepishly, 'that you were unable to phone your young lady last night. There seems to be something fundamentally inexplicable about the British telephone system, and my time machine doesn't like it. There's never any problem with the plumbing, the electricity, or even the gas. The connection interfaces are taken care of at some quantum level I don't entirely understand, and it's never been a problem.

'The phone on the other hand is definitely a problem. Every time I use the time machine, which is, of course, hardly at all, partly because of this very problem with the phone, the phone goes haywire and I have to get some lout from the phone company to come and fix it, and he starts asking stupid questions the answers to which he has no hope of understanding.

'Anyway, the point is that I have a very strict rule that I must not change anything in the past at all – ' Reg sighed – 'whatever the temptation.'

'What temptation?' said Dirk, sharply.

'Oh, it's just a little, er, thing I'm interested in,' said Reg, vaguely, 'it is perfectly harmless because I stick very strictly to the rule. It makes me sad, though.'

'But you broke your own rule!' insisted Dirk. 'Last night! You changed something in the past—'

'Well, yes,' said Reg, a little uncomfortably, 'but that was different. Very different. If you had seen the look on the poor child's face. So miserable. She thought the world should be a marvellous place, and all those appalling old dons were pouring their withering scorn on her just because it wasn't marvellous for them anymore.

'I mean,' he added, appealing to Richard, 'remember Cawley. What a bloodless old goat. Someone should get some humanity into him even if they have to knock it in with a brick. No, that was perfectly justifiable. Otherwise, I make it a very strict rule—'

Richard looked at him with dawning recognition of something.

'Reg,' he said politely, 'may I give you a little advice?'

'Of course you may, my dear fellow, I should adore you to,' said Reg.

'If our mutual friend here offers to take you for a stroll along the banks of the River Cam, *don't go*.'

'What on earth do you mean?'

'He means,' said Dirk earnestly, 'that he thinks there may be something a little disproportionate between what you actually did, and your stated reasons for doing it.'

'Oh. Well, odd way of saying it—'

'Well, he's a very odd fellow. But you see, there sometimes may be other reasons for things you do which you are not necessarily aware of. As in the case of post-hypnotic suggestion – or possession.'

Reg turned very pale.

'Possession—' he said.

'Professor – Reg – I believe there was some reason you wanted to see me. What exactly was it?'

'Cambridge! This is ... Cambridge!' came the lilting squawk of the station public-address system.

Crowds of noisy revellers spewed out on to the platform barking and honking at each other.

'Where's Rodney?' said one, who had clambered with difficulty from the carriage in which the bar was situated. He and his companion looked up and down the platform, totteringly. The large figure of Michael Wenton-Weakes loomed silently past them and out to the exit.

They jostled their way down the side of the train, looking in through the dirty carriage windows. They suddenly saw their missing companion still sitting, trance-like, in his seat in the now almost empty compartment. They banged on the window and hooted at him. For a moment or two he didn't react, and when he did he woke suddenly in a puzzled way as if seeming not to know where he was.

'He's pie-eyed!' his companions bawled happily, bundling themselves on to the train again and bundling Rodney back off.

He stood woozily on the platform and shook his head. Then glancing up he saw through the railings the large bulk of Michael Wenton-Weakes heaving himself and a large heavy bag into a taxicab, and he stood for a moment transfixed.

''Straordinary thing,' he said, 'that man. Telling me a long story about some kind of shipwreck.'

'Har har,' gurgled one of his two companions, 'get any money off you?'

'What?' said Rodney, puzzled. 'No. No, I don't think so. Except it wasn't a shipwreck, more an accident, an explosion—? He seems to think he caused it in some way. Or rather there was an accident, and he caused an explosion trying to put it right and killed everybody. Then he said there was an awful lot of rotting mud for years and years, and then slimy things with legs. It was all a bit peculiar.'

'Trust Rodney! Trust Rodney to pick a madman!'

'I think he must have been mad. He suddenly went off on a tangent about some bird. He said the bit about the bird was all nonsense. He wished he could get rid of the bit about the bird. But then he said it would be put right. It would all be put right. For some reason I didn't like it when he said that.'

'Should have come along to the bar with us. Terribly funny, we—'

'I also didn't like the way he said goodbye. I didn't like that at all.'

232

28

'You remember,' said Reg, 'when you arrived this afternoon I said that times recently had been dull, but for . . .
interesting reasons?'

'I remember it vividly,' said Dirk, 'it happened a mere
ten minutes ago. You were standing exactly there as I
recall. Indeed you were wearing the very clothes with
which you are currently apparelled, and—'

'Shut up, Dirk,' said Richard, 'let the poor man talk,
will you?'

Dirk made a slight, apologetic bow.

'Quite so,' said Reg. 'Well, the truth is that for many
weeks, months even, I have not used the time machine
at all, because I had the oddest feeling that someone or
something was trying to make me do it. It started as the
very faintest urge, and then it seemed to come at me in
stronger and stronger waves. It was extremely disturbing. I had to fight it very hard indeed because it was
trying to make me do something I actually wanted to
do. I don't think I would have realised that it was
something outside of me creating this pressure and not
just my own wishes asserting themselves if it wasn't for
the fact that I was so wary of allowing myself to do any
such thing. As soon as I began to realise that it was
something else trying to invade me, things got really bad
and the furniture began to fly about. Quite damaged my
little Georgian writing desk. Look at the marks on
the—'

'Is that what you were afraid of last night, upstairs?' asked Richard.

'Oh yes,' said Reg in a hushed voice, 'most terribly afraid. But it was only that rather nice horse, so that was all right. I expect it just wandered in when I was out getting some powder to cover up my suntan.'

'Oh?' said Dirk. 'And where did you go for that?' he asked. 'I can't think of many chemists that a horse would be likely to visit.'

'Oh, there's a planet off in what's known here as the Pleiades where the dust is exactly the right—'

'You went,' said Dirk in a whisper, 'to another planet? To get face powder?'

'Oh, it's no distance,' said Reg cheerfully. 'You see, the actual distance between two points in the whole of the space/time continuum is almost infinitely smaller than the apparent distance between adjacent orbits of an electron. Really, it's a lot less far than the chemist, and there's no waiting about at the till. I never have the right change, do you? Go for the quantum jump is always my preference. Except of course that you then get all the trouble with the telephone. Nothing's ever that easy, is it?'

He looked bothered for a moment.

'I think you may be right in what I think you're thinking, though,' he added quietly.

'Which is?'

'That I went through a rather elaborate bit of business to achieve a very small result. Cheering up a little girl, charming, delightful and sad though she was, doesn't seem to be enough explanation for – well, it was a fairly major operation in time-engineering, now that I come to face up to it. There's no doubt that it would have been simpler to compliment her on her dress. Maybe the ... ghost – we are talking of a ghost here, aren't we?'

234

'I think we are, yes,' said Dirk slowly.

'A ghost?' said Richard. 'Now come on—'

'Wait!' said Dirk, abruptly. 'Please continue,' he said to Reg.

'It's possible that the ... ghost caught me off my guard. I was fighting so strenuously against doing one thing that it easily tripped me into another—'

'And now?'

'Oh, it's gone completely. The ghost left me last night.'

'And where, we wonder,' said Dirk, turning his gaze on Richard, 'did it go?'

'No, please,' said Richard, 'not this. I'm not even sure I've agreed we're talking about time machines yet, and now suddenly it's ghosts?'

'So what was it,' hissed Dirk, 'that got into you to make you climb the wall?'

'Well, you suggested that I was under post-hypnotic suggestion from someone—'

'I did not! I demonstrated the power of post-hypnotic suggestion to you. But I believe that hypnosis and possession work in very, very similar ways. You can be made to do all kinds of absurd things, and will then cheerfully invent the most transparent rationalisations to explain them to yourself. But – you cannot be made to do something that runs against the fundamental grain of your character. You will fight. You will resist!'

Richard remembered then the sense of relief with which he had impulsively replaced the tape in Susan's machine last night. It had been the end of a struggle which he had suddenly won. With the sense of another struggle that he was now losing he sighed and related this to the others.

'Exactly!' exclaimed Dirk. 'You wouldn't do it! Now we're getting somewhere! You see, hypnosis works best

235

when the subject has some fundamental sympathy with what he or she is being asked to do. Find the right subject for your task and the hypnosis can take a very, very deep hold indeed. And I believe the same to be true of possession. So. What do we have?

'We have a ghost that wants something done and is looking for the right person to take possession of to do that for him. Professor—'

'Reg—' said Reg.

'Reg – may I ask you something that may be terribly personal? I will understand perfectly if you don't want to answer, but I will just keep pestering you until you do. Just my methods, you see. You said there was something that you found to be a terrible temptation to you. That you wanted to do but would not allow yourself, and that the ghost was trying to make you do? Please. This may be difficult for you, but I think it would be very helpful if you would tell us what it is.'

'I will not tell you.'

'You must understand how important—'

'I'll show you instead,' said Reg.

Silhouetted in the gates of St Cedd's stood a large figure carrying a large heavy black nylon bag. The figure was that of Michael Wenton-Weakes, the voice that asked the porter if Professor Chronotis was currently in his room was that of Michael Wenton-Weakes, the ears that heard the porter say he was buggered if he knew because the phone seemed to be on the blink again was that of Michael Wenton-Weakes, but the spirit that gazed out of his eyes was his no longer.

He had surrendered himself completely. All doubt, disparity and confusion had ceased.

A new mind had him in full possession.

The spirit that was not Michael Wenton-Weakes surveyed the college which lay before it, to which it had grown accustomed in the last few frustrating, infuriating weeks.

Weeks! Mere microsecond blinks.

Although the spirit – the ghost – that now inhabited Michael Wenton-Weakes' body had known long periods of near oblivion, sometimes even for centuries at a stretch, the time for which it had wandered the earth was such that it seemed only minutes ago that the creatures which had erected these walls had arrived. Most of his personal eternity – not really eternity, but a few billion years could easily seem like it – had been spent wandering across interminable mud, wading through ceaseless seas, watching with stunned horror when the slimy things with legs suddenly had begun to crawl from those rotting seas – and here they were, suddenly walking around as if they owned the place and complaining about the phones.

Deep in a dark and silent part of himself he knew that he was now mad, had been driven mad almost immediately after the accident by the knowledge of what he had done and of the existence he faced, by the memories of his fellows who had died and who for a while had haunted him even as he had haunted the Earth.

He knew that what he now had been driven to would have revolted the self he only infinitesimally remembered, but that it was the only way for him to end the ceaseless nightmare in which each second of billions of years had been worse than the previous one.

He hefted the bag and started to walk.

29

Deep in the rain forest it was doing what it usually does in rain forests, which was raining: hence the name.

It was a gentle, persistent rain, not the heavy slashing which would come later in the year, in the hot season. It formed a fine dripping mist through which the occasional shaft of sunlight would break, be softened and pass through on its way towards the wet bark of a calvaria tree on which it would settle and glisten. Sometimes it would do this next to a butterfly or a tiny motionless sparkling lizard, and then the effect would be almost unbearable.

Away up in the high canopy of the trees an utterly extraordinary thought would suddenly strike a bird, and it would go flapping wildly through the branches and settle at last in a different and altogether better tree where it would sit and consider things again more calmly until the same thought came along and struck it again, or it was time to eat.

The air was full of scents – the light fragrance of flowers, and the heavy odour of the sodden mulch with which the floor of the forest was carpeted.

Confusions of roots tangled through the mulch, moss grew on them, insects crawled.

In a space in the forest, on an empty patch of wet ground between a circle of craning trees, appeared quietly and without fuss a plain white door. After a few seconds it opened a little way with a slight squeak. A tall thin man looked out, looked around, blinked in surprise, and quietly pulled the door closed again.

A few seconds later the door opened again and Reg looked out.

'It's real,' he said, 'I promise you. Come out and see for yourself.' Walking out into the forest, he turned and beckoned the other two to follow him.

Dirk stepped boldly through, seemed disconcerted for about the length of time it takes to blink twice, and then announced that he saw exactly how it worked, that it was obviously to do with the unreal numbers that lay between minimum quantum distances and defined the fractal contours of the enfolded Universe and he was only astonished at himself for not having thought of it himself.

'Like the catflap,' said Richard from the doorway behind him.

'Er, yes, quite so,' said Dirk, taking off his spectacles and leaning against a tree wiping them, 'you spotted of course that I was lying. A perfectly natural reflex in the circumstances as I think you'll agree. Perfectly natural.' He squinted slightly and put his spectacles back on. They began to mist up again almost immediately.

'Astounding,' he admitted.

Richard stepped through more hesitantly and stood rocking for a moment with one foot still on the floor in Reg's room and the other on the wet earth of the forest. Then he stepped forward and committed himself fully.

His lungs instantly filled with the heady vapours and his mind with the wonder of the place. He turned and looked at the doorway through which he had walked. It was still a perfectly ordinary door frame with a perfectly ordinary little white door swinging open in it, but it was standing free in the open forest, and through it could clearly be seen the room he had just stepped out of.

He walked wonderingly round the back of the door, testing each foot on the muddy ground, not so much for fear of slipping as for fear that it might simply not be there. From behind it was just a perfectly ordinary open door frame, such as you might fail to find in any perfectly ordinary rain forest. He walked through the door from behind, and looking back again could once more see, as if he had just stepped out of them again, the college rooms of Professor Urban Chronotis of St Cedd's College, Cambridge, which must be thousands of miles away. Thousands? Where were they?

He peered off through the trees and thought he caught a slight shimmer in the distance, between the trees.

'Is that the sea?' he asked.

'You can see it a little more clearly from up here,' called Reg, who had walked on a little way up a slippery incline and was now leaning, puffing, against a tree. He pointed.

The other two followed him up, pulling themselves noisily through the branches and causing a lot of cawing and complaining from unseen birds high above.

'The Pacific?' asked Dirk.

'The Indian Ocean,' said Reg.

Dirk wiped his glasses again and had another look.

'Ah, yes, of course,' he said.

'Not Madagascar?' said Richard. 'I've been there—'

'Have you?' said Reg. 'One of the most beautiful and astonishing places on Earth, and one that is also full of the most appalling . . . temptations for me. No.'

His voice trembled slightly, and he cleared his throat.

'No,' he continued, 'Madagascar is – let me see, which direction are we – where's the sun? Yes. That way. Westish. Madagascar is about five hundred miles roughly west of here. The island of Réunion lies roughly in-between.'

'Er, what's the place called?' said Dirk suddenly, rapping his knuckles on the tree and frightening a lizard. 'Place where that stamp comes from, er – Mauritius.'

'Stamp?' said Reg.

'Yes, you must know,' said Dirk, 'very famous stamp. Can't remember anything about it, but it comes from here. Mauritius. Famous for its very remarkable stamp, all brown and smudged and you could buy Blenheim Palace with it. Or am I thinking of British Guiana?'

'Only you,' said Richard, 'know what you are thinking of.'

'Is it Mauritius?'

'It is,' said Reg, 'it is Mauritius.'

'But you don't collect stamps?'

'No.'

'What on *earth's* that?' said Richard suddenly, but Dirk carried on with his thought to Reg. 'Pity, you could get some nice first day covers, couldn't you?'

Reg shrugged. 'Not really interested,' he said.

Richard slithered back down the slope behind them.

'So what's the great attraction here?' said Dirk. 'It's not, I have to confess, what I was expecting. Very nice in its way, of course, all this nature, but I'm a city boy myself, I'm afraid.' He cleaned his glasses once again and pushed them back up his nose.

He started backwards at what he saw, and heard a strange little chuckle from Reg. Just in front of the door back into Reg's room, the most extraordinary confrontation was taking place.

A large cross bird was looking at Richard and Richard was looking at a large cross bird. Richard was looking at the bird as if it was the most extraordinary thing he had ever seen in his life, and the bird was looking at Richard as if defying him to find its beak even remotely funny.

Once it had satisfied itself that Richard did not intend

241

to laugh, the bird regarded him instead with a sort of grim irritable tolerance and wondered if he was just going to stand there or actually do something useful and feed it. It padded a couple of steps back and a couple of steps to the side and then just a single step forward again, on great waddling yellow feet. It then looked at him again, impatiently, and squarked an impatient squark.

The bird then bent forward and scraped its great absurd red beak across the ground as if to give Richard the idea that this might be a good area to look for things to give it to eat.

'It eats the nuts of the calvaria tree,' called out Reg to Richard.

The big bird looked sharply up at Reg in annoyance, as if to say that it was perfectly clear to any idiot what it ate. It then looked back at Richard once more and stuck its head on one side as if it had suddenly been struck by the thought that perhaps it was an idiot it had to deal with, and that it might need to reconsider its strategy accordingly.

'There are one or two on the ground behind you,' called Reg softly.

In a trance of astonishment Richard turned awkwardly and saw one or two large nuts lying on the ground. He bent and picked one up, glancing up at Reg, who gave him a reassuring nod.

Tentatively Richard held the thing out to the bird, which leant forward and pecked it sharply from between his fingers. Then, because Richard's hand was still stretched out, the bird knocked it irritably aside with its beak.

Once Richard had withdrawn to a respectful distance, it stretched its neck up, closed its large yellow eyes and seemed to gargle gracelessly as it shook the nut down its neck into its maw.

It appeared then to be at least partially satisfied. Whereas before it had been a cross dodo, it was at least now a cross, fed dodo, which was probably about as much as it could hope for in this life.

It made a slow, waddling, on-the-spot turn and padded back into the forest whence it had come, as if defying Richard to find the little tuft of curly feathers stuck up on top of its backside even remotely funny.

'I only come to look,' said Reg in a small voice, and glancing at him Dirk was discomfited to see that the old man's eyes were brimming with tears which he quickly brushed away. 'Really, it is not for me to interfere—'

Richard came scurrying breathlessly up to them.

'Was that a *dodo*?' he exclaimed.

'Yes,' said Reg, 'one of only three left at this time. The year is 1676. They will all be dead within four years, and after that no one will ever see them again. Come,' he said, 'let us go.'

Behind the stoutly locked outer door in the corner staircase in the Second Court of St Cedd's College, where only a millisecond earlier there had been a slight flicker as the inner door departed, there was another slight flicker as the inner door now returned.

Walking through the dark evening towards it the large figure of Michael Wenton-Weakes looked up at the corner windows. If any slight flicker had been visible, it would have gone unnoticed in the dim dancing firelight that spilled from the window.

The figure then looked up into the darkness of the sky, looking for what it knew to be there though there was not the slightest chance of seeing it, even on a clear night which this was not. The orbits of Earth were now so cluttered with pieces of junk and debris that one more item among them – even such a large one as this was – would pass perpetually unnoticed. Indeed, it had done so, though its influence had from time to time exerted itself. From time to time. When the waves had been strong. Not for nearly two hundred years had they been so strong as now they were again.

And all at last was now in place. The perfect carrier had been found.

The perfect carrier moved his footsteps onwards through the court.

The Professor himself had seemed the perfect choice at first, but that attempt had ended in frustration, fury, and then – inspiration! Bring a Monk to Earth! They were designed to believe anything, to be completely malleable. It could be suborned to undertake the task with the greatest of ease.

Unfortunately, however, this one had proved to be completely hopeless. Getting it to believe something was very easy. Getting it to continue to believe the same thing for more than five minutes at a time had proved to be an even more impossible task than that of getting the Professor to do what he fundamentally wanted to do but wouldn't allow himself.

Then another failure and then, miraculously, the perfect carrier had come at last.

The perfect carrier had already proved that it would have no compunction in doing what would have to be done.

Damply, clogged in mist, the moon struggled in a corner of the sky to rise. At the window, a shadow moved.

30

From the window overlooking Second Court Dirk watched the moon. 'We shall not,' he said, 'have long to wait.'

'To wait for what?' said Richard.

Dirk turned.

'For the ghost,' he said, 'to return to us. Professor,' he added to Reg, who was sitting anxiously by the fire, 'do you have any brandy, French cigarettes or worry beads in your rooms?'

'No,' said Reg.

'Then I shall have to fret unaided,' said Dirk and returned to staring out of the window.

'I have yet to be convinced,' said Richard, 'that there is not some other explanation than that of . . . ghosts to—'

'Just as you required actually to see a time machine in operation before you could accept it,' returned Dirk. 'Richard, I commend you on your scepticism, but even the sceptical mind must be prepared to accept the unacceptable when there is no alternative. If it looks like a duck, and quacks like a duck, we have at least to consider the possibility that we have a small aquatic bird of the family *Anatidae* on our hands.'

'Then what *is* a ghost?'

'I think that a ghost . . .' said Dirk, 'is someone who died either violently or unexpectedly with unfinished business on his, her – or its – hands. Who cannot rest until it has been finished, or put right.'

He turned to face them again.

'Which is why,' he said, 'a time machine would have such a fascination for a ghost once it knew of its existence. A time machine provides the means to put right what, in the ghost's opinion, went wrong in the past. To free it.

'Which is why it will be back. It tried first to take possession of Reg himself, but he resisted. Then came the incident with the conjuring trick, the face powder and the horse in the bathroom which I – ' he paused – 'which even I do not understand, though I intend to if it kills me. And then you, Richard, appear on the scene. The ghost deserts Reg and concentrates instead on you. Almost immediately there occurs an odd but significant incident. You do something that you then wish you hadn't done.

'I refer, of course, to the phone call you made to Susan and left on her answering machine.

'The ghost seizes its chance and tries to induce you to undo it. To, as it were, go back into the past and erase that message – to change the mistake you had made. Just to see if you would do it. Just to see if it was in your character.

'If it had been, you would now be totally under its control. But at the very last second your nature rebelled and you would not do it. And so the ghost gives you up as a bad job and deserts you in turn. It must find someone else.

'How long has it been doing this? I do not know. Does this now make sense to you? Do you recognise the truth of what I am saying?'

Richard turned cold.

'Yes,' he said, 'I think you must be absolutely right.'

'And at what moment, then,' said Dirk, 'did the ghost leave you?'

Richard swallowed.

'When Michael Wenton-Weakes walked out of the room,' he said.

'So I wonder,' said Dirk quietly, 'what possibilities the ghost saw in him. I wonder whether this time it found what it wanted. I believe we shall not have long to wait.'

There was a knock on the door.

When it opened, there stood Michael Wenton-Weakes. He said simply, 'Please, I need your help.'

Reg and Richard stared at Dirk, and then at Michael.

'Do you mind if I put this down somewhere?' said Michael. 'It's rather heavy. Full of scuba-diving equipment.'

'Oh, I see,' said Susan, 'oh well, thanks, Nicola, I'll try that fingering. I'm sure he only put the E flat in there just to annoy people. Yes, I've been at it solidly all afternoon. Some of those semiquaver runs in the second movement are absolute bastards. Well, yes, it helped take my mind off it all. No, no news. It's all just mystifying and absolutely horrible. I don't want even to – look, maybe I'll give you a call again later and see how you're feeling. I know, yes, you never know which is worse, do you, the illness, the antibiotics, or the doctor's bedside manner. Look after yourself, or at least, make sure Simon does. Tell him to bring you gallons of hot lemon. OK. Well, I'll talk to you later. Keep warm. Bye now.'

She put the phone down and returned to her cello. She had hardly started to reconsider the problem of the irritating E flat when the phone went again. She had simply left it off the hook for the afternoon, but had forgotten to do so again after making her own call.

With a sigh she propped up the cello, put down the bow, and went to the phone again.

'Hello?' she demanded.

Again, there was nothing, just a distant cry of wind. Irritably, she slammed the receiver back down once more.

She waited a few seconds for the line to clear, and then was about to take the phone off the hook once more when she realised that perhaps Richard might need her.

She hesitated.

She admitted to herself that she hadn't been using the answering machine, because she usually just put it on for Gordon's convenience, and that was something of which she did not currently wish to be reminded.

Still, she put the answering machine on, turned the volume right down, and returned again to the E flat that Mozart had put in only to annoy cellists.

In the darkness of the offices of Dirk Gently's Holistic Detective Agency, Gordon Way clumsily fumbled the telephone receiver back on to its rest and sat slumped in the deepest dejection. He didn't even stop himself slumping all the way through the seat until he rested lightly on the floor.

Miss Pearce had fled the office the first time the telephone had started actually using itself, her patience with all this sort of thing finally exhausted again, since which time Gordon had had the office to himself. However, his attempts to contact anybody had failed completely.

Or rather, his attempts to contact Susan, which was all he cared about. It was Susan he had been speaking to when he died and he knew he had somehow to speak to her again. But she had left her phone off the hook most of the afternoon and even when she had answered she could not hear him.

He gave up. He roused himself from the floor, stood

up, and slipped out and down into the darkening streets. He drifted aimlessly for a while, went for a walk on the canal, which was a trick that palled very quickly, and then wandered back up to the street again.

The houses with light and life streaming from them upset him most particularly since the welcome they seemed to extend would not be extended to him. He wondered if anyone would mind if he simply slipped into their house and watched television for the evening. He wouldn't be any trouble.

Or a cinema.

That would be better, he could go to the cinema.

He turned with more positive, if still insubstantial, footsteps into Noel Road and started to walk up it.

Noel Road, he thought. It rang a vague bell. He had a feeling that he had recently had some dealings with someone in Noel Road. Who was it?

His thoughts were interrupted by a terrible scream of horror that rang through the street. He stood stock still. A few seconds later a door flew open a few yards from him and a woman ran out of it, wild-eyed and howling.

31

Richard had never liked Michael Wenton-Weakes and he liked him even less with a ghost in him. He couldn't say why, he had nothing against ghosts personally, didn't think a person should be judged adversely simply for being dead, but – he didn't like it.

Nevertheless, it was hard not to feel a little sorry for him.

Michael sat forlornly on a stool with his elbow resting on the large table and his head resting on his fingers. He looked ill and haggard. He looked deeply tired. He looked pathetic. His story had been a harrowing one, and concluded with his attempts to possess first Reg and then Richard.

'You were,' he concluded, 'right. Entirely.'

He said this last to Dirk, and Dirk grimaced as if trying not to beam with triumph too many times in a day.

The voice was Michael's and yet it was not Michael's. Whatever timbre a voice acquires through a billion or so years of dread and isolation, this voice had acquired it, and it filled those who heard it with a dizzying chill akin to that which clutches the mind and stomach when standing on a cliff at night.

He turned his eyes on Reg and on Richard, and the effect of the eyes, too, was one that provoked pity and terror. Richard had to look away.

'I owe you both an apology,' said the ghost within

Michael, 'which I offer you from the depths of my heart, and only hope that as you come to understand the desperation of my predicament, and the hope which this machine offers me, you will understand why I have acted as I have, and that you will find it within yourselves to forgive me. And to help me. I beg you.'

'Give the man a whisky,' said Dirk gruffly.

'Haven't got any whisky,' said Reg. 'Er, port? There's a bottle or so of Margaux I could open. Very fine one. Should be chambréd for an hour, but I can do that of course, it's very easy, I—'

'Will you help me?' interrupted the ghost.

Reg bustled to fetch some port and some glasses.

'Why have you taken over the body of this man?' said Dirk.

'I need to have a voice with which to speak and a body with which to act. No harm will come to him, no harm—'

'Let me ask the question again. Why have you taken over the body of this man?' insisted Dirk.

The ghost made Michael's body shrug.

'He was willing. Both of these two gentlemen quite understandably resisted being ... well, hypnotised – your analogy is fair. This one? Well, I think his sense of self is at a low ebb, and he has acquiesced. I am very grateful to him and will not do him any harm.'

'His sense of self,' repeated Dirk thoughtfully, 'is at a low ebb.'

'I suppose that is probably true,' said Richard quietly to Dirk. 'He seemed very depressed last night. The one thing that was important to him had been taken away because he, well, he wasn't really very good at it. Although he's proud I expect he was probably quite receptive to the idea of actually being wanted for something.'

'Hmmm,' said Dirk, and said it again. He said it a third time with feeling. Then he whirled round and barked at the figure on the stool.

'Michael Wenton-Weakes!'

Michael's head jolted back and he blinked.

'Yes?' he said, in his normal lugubrious voice. His eyes followed Dirk as he moved.

'You can hear me,' said Dirk, 'and you can answer for yourself?'

'Oh, yes,' said Michael, 'most certainly I can.'

'This . . . being, this spirit. You know he is in you? You accept his presence? You are a willing party to what he wishes to do?'

'That is correct. I was much moved by his account of himself, and am very willing to help him. In fact I think it is right for me to do so.'

'All right,' said Dirk with a snap of his fingers, 'you can go.'

Michael's head slumped forward suddenly, and then after a second or so it slowly rose again, as if being pumped up from inside like a tyre.

The ghost was back in possession.

Dirk took hold of a chair, spun it round and sat astride it facing the ghost in Michael, peering intently into its eyes.

'Again,' he said, 'tell me again. A quick snap account.'

Michael's body tensed slightly. It reached out to Dirk's arm.

'Don't – touch me!' snapped Dirk. 'Just tell me the facts. The first time you try and make me feel sorry for you I'll poke you in the eye. Or at least, the one you've borrowed. So leave out all the stuff that sounded like . . . er—'

'Coleridge,' said Richard suddenly, 'it sounded exactly

252

like Coleridge. It was like "The Rime of the Ancient Mariner". Well, bits of it were.'

Dirk frowned. 'Coleridge?' he said.

'I tried to tell him my story,' admitted the ghost, 'I—'

'Sorry,' said Dirk, 'you'll have to excuse me – I've never cross-examined a four-billion-year-old ghost before. Are we talking Samuel Taylor here? Are you saying you told your story to Samuel Taylor Coleridge?'

'I was able to enter his mind at . . . certain times. When he was in an impressionable state.'

'You mean when he was on laudanum?' said Richard.

'That is correct. He was more relaxed then.'

'I'll say,' snorted Reg, 'I sometimes encountered him when he was quite astoundingly relaxed. Look, I'll make some coffee.' He disappeared into the kitchen, where he could be heard laughing to himself.

'It's another world,' muttered Richard to himself, sitting down and shaking his head.

'But unfortunately when he was fully in possession of himself I, so to speak, was not,' said the ghost, 'and so that failed. And what he wrote was very garbled.'

'Discuss,' said Richard, to himself, raising his eyebrows.

'Professor,' called out Dirk, 'this may sound absurd. Did – Coleridge ever try to . . . er . . . use your time machine? Feel free to discuss the question in any way which appeals to you.'

'Well, do you know,' said Reg, looking round the door, 'he did come in prying around on one occasion, but I think he was in a great deal too relaxed a state to do anything.'

'I see,' said Dirk. 'But why,' he added turning back to the strange figure of Michael slumped on its stool, 'why has it taken you so long to find someone?'

'For long, long periods I am very weak, almost totally nonexistent, and unable to influence anything at all. And then, of course, before that time there was no time machine here, and . . . no hope for me at all—'

'Perhaps ghosts exist like wave patterns,' suggested Richard, 'like interference patterns between the actual with the possible. There would be irregular peaks and troughs, like in a musical waveform.'

The ghost snapped Michael's eyes around to Richard.

'You . . .' he said, 'you wrote that article . . .'

'Er, yes—'

'It moved me very greatly,' said the ghost, with a sudden remorseful longing in his voice which seemed to catch itself almost as much by surprise as it did its listeners.

'Oh. I see,' said Richard. 'Well, thank you. You didn't like it so much last time you mentioned it. Well, I know that wasn't you as such—'

Richard sat back frowning to himself.

'So,' said Dirk, 'to return to the beginning—'

The ghost gathered Michael's breath for him and started again. 'We were on a ship—' it said.

'A spaceship.'

'Yes. Out from Salaxala, a world in . . . well, very far from here. A violent and troubled place. We – a party of some nine dozen of us – set out, as people frequently did, to find a new world for ourselves. All the planets in this system were completely unsuitable for our purpose, but we stopped on this world to replenish some necessary mineral supplies.

'Unfortunately our landing ship was damaged on its way into the atmosphere. Damaged quite badly, but still quite reparable.

'I was the engineer on board and it fell to me to supervise the task of repairing the ship and preparing it to return to our main ship. Now, in order to understand what happened next you must know something of the nature of a highly automated society. There is no task that cannot be done more easily with the aid of advanced computerisation. And there were some very specific problems associated with a trip with an aim such as ours—'

'Which was?' said Dirk sharply.

The ghost in Michael blinked as if the answer was obvious.

'Well, to find a new and better world on which we could all live in freedom, peace and harmony forever, of course,' he said.

Dirk raised his eyebrows.

'Oh, that,' he said. 'You'd thought this all out carefully, I assume.'

'We'd had it thought out for us. We had with us some very specialised devices for helping us to continue to believe in the purpose of the trip even when things got difficult. They generally worked very well, but I think we probably came to rely on them too much.'

'What on earth were they?' said Dirk.

'It's probably hard for you to understand how reassuring they were. And that was why I made my fatal mistake. When I wanted to know whether or not it was safe to take off, I didn't want to know that it might *not* be safe. I just wanted to be reassured that it *was*. So instead of checking it myself, you see, I sent out one of the Electric Monks.'

32

The brass plaque on the red door in Peckender Street glittered as it reflected the yellow light of a street lamp. It glared for a moment as it reflected the violent flashing light of a passing police car sweeping by.

It dimmed slightly as a pale, pale wraith slipped silently through it. It glimmered as it dimmed, because the wraith was trembling with such terrible agitation.

In the dark hallway the ghost of Gordon Way paused. He needed something to lean on for support, and of course there was nothing. He tried to get a grip on himself, but there was nothing to get a grip on. He retched at the horror of what he had seen, but there was, of course, nothing in his stomach. He half stumbled, half swam up the stairs, like a drowning man trying to grapple for a grip on the water.

He staggered through the wall, through the desk, through the door, and tried to compose and settle himself in front of the desk in Dirk's office.

If anyone had happened into the office a few minutes later – a night cleaner perhaps, if Dirk Gently had ever employed one, which he didn't on the grounds that they wished to be paid and he did not wish to pay them, or a burglar, perhaps, if there had been anything in the office worth burgling, which there wasn't – they would have seen the following sight and been amazed by it.

The receiver of the large red telephone on the desk

suddenly rocked and tumbled off its rest on to the desk top.

A dialling tone started to burr. Then, one by one, seven of the large, easily pushed buttons depressed themselves, and after the very long pause which the British telephone system allows you within which to gather your thoughts and forget who it is you're phoning, the sound of a phone ringing at the other end of the line could be heard.

After a couple of rings there was a click, a whirr, and a sound as of a machine drawing breath. Then a voice started to say, 'Hello, this is Susan. I can't come to the phone right at the moment because I'm trying to get an E flat right, but if you'd like to leave your name . . .'

'So then, on the say so of an – I can hardly bring myself to utter the words – Electric Monk,' said Dirk in a voice ringing with derision, 'you attempt to launch the ship and to your utter astonishment it explodes. Since when—?'

'Since when,' said the ghost, abjectly, 'I have been alone on this planet. Alone with the knowledge of what I had done to my fellows on the ship. All, all alone . . .'

'Yes, skip that, I said,' snapped Dirk angrily. 'What about the main ship? That presumably went on and continued its search for—'

'No.'

'Then what happened to it?'

'Nothing. It's still there.'

'Still *there*?'

Dirk leapt to his feet and whirled off to pace the room, his brow furiously furrowed.

'Yes.' Michael's head drooped a little, but he looked up pitieously at Reg and at Richard. 'All of us were aboard the landing craft. At first I felt myself to be haunted by the ghosts of the rest, but it was only in my imagination. For millions of years, and then billions, I stalked the mud utterly alone. It is impossible for you to conceive of even the tiniest part of the torment of such eternity. Then,' he added, 'just recently life arose on the planet. Life. Vegetation, things in the sea, then, at last, you. Intelligent life. I turn to you to release me from the torment I have endured.'

Michael's head sank abjectly on to his chest for some few seconds. Then slowly, wobblingly, it rose and stared at them again, with yet darker fires in his eyes.

'Take me back,' he said, 'I beg you, take me back to the landing craft. Let me undo what was done. A word from me, and it can be undone, the repairs properly made, the landing craft can then return to the main ship, we can be on our way, my torment will be extinguished, and I will cease to be a burden to you. I beg you.'

There was a short silence while his plea hung in the air.

'But that can't work, can it?' said Richard. 'If we do that, then this won't have happened. Don't we generate all sorts of paradoxes?'

Reg stirred himself from thought. 'No worse than many that exist already,' he said. 'If the Universe came to an end every time there was some uncertainty about what had happened in it, it would never have got beyond the first picosecond. And many of course don't. It's like a human body, you see. A few cuts and bruises here and there don't hurt it. Not even major surgery if it's done properly. Paradoxes are just the scar tissue. Time and space heal themselves up around them and people simply remember a version of events which makes as much sense as they require it to make.

'That isn't to say that if you get involved in a paradox a few things won't strike you as being very odd, but if you've got through life without that already happening to you, then I don't know which Universe you've been living in, but it isn't this one.'

'Well, if that's the case,' said Richard, 'why were you so fierce about not doing anything to save the dodo?'

Reg sighed. 'You don't understand at all. The dodo wouldn't have died if I hadn't worked so hard to save the coelacanth.'

'The coelacanth? The prehistoric fish? But how could one possibly affect the other?'

'Ah. Now there you're asking. The complexities of cause and effect defy analysis. Not only is the continuum like a human body, it is also very like a piece of badly put up wallpaper. Push down a bubble somewhere, another one pops up somewhere else. There are no more dodos because of my interference. In the end I imposed the rule on myself because I simply couldn't bear it any more. The only thing that really gets hurt when you try and change time is yourself.' He smiled bleakly, and looked away.

Then he added, after a long moment's reflection, 'No, it can be done. I'm just cynical because it's gone wrong so many times. This poor fellow's story is a very pathetic one, and it can do no harm to put an end to his misery. It happened so very, very long ago on a dead planet. If we do this we will each remember whatever it is that has happened to us individually. Too bad if the rest of the world doesn't quite agree. It will hardly be the first time.'

Michael's head bowed.

'You're very silent, Dirk,' said Richard.

Dirk glared angrily at him. 'I want to see this ship,' he demanded.

In the darkness, the red telephone receiver slipped and slid fitfully back across the desk. If anybody had been there to see it they might just have discerned a shape that moved it.

It shone only very faintly, less than would the hands of a luminous watch. It seemed more as if the darkness around it was just that much darker and the ghostly shape sat within it like thickened scar tissue beneath the surface of the night.

Gordon grappled one last time with the recalcitrant receiver. At length he got a final grip and slipped it up on to the top of the instrument.

From there it fell back on to its rest and disconnected the call. At the same moment the ghost of Gordon Way, his last call finally completed, fell back to his own rest and vanished.

33

Swinging slowly round in the shadow of the Earth, just one more piece of debris among that which floated now forever in high orbit, was one dark shape that was larger and more regularly formed than the rest. And far, far older.

For four billion years it had continued to absorb data from the world below it, scanning, analysing, processing. Occasionally it sent pieces back if it thought they would help, if it thought they might be received. But otherwise, it watched, it listened, it recorded. Not the lapping of a wave nor the beating of a heart escaped its attention.

Otherwise, nothing inside it had moved for four billion years, except for the air which circulated still, and the motes of dust within the air that danced and danced and danced and danced . . . and danced.

It was only a very slight disturbance that occurred now. Quietly, without fuss, like a dew drop precipitating from the air on to a leaf, there appeared in a wall which had stood blank and grey for four billion years, a door. A plain, ordinary white-panelled door with a small dented brass handle.

This quiet event, too, was recorded and incorporated in the continual stream of data processing that the ship ceaselessly performed. Not only the arrival of the door, but the arrival of those behind the door, the way they looked, the way they moved, the way they felt about being there. All processed, all recorded, all transformed.

After a moment or two had passed, the door opened.

Within it could be seen a room unlike any on the ship. A room of wooden floors, of shabby upholstery, a room in which a fire danced. And as the fire danced, its data danced within the ship's computers, and the motes of dust in the air also danced with it.

A figure stood in the doorway – a large lugubrious figure with a strange light that danced now in its eyes. It stepped forward across the threshold into the ship, and its face was suddenly suffused with a calm for which it had longed but had thought never again to experience.

Following him stepped out a smaller, older man with hair that was white and wayward. He stopped and blinked with wonder as he passed from out of the realm of his room and into the realm of the ship. Following him came a third man, impatient and tense, with a large leather overcoat that flapped about him. He, too, stopped and was momentarily bewildered by something he didn't understand. With a look of deepest puzzlement on his face he walked forward and looked around at the grey and dusty walls of the ancient ship.

At last came a fourth man, tall and thin. He stooped as he walked out of the door, and then instantly stopped as if he had walked into a wall.

He had walked into a wall, of a kind.

He stood transfixed. If anyone had been looking at his face at that moment, it would have been abundantly clear to them that the single most astonishing event of this man's entire existence was currently happening to him.

When slowly he began to move it was with a curious gait, as if he was swimming very slowly. Each tiniest movement of his head seemed to bring fresh floods of awe and astonishment into his face. Tears welled in his eyes, and he became breathless with gasping wonder.

Dirk turned to look at him, to hurry him along.

'What's the matter?' he called above the noise.

'The . . . music . . .' whispered Richard.

The air was full of music. So full it seemed there was room for nothing else. And each particle of air seemed to have its own music, so that as Richard moved his head he heard a new and different music, though the new and different music fitted quite perfectly with the music that lay beside it in the air.

The modulations from one to another were perfectly accomplished – astonishing leaps to distant keys made effortlessly in the mere shifting of the head. New themes, new strands of melody, all perfectly and astoundingly proportioned, constantly involved themselves into the continuing web. Huge slow waves of movement, faster dances that thrilled through them, tiny scintillating scampers that danced on the dances, long tangled tunes whose ends were so like their beginnings that they twisted around upon themselves, turned inside out, upside down, and then rushed off again on the back of yet another dancing melody in a distant part of the ship.

Richard staggered against the wall.

Dirk hurried to grab him.

'Come on,' he said, brusquely, 'what's the matter? Can't you stand the music? It's a bit loud, isn't it? For God's sake, pull yourself together. There's something here I still don't understand. It's not right. Come on—'

He tugged Richard after him, and then had to support him as Richard's mind sank further and further under the overwhelming weight of music. The visions that were woven in his mind by the million thrilling threads of music as they were pulled through it, were increasingly a welter of chaos, but the more the chaos burgeoned the more it fitted with the other chaos, and the next greater chaos, until it all became a vast exploding ball of harmony expanding in his mind faster than any mind could deal with.

And then it was all much simpler.

A single tune danced through his mind and all his attention rested upon it. It was a tune that seethed through the magical flood, shaped it, formed it, lived through it hugely, lived through it minutely, was its very essence. It bounced and trilled along, at first a little tripping tune, then it slowed, then it danced again but with more difficulty, seemed to founder in eddies of doubt and confusion, and then suddenly revealed that the eddies were just the first ripples of a huge new wave of energy surging up joyfully from beneath.

Richard began very, very slowly to faint.

He lay very still.

He felt he was an old sponge steeped in paraffin and left in the sun to dry.

He felt like the body of an old horse burning hazily in the sun. He dreamed of oil, thin and fragrant, of dark heaving seas. He was on a white beach, drunk with fish, stupefied with sand, bleached, drowsing, pummelled with light, sinking, estimating the density of vapour clouds in distant nebulae, spinning with dead delight. He was a pump spouting fresh water in the springtime, gushing into a mound of reeking newmown grass. Sounds, almost unheard, burned away like distant sleep.

He ran and was falling. The lights of a harbour spun into night. The sea like a dark spirit slapped infinitesimally at the sand, glimmering, unconscious. Out where it was deeper and colder he sank easily with the heavy sea swelling like oil around his ears, and was disturbed only by a distant burr burr as of the phone ringing.

He knew he had been listening to the music of life itself. The music of light dancing on water that rippled with the wind and the tides, of the life that moved through the water, of the life that moved on the land, warmed by the light.

He continued to lie very still. He continued to be disturbed by a distant burr burr as of a phone ringing.

Gradually he became aware that the distant burr burr as of a phone ringing was a phone ringing.

He sat up sharply.

He was lying on a small crumpled bed in a small untidy panelled room that he knew he recognised but couldn't place. It was cluttered with books and shoes. He blinked at it and was blank.

The phone by the bed was ringing. He picked it up.

'Hello?' he said.

'Richard!' It was Susan's voice, utterly distraught. He shook his head and had no recollection of anything useful.

'Hello?' he said again.

'Richard, is that you? *Where are you?*'

'Er, hold on, I'll go and look.'

He put the receiver down on the crumpled sheets, where it lay squawking, climbed shakily off the bed, staggered to the door and opened it.

Here was a bathroom. He peered at it suspiciously. Again, he recognised it but felt that there was something missing. Oh yes. There should be a horse in it. Or at least, there had been a horse in it the last time he had seen it. He crossed the bathroom floor and went out of the other door. He found his way shakily down the stairs and into Reg's main room.

He was surprised by what he saw when he got there.

34

The storms of the day before, and of the day before that, and the floods of the previous week, had now abated. The skies still bulged with rain, but all that actually fell in the gathering evening gloom was a dreary kind of prickle.

Some wind whipped across the darkening plain, blundered through the low hills and gusted across a shallow valley where stood a structure, a kind of tower, alone in a nightmare of mud, and leaning.

It was a blackened stump of a tower. It stood like an extrusion of magma from one of the more pestilential pits of hell, and it leaned at a peculiar angle, as if oppressed by something altogether more terrible than its own considerable weight. It seemed a dead thing, long ages dead.

The only movement was that of a river of mud that moved sluggishly along the bottom of the valley past the tower. A mile or so further on, the river ran down a ravine and disappeared underground.

But as the evening darkened it became apparent that the tower was not entirely without life. There was a single dim red light guttering deep within it.

It was this scene that Richard was surprised to see from a small white doorway set in the side of the valley wall, a few hundred yards from the tower.

'Don't step out!' said Dirk, putting up an arm. 'The atmosphere is poisonous. I'm not sure what's in it but it would certainly get your carpets nice and clean.'

Dirk was standing in the doorway watching the valley with deep mistrust.

'Where are we?' asked Richard.

'Bermuda,' said Dirk. 'It's a bit complicated.'

'Thank you,' said Richard and walked groggily back across the room.

'Excuse me,' he said to Reg, who was busy fussing round Michael Wenton-Weakes, making sure that the scuba diving suit he was wearing fitted snuggly everywhere, that the mask was secure and that the regulator for the air supply was working properly.

'Sorry, can I just get past?' said Richard. 'Thanks.'

He climbed back up the stairs, went back into Reg's bedroom, sat shakily on the edge of the bed and picked up the phone again.

'Bermuda,' he said, 'it's a bit complicated.'

Downstairs, Reg finished smearing Vaseline on all the joins of the suit and the few pieces of exposed skin around the mask, and then announced that all was ready.

Dirk swung himself away from the door and stood aside with the utmost bad grace.

'Well then,' he said, 'be off with you. Good riddance. I wash my hands of the whole affair. I suppose we will have to wait here for you to send back the empty, for what it's worth.' He stalked round the sofa with an angry gesture. He didn't like this. He didn't like any of it. He particularly didn't like Reg knowing more about space/time than he did. It made him angry that he didn't know why he didn't like it.

'My dear fellow,' said Reg in a conciliatory tone, 'consider what a very small effort it is for us to help the poor soul. I'm sorry if it seems to you an anticlimax after all your extraordinary feats of deduction. I know you feel that a mere errand of mercy seems not enough for you, but you should be more charitable.'

'Charitable, ha!' said Dirk. 'I pay my taxes, what more do you want?'

He threw himself on to the sofa, ran his hands through his hair and sulked.

The possessed figure of Michael shook hands with Reg and said a few words of thanks. Then he walked stiffly to the door, turned and bowed to them both.

Dirk flung his head round and glared at him, his eyes flashing behind their spectacles and his hair flying wildly. The ghost looked at Dirk, and for a moment shivered inside with apprehension. A superstitious instinct suddenly made the ghost wave. He waved Michael's hand round in a circle, three times, and then said a single word.

'Goodbye,' he said.

With that he turned again, gripped the sides of the doorway and stepped resolutely out into the mud, and into the foul and poisonous wind.

He paused for a moment to be sure that his footing was solid, that he had his balance, and then without another look back he walked away from them, out of the reach of the slimy things with legs, towards his ship.

'Now, what on earth did *that* mean?' said Dirk, irritably mimicking the odd triple wave.

Richard came thundering down the stairs, threw open the door and plunged into the room, wild-eyed.

'Ross has been murdered!' he shouted.

'Who the hell's Ross?' shouted Dirk back at him.

'Whatsisname Ross, for God's sake,' exclaimed Richard, 'the new editor of *Fathom*.'

'What's *Fathom*?' shouted Dirk again.

'Michael's bloody magazine, Dirk! Remember? Gordon chucked Michael off the magazine and gave it to this Ross guy to run instead. Michael hated him for that. Well, last night Michael went and bloody murdered him!'

He paused, panting. 'At least,' he said, 'he was murdered. And Michael was the only one with any reason to.'

He ran to the door, looked out at the retreating figure disappearing into the gloom, and spun round again.

'Is he coming back?' said Richard.

Dirk leapt to his feet and stood blinking for a moment.

'That's it . . .' he said, '*that's* why Michael was the perfect subject. *That's* what I should have been looking for. The thing the ghost made him do in order to establish his hold, the thing he had to be fundamentally *willing* to do, the thing that would match the ghost's own purpose. Oh my dear God. He thinks we've supplanted them and that's what he wants to reverse.

'He thinks this is their world not ours. *This* was where they were going to settle and build their blasted paradise. It matches every step of the way.

'You see,' he said, turning on Reg, 'what we have done? I would not be surprised to discover that the accident your poor tormented soul out there is trying to reverse is the very thing which started life on this planet!'

He turned his eyes suddenly from Reg, who was white and trembling, back to Richard.

'When did you hear this?' he said, puzzled.

'Er, just now,' said Richard, 'on . . . on the phone. Upstairs.'

'What?'

'It was Susan, I don't know how – said she had a message on her answering machine telling her about it. She said the message . . . was from – she said it was from Gordon, but I think she was hysterical. Dirk, what the hell is happening? Where are we?'

'We are four billion years in the past,' said Reg in a shaking voice, 'please don't ask me why it is that the phone works when we are anywhere in the Universe other than where it's actually connected, that's a matter you will have to take up with British Telecom, but—'

'Damn and blast British Telecom,' shouted Dirk, the words coming easily from force of habit. He ran to the door and peered again at the dim shadowy figure trudging through the mud towards the Salaxalan ship, completely beyond their reach.

'How long,' said Dirk, quite calmly, 'would you guess that it's going to take that fat self-deluding bastard to reach his ship? Because that is how long we have.

'Come. Let us sit down. Let us think. We have two minutes in which to decide what we are going to do. After that, I very much suspect that the three of us, and everything we have ever known, including the coelacanth and the dodo, dear Professor, will cease ever to have existed.'

He sat heavily on the sofa, then stood up again and removed Michael's discarded jacket from under him. As he did so, a book fell out of the pocket.

35

'I think it's an appalling act of desecration,' said Richard to Reg, as they sat hiding behind a hedge.

The night was full of summer smells from the cottage garden, and the occasional whiff of sea air which came in on the light breezes that were entertaining themselves on the coast of the Bristol Channel.

There was a bright moon playing over the sea off in the distance, and by its light it was also possible to see some distance over Exmoor stretching away to the south of them.

Reg sighed.

'Yes, maybe,' he said, 'but I'm afraid he's right, you know, it must be done. It was the only sure way. All the instructions were clearly contained in the piece once you knew what you were looking for. It has to be suppressed. The ghost will always be around. In fact two of him now. That is, assuming this works. Poor devil. Still, I suppose he brought it on himself.'

Richard fretfully pulled up some blades of grass and twisted them between his fingers.

He held them up to the moonlight, turned them to different angles, and watched the way light played on them.

'Such music,' he said. 'I'm not religious, but if I were I would say it was like a glimpse into the mind of God. Perhaps it was and I ought to be religious. I have to keep reminding myself that they didn't create the music, they only created the instrument which could read the score. And the score was life itself. And it's all up there.'

He glanced into the sky. Unconsciously he started to quote:

'Could I revive within me
Her symphony and song
To such a deep delight 'twould win me
That with music loud and long
I would build that dome in air,
That sunny dome, those caves of ice!'

'Hmmm,' said Reg to himself, 'I wonder if he arrived early enough.'

'What did you say?'

'Oh, nothing. Just a thought.'

'Good God, he can talk, can't he?' Richard exclaimed suddenly. 'He's been in there over an hour now. I wonder what's going on.'

He got up and looked over the hedge at the small farm cottage basking in the moonlight behind them. About an hour earlier Dirk had walked boldly up to the front door and rapped on it.

When the door had opened, somewhat reluctantly, and a slightly dazed face had looked out, Dirk had doffed his absurd hat and said in a loud voice, 'Mr Samuel Coleridge?

'I was just passing by, on my way from Porlock, you understand, and I was wondering if I might trouble you to vouchsafe me an interview? It's just for a little parish broadsheet I edit. Won't take much of your time I promise, I know you must be busy, famous poet like you, but I do so admire your work, and . . .'

The rest was lost, because by that time Dirk had effected his entry and closed the door behind him.

'Would you excuse me a moment?' said Reg.

'What? Oh sure,' said Richard, 'I'm just going to have a look and see what's happening.'

While Reg wandered off behind a tree Richard pushed open the little gate and was just about to make his way up the path when he heard the sound of voices approaching the front door from within.

He hurriedly darted back, as the front door started to open.

'Well, thank you very much indeed, Mr Coleridge,' said Dirk, as he emerged, fiddling with his hat and bowing, 'you have been most kind and generous with your time, and I do appreciate it very much, as I'm sure will my readers. I'm sure it will work up into a very nice little article, a copy of which you may rest assured I will send you for you to peruse at your leisure. I will most certainly welcome your comments if you have any, any points of style, you know, hints, tips, things of that nature. Well, thank you again, so much, for your time, I do hope I haven't kept you from anything important—'

The door slammed violently behind him.

Dirk turned with another in a long succession of triumphant beams and hurried down the path to Richard.

'Well, that's put a stop to that,' he said, patting his hands together. 'I think he'd made a start on writing it down, but he won't remember another word, that's for certain. Where's the egregious Professor? Ah, there you are. Good heavens, I'd no idea I'd been that long. A most fascinating and entertaining fellow, our Mr Coleridge, or at least I'm sure he would have been if I'd given him the chance, but I was rather too busy being fascinating myself.

'Oh, but I did do as you asked, Richard, I asked him at the end about the albatross and he said what albatross? So I said, oh it wasn't important, the albatross did not signify. He said what albatross didn't signify, and I said never mind the albatross, it didn't matter, and he said it did matter – someone comes to his house in the middle of the night raving about albatrosses, he wanted to know why. I said blast the bloody albatross and he said he had a good mind to and he wasn't certain that that didn't give him an idea for a poem he was working on. Much better, he said, than being hit by an asteroid, which he thought was stretching credulity a bit. And so I came away.

'Now. Having saved the entire human race from extinction I could do with a pizza. What say you to such a proposal?'

Richard didn't offer an opinion. He was staring instead with some puzzlement at Reg.

'Something troubling you?' said Reg, taken aback.

'That's a good trick,' said Richard, 'I could have sworn you didn't have a beard before you went behind the tree.'

'Oh – ' Reg fingered the luxuriant three-inch growth – 'yes,' he said, 'just carelessness,' he said, 'carelessness.'

'What have you been up to?'

'Oh, just a few adjustments. A little surgery, you understand. Nothing drastic.'

A few minutes later as he ushered them into the extra door that a nearby cowshed had mysteriously acquired, he looked back up into the sky behind them, just in time to see a small light flare up and disappear.

'Sorry, Richard,' he muttered, and followed them in.

36

'Thank you, no,' said Richard firmly, 'much as I would love the opportunity to buy you a pizza and watch you eat it, Dirk, I want to go straight home. I have to see Susan. Is that possible, Reg? Just straight to my flat? I'll come up to Cambridge next week and collect my car.'

'We are already there,' said Reg, 'simply step out of the door, and you are home in your own flat. It is early on Friday evening and the weekend lies before you.'

'Thanks. Er, look, Dirk, I'll see you around, OK? Do I owe you something? I don't know.'

Dirk waved the matter aside airily. 'You will hear from my Miss Pearce in due course,' he said.

'Fine, OK, well I'll see you when I've had some rest. It's been, well, unexpected.'

He walked to the door and opened it. Stepping outside he found himself halfway up his own staircase, in the wall of which the door had materialised.

He was about to start up the stairs when he turned again as a thought struck him. He stepped back in, closing the door behind him.

'Reg, could we make one tiny detour?' he said. 'I think it would be a good move if I took Susan out for a meal tonight, only the place I have in mind you have to book in advance. Could you manage three weeks for me?'

'Nothing could be easier,' said Reg, and made a subtle adjustment to the disposition of the beads on the abacus.

'There,' he said, 'We have travelled backwards in time three weeks. You know where the phone is.'

Richard hurried up the internal staircase to Reg's bedroom and phoned L'Esprit d'Escalier. The maître d' was charmed and delighted to take his reservation, and looked forward to seeing him in three weeks' time. Richard went back downstairs shaking his head in wonder.

'I need a weekend of solid reality,' he said. 'Who was that just going out of the door?'

'That,' said Dirk, 'was your sofa being delivered. The man asked if we minded him opening the door so they could manoeuvre it round and I said we would be delighted.'

It was only a few minutes later that Richard found himself hurrying up the stairs to Susan's flat. As he arrived at her front door he was pleased, as he always was, to hear the deep tones of her cello coming faintly from within. He quietly let himself in and then as he walked to the door of her music room he suddenly froze in astonishment. The tune she was playing was one he had heard before. A little tripping tune, that slowed, then danced again but with more difficulty . . .

His face was so amazed that she stopped playing the instant she saw him.

'What's wrong?' she said, alarmed.

'Where did you get that music?' said Richard in a whisper.

She shrugged. 'Well, from the music shop,' she said, puzzled. She wasn't being facetious, she simply didn't understand the question.

'What is it?'

'It's from a cantata I'm playing in in a couple of weeks,' she said, 'Bach, number six.'

'Who wrote it?'

'Well, Bach I expect. If you think about it.'

'Who?'

'Watch my lips. Bach. B-A-C-H. Johannes Sebastian. Remember?'

'No, never heard of him. Who is he? Did he write anything else?'

Susan put down her bow, propped up her cello, stood up and came over to him.

'Are you all right?' she said.

'Er, it's rather hard to tell. What's . . .'

He caught sight of a pile of music books sitting in a corner of the room with the same name on the top one. BACH. He threw himself at the pile and started to scrabble through it. Book after book – J. S. BACH. Cello sonatas. Brandenburg Concertos. A Mass in B Minor.

He looked up at her in blank incomprehension.

'I've never seen any of this before,' he said.

'Richard my darling,' she said, putting her hand to his cheek, 'what on earth's the matter? It's just Bach sheet music.'

'But don't you understand?' he said, shaking a handful of the stuff. 'I've never, ever seen any of this before!'

'Well,' she said with mock gravity, 'perhaps if you didn't spend all your time playing with computer music . . .'

He looked at her with wild surprise, then slowly he sat back against the wall and began to laugh hysterically.

On Monday afternoon Richard phoned Reg.

'Reg!' he said. 'Your phone is working. Congratulations.'

'Oh yes, my dear fellow,' said Reg, 'how delightful to hear from you. Yes. A very capable young man arrived and fixed the phone a little earlier. I don't think it will go wrong again now. Good news, don't you think?'

'Very good. You got back safely then.'

'Oh yes, thank you. Oh, we had high excitement here when we returned from dropping you off. Remember the horse? Well he turned up again with his owner. They'd had some unfortunate encounter with the constabulary and wished to be taken home. Just as well. Dangerous sort of chap to have on the loose I think. So. How are you then?

'Reg . . . The music—'

'Ah, yes, I thought you'd be pleased. Took a bit of work, I can tell you. I saved only the tiniest tiniest scrap, of course, but even so I cheated. It was rather more than one man could actually do in a lifetime, but I don't suppose anybody will look at that too seriously.'

'Reg, can't we get some more of it?'

'Well, no. The ship has gone, and besides—'

'We could go back in time—'

'No, well, I told you. They've fixed the phone so it won't go wrong again.'

'So?'

'Well, the time machine won't work now. Burnt out. Dead as a dodo. I think that's it I'm afraid. Probably just as well, though, don't you think?'

On Monday, Mrs Sauskind phoned Dirk Gently's Holistic Detective Agency to complain about her bill.

'I don't understand what all this is about,' she said, 'it's complete nonsense. What's the meaning of it?'

'My dear Mrs Sauskind,' he said, 'I can hardly tell you how much I have been looking forward to having this exact same conversation with you yet again. Where shall we begin today? Which particular item is it that you would like to discuss?'

'None of them, thank you very much, Mr Gently. I do not know who you are or why you should think my cat is missing. Dear Roderick passed away in my arms two years ago and I have not wished to replace him.'

'Ah, well Mrs Sauskind,' said Dirk, 'what you probably fail to appreciate is that it is as a direct result of my efforts that – if I might explain about the interconnectedness of all—' He stopped. It was pointless. He slowly dropped the telephone back on its cradle.

'Miss Pearce!' he called out. 'Kindly send out a revised bill would you to our dear Mrs Sauskind. The new bill reads "To: saving human race from total extinction – no charge."'

He put on his hat and left for the day.